MURDER AT NORTH STAR SUMMIT

A Mistwood Mysteries Novel

Book 2

TINA VAN HOVEN

Copyright © 2026 by AUGUSTINA JACOBSON

All rights are reserved. No part of this book may be used or reproduced in any manner without written permission except in the case of brief quotations used in articles or reviews.

Murder on North Star Summit is a work of fiction. Names, characters, places, and incidents are products of the writer's imagination or have been used fictitiously and are not to be construed as real. Any resemblance to persons living or dead, actual events, places, incidents, or organizations is coincidental.

Cover by Elizabeth Mackey

Edited by Proof Perfect Editing

Formatting by Kalie Gerwig : Good Girl Author Services

ISBN: 978-1-951534-41-7

Contents

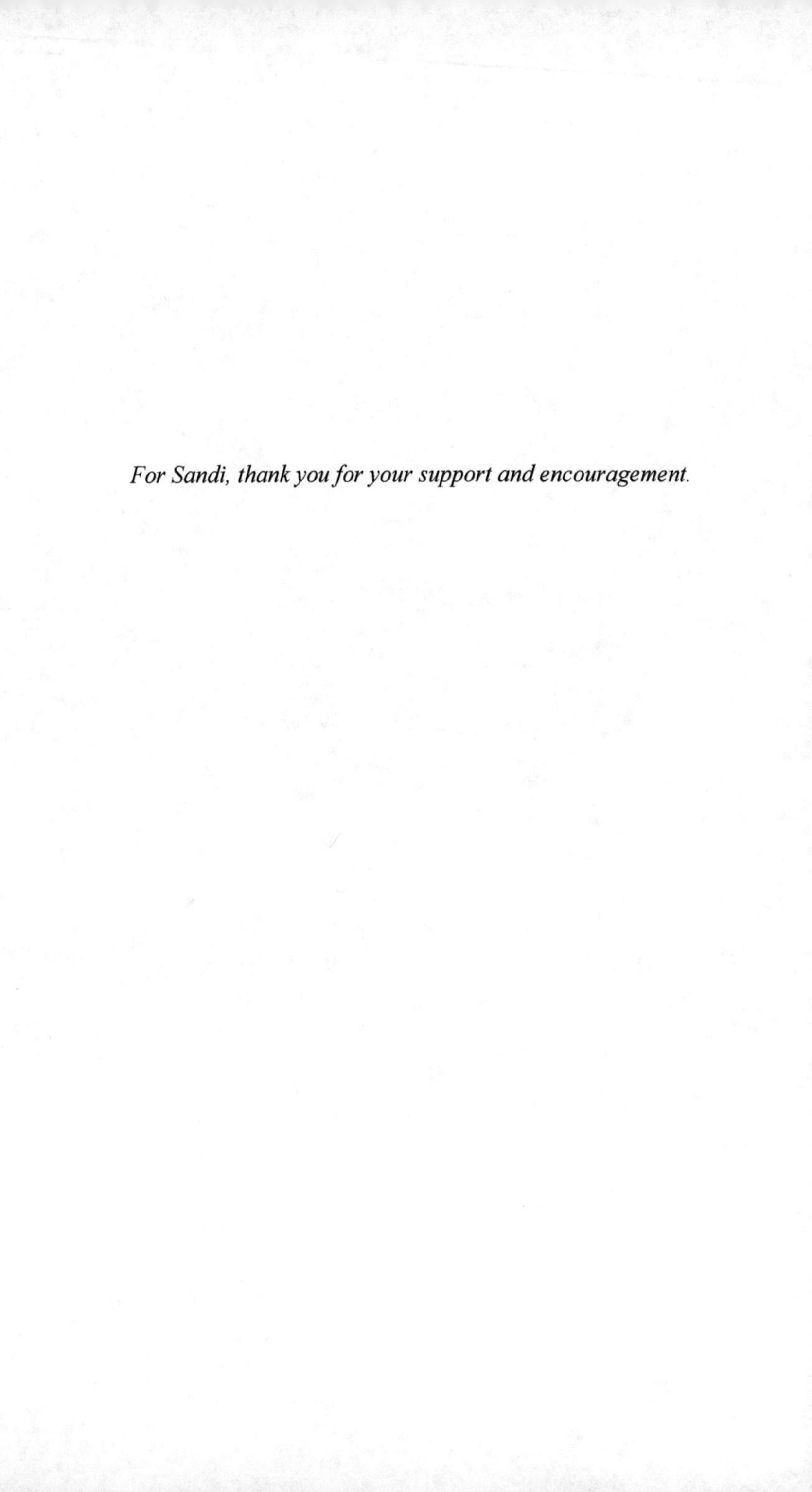

For Sandi, thank you for your support and encouragement.

CHAPTER ONE

The Invitation

The second week of November settled over Mistwood with a quiet, creeping certainty.

Winter had arrived early. A thin crust of frost glazed the surface of Mistwood Lake, catching the pale morning light and turning the water into a sheet of dull silver. Along the far shore, pine trees stood dark and still, their branches dusted with the season's first snow. Higher up, the mountains wore a heavier coat, white clinging to their ridges and pooling in the shadows of the slopes that would soon be crowded with skiers.

In town, the change was already underway. Pickup trucks rolled past the main street cafe, their beds loaded with lumber and equipment bound for the mountains. Construction crews leaned out of open windows, shouting over engines as they headed toward North Star Summit to finish last-minute repairs before the season opened. Ski instructors, identifiable by their bright jackets and easy confidence, drifted back into town after months away, bringing with them the restless energy of a place on the verge of transformation.

Locals moved with purpose. They stocked shelves, hauled firewood, and double-checked furnace systems that had sat idle through the warmer months. The grocery store saw a steady stream of customers filling carts with canned goods, flour, and enough coffee to survive a siege.

Conversations lingered in aisles and on sidewalks, all circling back to the same topic.

Snow was coming. More than this. Soon.

At the edge of town, March House stood warm and welcoming against the chill.

Once a quiet bed-and-breakfast with a reputation for creaky floors and odd drafts, it had taken on new life over the past month. Light spilled from its solarium, golden and inviting, and the faint curl of steam rising from its chimney hinted at heat and activity within.

Inside, the coffee shop was already in full swing. The hiss of the espresso machine cut through the hum of conversation, followed by the sharp knock of a portafilter against metal. The rich scent of coffee mingled with cinnamon and butter, drifting through the space and wrapping itself around every customer who stepped inside.

Every table was occupied. Locals clustered near the solarium windows, mugs in hand, watching the lake as if it might change again while they looked away. A pair of construction workers argued quietly over blueprints spread across a small, round table. Two ski instructors compared notes about the condition of the slopes, their voices low but animated.

Behind the counter, Emma Carter moved with practiced efficiency. She had taken to the job as if she had been born into it. Orders were called, drinks assembled, and pastries plated with a speed that kept the line from growing too long. Her dark hair was pulled back, not a strand out of place, and her expression remained focused even as she balanced three tasks at once.

"Two lattes, one extra hot, one with oat milk," she called, already reaching for the cups before the words had fully left her mouth.

Jessica Alvarez worked beside her, slower but no less capable. Where Emma was precise, Jess was expressive. She leaned over each cup with careful attention, coaxing delicate designs into the foam. A swirl became a leaf, then a feather, then something that might have been a small, abstract bird if one tilted their head just right.

"Art takes time," Jess muttered under her breath when Emma shot her a look. "People appreciate beauty."

"They appreciate getting their coffee before lunch," Emma replied without missing a beat.

Jess smirked, but handed off the finished drink.

In the kitchen, Olivia wiped her hands on a towel and checked the oven. The second batch of cinnamon rolls had risen perfectly. Their tops were golden and soft. She opened the oven door, and a wave of heat rushed out to meet her, carrying the sweet, comforting scent of sugar and spice.

For a moment, she allowed herself to breathe it in. This was hers. The shop, the kitchen, the rhythm of the morning. It had taken weeks of work, long hours, and more than one moment of doubt, but it was real now. Alive in a way March House had not been in years.

She slid the tray out and set it on the counter, already reaching for the glaze.

"You're going to spoil them," came a voice from behind her.

Olivia didn't turn. "They're cinnamon rolls," she said, pouring the glaze in slow, even lines. "That's the point."

A soft huff answered her. "If you say so. Though I maintain that subtlety is a virtue."

Olivia finally glanced over her shoulder. Sir Alistair stood near the doorway, hands clasped behind his back, his expression one of mild disapproval. His attire remained as immaculate as ever, despite the fact that he had not existed in the physical sense for well over a century.

"Coffee is a barbaric colonial beverage," he added, continuing a conversation he had been having for days.

"You've mentioned," Olivia said. "Several times."

He inclined his head, satisfied.

Near the front of the kitchen, a figure in a beaded dress lounged against the wall, watching the activity with open amusement. "I don't know," Monique said, examining her nails. "I think it's charming. All this fuss over a drink. In my day, we had better things to worry about."

Olivia raised an eyebrow. "You mean prohibition?"

Monique smiled. "Exactly. Much more interesting."

A sudden movement near the back door drew Olivia's attention.

Simon, the Civil War soldier, had taken up position beside it, standing ramrod straight, eyes fixed on the entrance as if expecting an attack at any moment.

"You're blocking the door," Olivia said.

"I am guarding the perimeter," he replied, without looking at her.

"There is no perimeter."

"There is always a perimeter."

Olivia pressed her lips together, fighting the urge to laugh.

"Customers can't see you," she reminded him. "But they can feel the door not opening all the way. Which raises questions."

He hesitated, then shifted a few inches to the side.

It was progress.

Olivia turned back to her work, shaking her head slightly.

"Behave," she added, more out of habit than expectation. The ghosts, for once, seemed inclined to listen.

The morning continued at a steady pace. Orders came and went. Cups clinked. The door opened and closed in a constant rhythm, letting in brief gusts of cold air that vanished almost as quickly as they arrived.

Olivia carried a tray of fresh pastries out to the counter, setting them beside the register just as the bell above the door chimed again.

She glanced up, expecting another regular. Instead, she found herself looking at a delivery driver she didn't recognize.

"Morning," he said, stepping inside and stamping his boots against the mat. "Got something for Olivia March?"

"That's me."

He nodded and reached into his bag, pulling out a single envelope. It was thick, cream-colored, and sealed with a crisp, embossed emblem Olivia didn't immediately recognize.

"Sign here," he said, offering a small electronic pad.

She did, her curiosity already stirring.

"Thanks," the driver added, handing over the envelope before turning back toward the door.

The bell chimed again as he left, and the cold air slipped in behind him before the warmth reclaimed the space.

Olivia turned the envelope over in her hands. Her name was written in neat, formal script.

There was no return address.

"Secret admirer?" Jess called from behind the counter.

"Doubtful," Olivia replied.

She slid a finger beneath the seal and broke it open. Inside, a single folded card waited.

She pulled it free and unfolded it, her eyes scanning the text. North Star Summit Lodge Winter Business Summit Invitation

Her brow lifted slightly as she read on.

The invitation was formal but direct. A three-day summit, hosted at the lodge, was designed for Mistwood business owners whose work depended on the winter tourism season. Meetings, networking opportunities, and presentations from resort management. A chance to connect. To grow. To secure partnerships that could shape the coming months.

Olivia read it twice, slower the second time. Restaurants, hotels, rental shops, tour companies, outfitters. And now, apparently, her bed-and-breakfast and coffee shop.

"Well?" Emma asked, glancing over as she filled another order.

Olivia lowered the card.

"It's from North Star Summit," she said.

Jess leaned in immediately. "Fancy."

"They're hosting a business summit. Three days."

Emma's interest sharpened. "That could be good."

Olivia nodded slowly. It could be more than good. The lodge drew most of the winter traffic in Mistwood. If she could connect with the right people, secure a catering contract, or even just ensure March House became a recommended stop for visitors, it could change everything. The coffee shop was doing well now. But winter would decide whether it lasted.

She looked back at the invitation. Three days at the lodge. Three days away from March House. From the constant presence of voices that only she could hear. From doors that opened when no one touched them. From objects that moved just enough to be noticed if one paid attention. Three days of quiet. The thought settled in her chest with unexpected weight.

"You're going," Jess said, as if it were already decided.

Olivia glanced at her. "I haven't said that."

"You're going." Emma agreed. "This is exactly the kind of opportunity we need."

Olivia looked around the shop. At the crowded tables. The steady line. The life that had taken root here. Then she thought of the mountains. Of the lodge. Of the chance to step away, even for a short while.

"I am," she said, the decision forming as the words left her mouth. "I'm going."

Monique perked up immediately. "A trip? How exciting."

Sir Alistair frowned. "I see no reason to abandon a perfectly functional establishment."

Simon said nothing, but his posture stiffened, as if preparing for a departure.

Olivia folded the invitation and slipped it into her apron pocket. "For three days," she said, mostly to herself. "Everything will be fine for three days."

Emma gave her a reassuring nod. "We've got this."

Jess grinned. "Go. Network. Impress important people."

Olivia smiled, a mix of anticipation and something she couldn't quite name settling beneath it.

Outside, the lake held its fragile layer of ice. The mountains waited. And somewhere beyond them, the lodge stood ready. For the summit. For opportunity. For whatever else might be waiting in the snow.

CHAPTER TWO

Holding Down the Fort

By the time the morning rush eased, March House had settled into that narrow stretch between chaos and calm.

The coffee shop still hummed with life, but it was no longer the frenzied storm of sunrise. The line at the counter had shrunk to a manageable trickle. Conversation drifted through the front rooms in a softer current. Cups clinked against saucers. Chairs scraped lightly across old hardwood floors. Somewhere near the front windows, two retired teachers debated the probability of a hard freeze before Thanksgiving with the solemn intensity of diplomats negotiating a treaty.

Olivia carried the invitation from North Star Summit into the kitchen, where the air was warmer and more fragrant than in the cafe. Butter, coffee, toasted bread, and maple syrup had woven themselves into the walls over the past hour. The big center table was crowded with breakfast trays, folded napkins, and small bowls of jam arranged with the kind of careful precision that suggested Lark had been at work long before dawn.

Lark stood at the counter, slicing strawberries into a ceramic bowl. She had tied her hair up in a loose scarf that managed to look both practical and artistically accidental. Bangles chimed softly against her wrist each time she reached for something. Even in the middle of a busy morning, she moved with her usual effortless grace, as if the kitchen were a stage and she alone knew where every mark had been placed.

"You're late," she said without turning.

Olivia glanced at the clock. "It's ten-thirty."

"Exactly. Tragic."

Olivia set the invitation on the counter beside the fruit bowl. "I was a little busy building a caffeine empire."

Lark looked down at the envelope, then at Olivia. Her eyes brightened at once. "What's that?"

Olivia picked it up and handed it over. "An invitation."

Lark dried her fingers on a towel and opened it with the ceremony usually reserved for royal decrees or very juicy gossip. She scanned the card, then broke into a grin. "Oh, this is perfect."

Olivia leaned back against the worktable, arms folded across her chest. "That was fast."

"It's the mountain," Lark said, as if that explained everything. "It's official. It's exclusive. It involves people in knitwear pretending not to judge each other's business cards. This is Mistwood's version of high society."

Olivia laughed despite herself.

Lark looked up from the invitation. "You're going." It was not phrased as a question.

"I think I should."

"You absolutely should."

Olivia exhaled slowly. "I know it could help the coffee shop and the bed-and-breakfast. If I make the right connections, maybe I can get March House on the list of recommended places for visitors. Maybe even pick up a catering order or two."

Lark gave her a flat look. "Yes, yes, business growth, networking, all very important. I am not arguing that. I am arguing that you have been working nonstop since September, and you need to leave this house before you become one with the kitchen tiles."

Olivia frowned. "That feels dramatic."

Lark set the invitation down and pointed a strawberry knife at her. "You opened the shop in October. Before that, you were trying to save a haunted bed-and-breakfast from financial ruin, solve a murder, and figure out what to do with seven dead people who treat the afterlife like a long-term room rental situation. You need three days away."

Olivia opened her mouth, then closed it.

Unfortunately, Lark was right. Since September, everything in her life had been movement. Renovating. Hiring. Baking. Balancing expenses. Making room for guests. Dodging ghosts. Solving one murder had not exactly led to the quiet life she might once have imagined. If anything, it had made the quiet feel almost suspicious.

Lark smiled, softer now. "Go to the summit. Be impressive. Drink coffee made by other people for a change."

Olivia glanced toward the doorway that led into the cafe. "I'm not sure I trust anyone else to make it."

"That," Lark said, "is exactly why you need the break." She picked up the breakfast tray she had been assembling and added a small vase with one winter berry branch tucked inside. Olivia watched her carry it to the rolling cart, then return for the next one.

On the far side of the room, the ancient dumbwaiter door rattled once, then stilled.

Olivia pretended not to notice. Mostly because she knew exactly who was near it.

"Have you told the others yet?" Lark asked.

"Emma and Jess know."

"And?"

"They think I should go."

"Smart girls."

Olivia moved to the counter and reached for a clean mug, more out of habit than need. "We talked about the cafe already. Emma can handle the morning rush in her sleep. Jess might spend an extra thirty seconds on every cappuccino because she thinks foam is an artistic medium, but the drinks will still get out."

Lark laughed. "The latte leaves are becoming more elaborate."

"Yesterday she made a swan."

"Was it pretty?"

"It was infuriatingly pretty."

"That is a problem."

Olivia filled the mug with coffee from the pot kept warm near the stove and took a cautious sip. Lark started assembling another tray, adding a small pitcher of cream and two neatly folded cloth napkins.

"We'll be fine," Lark said. "Emma can oversee the cafe floor. Jess can manage drinks and keep the regulars entertained with sarcasm. I'll handle the bed-and-breakfast, the kitchen, and the staff."

Olivia raised an eyebrow. "That's all?"

Lark gave a modest shrug. "I do enjoy a light schedule."

Olivia smiled, but the practical side of her mind was already ticking through details. "Mrs. Holcomb in room three wants gluten-free muffins in the mornings. The Petersons keep asking for extra towels even though I'm convinced they're building some kind of private towel fortress upstairs. Mr. Weller likes his eggs with hot sauce, but only the green kind, not the red."

"I know."

"And the espresso machine has been making that odd sound again."

"I know."

"And if the furnace in the east wing starts clanking, it usually stops if you ignore it long enough." Lark paused with a tray in her hands and stared at Olivia with affectionate exasperation. "Darling. Breathe."

Olivia did, though somewhat reluctantly.

Lark set down the tray and stepped closer. "March House was standing before you arrived, even if barely. It will survive three days without you hovering in every room like a worried pastry ghost."

Olivia snorted. "That's rude."

"It's true."

From somewhere near the ceiling came a faint, offended huff.

Olivia glanced up.

Monique had drifted in through the wall near the pantry, her beaded dress shimmering faintly in the kitchen light. She pressed a dramatic hand to her chest and stared at Olivia as if personally betrayed.

"You're leaving?" she demanded.

Olivia closed her eyes for one brief second. There it was. The news had reached them.

Across the room, Simon appeared beside the back door so

abruptly that even Olivia jumped. His expression was grave. His posture was even more rigid than usual.

"For how long?" he asked.

"Three days," Olivia said under her breath.

Sir Alistair materialized near the stove with all the disapproving dignity of a man arriving to witness the collapse of civilization.

"Three days," he repeated. "Utterly reckless."

Lark, who had not seen or heard any of this, froze in the middle of reaching for a spoon.

Then she looked toward Olivia with resigned amusement. "Your invisible friends upset again?"

Olivia sighed into her coffee. "Very."

The air in the kitchen had shifted. Lark could not see them, but she could sense the difference. A subtle pressure settled over the room, as if the atmosphere had tightened a notch. The little hairs on Olivia's arms lifted in warning.

"Who started it?" Lark asked.

"The usual suspects."

Monique swept closer. "Abandonment in November. Honestly, if you were going to forsake us, spring would have been more flattering."

"I am not forsaking anyone."

"You are leaving the house. Voluntarily."

"It's a business summit."

Sir Alistair made a sound of pure disdain. "The household will collapse into anarchy."

"That seems unlikely."

"Without proper leadership?" he said. "Disaster is inevitable."

Simon frowned toward the windows. "Who will secure the premises?"

Olivia lowered her mug. "No one is storming the coffee shop."

"That is exactly what someone planning to storm the coffee shop would want us to believe."

Lark rubbed her hands together as if trying to shake off the static in the room. "Tell them I said the house is under control."

"They don't take orders from the living."

"That feels deeply unfair."

"It does."

Monique drifted toward the breakfast trays and peered at a bowl of grapes. “Well, I, for one feel wounded.”

“You don’t even eat.”

“That is not the point.”

Olivia pinched the bridge of her nose. “I am going away for three days, not sailing off to another continent.”

Sir Alistair looked unconvinced. “These things escalate.”

“Nothing is escalating.”

Something thumped lightly in the front hall.

Olivia glanced toward the sound, then frowned. “Please tell me nobody moved my keys again.”

Lark looked toward the doorway. “I didn’t.”

Olivia set down her mug and walked into the hall.

March House greeted her with familiar layers of sound and stillness. The inaudible murmur from the cafe drifted in from the front parlor. A grandfather clock ticked solemnly in the corner. Sunlight from the tall windows stretched across the patterned runner that led to the front door.

Her keys lay on the small table by the entrance. At least, they were supposed to. Instead, they lay on the floor beside it.

Olivia bent to pick them up. The worn leather keychain brushed her palm, along with the familiar weight of the car key attached to it.

From behind her, Lark said, “Are you planning to take Gus up the mountain?”

Olivia straightened and turned. “That was a remarkably loaded question.”

Lark leaned against the doorframe, arms folded. “I’m asking because North Star Summit is a mountain resort in November. There will be snow. Possibly ice. Probably tourists who believe all-wheel drive is a substitute for judgment.”

Olivia held up the keys. “Gus has survived worse.”

A smile tugged at Lark’s mouth. “That is true.”

Together they looked through the front window toward the gravel drive. Parked beside March House sat Izzy’s old Subaru Outback, dark green and perpetually dusted with either pine needles, road grit, or a fine coating of weather that never seemed to wash off completely. It was not pretty. It had long since moved past charming and settled comfortably into stubborn usefulness.

Gus. Reliable, loud in odd places, and somehow always a little damp-smelling after rain.

Olivia had driven it often enough by now that the quirks no longer surprised her. The driver's side window stuck in cold weather. The heater took a full five minutes to decide whether it wanted to participate in civilized society. The rear hatch occasionally required a second, firmer slam to close properly.

But it ran. It always ran.

Lark smiled as she followed Olivia's gaze. "Izzy named it Augustus, you know."

"I did wonder."

"She said it deserved a proper name because it had more character than most men she dated."

Olivia laughed. "That sounds like her."

"He's survived three winters, two blizzards, and that time Mrs. Henley backed into the mailbox."

Olivia winced. "I heard about that."

"You heard the polite version. The actual story involved a casserole, a corgi, and language unbecoming of a church treasurer."

Olivia slipped the keys into her pocket. "Then yes. I'm taking Gus."

Lark nodded approvingly. "Good. He knows the roads."

From behind them, Sir Alistair drifted into the hall and peered out at the Subaru with open suspicion. "That conveyance appears unsound."

"It's a car," Olivia said.

"It appears to be held together by resignation."

"It's held together by routine maintenance and grit."

Monique floated past him and gave the Subaru a thoughtful look. "I don't hate the color."

Simon emerged behind them all, his eyes narrowing at the driveway as though evaluating battlefield conditions. "Can it withstand a siege?"

Olivia turned. "Why does everything become a siege with you?"

He considered that. "Preparedness."

Before she could answer, the bell above the front door gave a sharp little jingle. A gust of cold air swept in.

Olivia looked up.

Luke Thatcher stepped inside, one hand on the door, the other shoved into the pocket of his jacket. He had that same guarded, slightly tired expression he always seemed to wear, as if the world insisted on disappointing him before breakfast and he had learned to plan accordingly.

He shut the door behind him and stamped the snow off his boots. His gaze moved from Olivia to Lark to the general, warm clutter of the house. "Morning."

"Deputy," Lark said brightly, with the exact tone she used when greeting delivery people, guests, or suspiciously attractive interruptions.

Luke ignored that and looked at Olivia. "Thought I'd check in."

Olivia crossed her arms. "On what?"

"Things."

"That's vague."

He shrugged. "After the last case, figured I should make sure nothing around here had caught fire, exploded, or turned into a crime scene."

Lark made a thoughtful noise. "And here I assumed you wanted coffee."

Luke's expression did not change, which told Olivia Lark was absolutely correct.

"I can check on things and want coffee," he said.

"That seems ambitious," Olivia replied.

His eyes shifted to the invitation still in Lark's hand, then to Olivia's pocket where the keys had just disappeared. A small duffel bag sat near the foot of the stairs, half-packed with sweaters and practical boots.

"You going somewhere?" he asked.

Olivia had the immediate, irrational urge to answer no simply to annoy him. Instead, she said, "North Star Summit."

His brow lifted. "The lodge?"

"They invited local business owners to a winter summit."

"For how long?"

"Three days."

For a brief second, something close to amusement touched his face. "You're voluntarily attending a networking event?"

Olivia gave him a flat look. "Try not to sound so shocked."

"I'm working on it."

Lark slipped neatly past them toward the cafe. "I'll get your coffee before you two start fencing with the kitchen knives."

"We're not fencing," Olivia called after her.

"Yet," Lark answered back.

Luke watched her disappear, then looked back at Olivia. "What are you driving up there?"

"Why?"

"General concern for public safety."

She narrowed her eyes. "Gus."

For the first time that morning, Luke actually smirked. "That thing still runs?"

Olivia smiled sweetly. "It runs better than your truck."

His smirk deepened. "Bold claim."

"It's true."

"My truck starts every morning."

"So does Gus."

"Does he also sound like a haunted farm implement climbing hills?"

Olivia tilted her head. "Interesting criticism from a man whose vehicle rattles every time it hits a pothole."

"That's character."

"That's neglect."

He opened his mouth to argue, then stopped, probably because Lark returned with a steaming cup and handed it to him before the debate could grow teeth.

Luke nodded his thanks, then took a sip. His expression changed by a fraction, enough for Olivia to recognize actual pleasure.

"Worth the trip?" she asked.

He gave her a sidelong glance. "Don't make this weird."

"Too late."

He looked toward the packed bag near the stairs, then back at her.

"For once," he said, "you might manage to avoid a dead body."

Olivia stared at him.

“What a lovely thing to say to someone heading into the mountains.”

“It’s optimism.”

“It’s rude optimism.”

He took another sip of coffee, entirely unrepentant. “You do have a track record.”

“I solved one murder.”

“You found it first.”

“I did not find it first. I was merely present.”

“You are present an awful lot when bad things happen.”

Olivia leaned one shoulder against the wall. “Then it should comfort you to know I plan to spend three full days minding my own business, meeting polite people, and discussing coffee service with resort managers.”

Luke’s eyes held hers a moment longer than necessary. “I’ll believe that when I see it.”

“Well, prepare to be dazzled.”

A silence settled between them, not awkward exactly, but edged with the familiar friction that seemed to spark every time they stood too close for too long.

From the staircase behind Olivia came the faint sound of someone clearing an invisible throat. She did not turn. The ghosts had, of course, gathered to witness this.

Monique lounged halfway up the stairs, looking delighted. Sir Alistair hovered near the newel post with the expression of a man attending theater of questionable quality. Bertie lay on the floor next to him, licking his paw.

Simon stood behind them both, still apparently concerned about the safety of the premises and now, perhaps, Olivia’s ability to travel without stumbling into homicide. Snowball sat beside him, flicking her tail.

Upstairs along the second-floor railing, Daisy, Flossie, JJ, and Walt were staring at Olivia with varying expressions of concern.

Lark, mercifully unaware of the audience, looked between Olivia and Luke with quiet amusement. “I’m sure everything will go smoothly.”

Luke lifted his coffee. “That makes one of us.”

Olivia pushed away from the wall. "It will be fine." She meant it. She wanted to mean it.

Three days at a winter business summit. Three days of meetings, resort chatter, and people whose biggest concern was occupancy rates and early-season reservations. Three days away from house ghosts, daily crisis management, and the strange heaviness that sometimes settled over Mistwood when the past refused to stay buried.

It sounded blissfully ordinary. And yet, standing there in the front hall of March House with Luke drinking coffee, Lark smiling knowingly, and eight dead spectators and a cat judging her travel plans, Olivia felt the faintest tug of unease. Not fear. Nothing so dramatic. Just the familiar sense that life in Mistwood rarely stayed simple for long.

She ignored it. Or tried to. Because the summit was an excellent opportunity. Because the cafe needed it. Because Lark was right, and she could not keep working herself into the ground. Because even if the ghosts acted as though she were abandoning them to wolves and social decline, the truth was plain. March House would be fine. The cafe would be fine. The world would continue turning without her for three days.

Luke set down his empty cup on the hall table and nodded toward the bag. "When do you leave?"

"Tomorrow morning."

He gave a brief nod, then headed for the door. At the threshold, he paused and looked back, eyes settling on Olivia again. "Try not to make trouble."

She gave him her driest smile. "I never make trouble."

He let out a breath that might have been a laugh. "That's not even remotely true."

Then he stepped outside into the cold, the door shutting behind him with a firm click.

The hall felt warmer once he was gone, though not quieter.

Monique drifted down two stairs and sighed dramatically. "He likes you."

Olivia groaned. "Please don't start."

Sir Alistair lifted his chin. "The man has poor posture and insufficient respect for silence."

"That," Olivia said, "is somehow worse."

Lark tilted her head. "Did one of them say something especially ridiculous?"

"All of them," Olivia said.

Lark smiled. "Then everything is normal."

Normal. In Mistwood, that word had become wonderfully flexible.

Olivia slipped a hand into her pocket and closed her fingers around Gus's keys. Tomorrow she'd drive up the mountain. She would leave March House in capable hands. She would attend the summit, talk business, and come home with new contacts and no complications.

That was the plan. And plans, she told herself, were still allowed to work. Even here.

CHAPTER THREE

The Drive to North Star Summit

Morning came to Mistwood with a pale, brittle light. The frost had thickened overnight.

Mistwood Lake no longer looked like water at all, but a dull mirror edged in white, the surface locked beneath a thin, fragile crust that would not hold weight but hinted at what was coming.

The trees along the shoreline stood stiff and silent, their branches traced in silver. Above them, the mountains rose in layered shadows, their higher slopes fully claimed by snow.

It was colder than the day before. The kind of cold that settled into wood and stone and refused to leave.

Olivia stepped out onto the front porch of March House and pulled her coat tighter around her. The air bit at her cheeks, sharp enough to wake her fully in a single breath. Behind her, the house hummed with early morning life. Voices drifted faintly from the cafe. Dishes clinked in the kitchen. Somewhere upstairs, a guest's footsteps crossed a creaking floorboard.

Normal. As normal as things ever were. She glanced back once before heading down the steps.

Lark stood just inside the doorway, a dish towel draped over one shoulder, watching her with a small, satisfied smile.

Emma moved behind the counter in the cafe, already managing the morning orders. Jess leaned over a cup, coaxing foam into another elaborate design that would take too long and still make people happy.

They had it handled. Olivia told herself that again as she crossed the gravel drive.

Gus waited where he always did. The dark green Subaru Outback looked exactly as it had the day before. Slightly weathered. Slightly stubborn. Entirely dependable. A dusting of frost coated the windshield, catching the morning light in a dull shimmer.

Olivia scraped it away with a sturdy, long-handled scraper, then opened the rear hatch.

Her overnight bag went in easily. It landed beside a collection of items that had long since taken up permanent residence in the cargo area. Boxes of baking supplies sat stacked along one side, labeled in a neat handwriting that still belonged to Izzy. Flour. Sugar. Baking soda. Things that had once been essential for a bed-and-breakfast that had run at full capacity through every season.

A folded pile of spare blankets rested beside them, thick and worn, the kind meant for emergencies or unexpected guests. Near the back corner, a canvas bag filled with coffee beans gave off a faint, rich scent that clung to the air even in the cold.

Olivia paused, one hand resting on the edge of the hatch.

Izzy had prepared for everything. Even now, months later, the car still carried the evidence of it. A life built around readiness. Around making sure no guest went without what they needed.

Olivia closed the hatch gently. "I'm just borrowing him," she murmured, more to the memory than anything else.

Gus, as expected, had no opinion.

She climbed into the driver's seat and shut the door. The interior greeted her with the familiar scent of coffee, old upholstery, and something faintly pine-scented that had never quite faded. The key turned in the ignition with a slight resistance, then the engine caught with a low, steady rumble.

Reliable. Always reliable.

Olivia adjusted the rearview mirror, glanced once more at March House, and pulled out onto the road.

Mistwood slipped past her in quiet increments. The main street was already awake. A few shops had opened their doors, their windows glowing against the cold. A delivery truck idled near the bakery. A pair of locals stood outside the hardware store, hands wrapped around coffee cups as they discussed the weather with the gravity it deserved.

Snow was coming. Everyone knew it.

Olivia drove past the last row of buildings and onto the road that curved toward the mountain.

The town fell away behind her. The road began its slow climb almost immediately.

Pines crowded closer on either side, their trunks dark against the pale ground. Patches of early snow clung to the shaded areas, tucked into dips and hollows where the sun had not yet reached. The higher she drove, the more frequent it became, until the edges of the road were lined in white.

Gus handled it without complaint. The engine held steady. The tires gripped the pavement with quiet confidence. The slight incline did nothing to slow him.

Olivia rested her hands lightly on the wheel, her eyes following the curve of the road as it wound upward.

When she'd first arrived in Mistwood, she had not trusted this car.

It had seemed too old. Too worn. Too prone to making odd noises at inconvenient times. The first time she had driven it up this road, she had expected something to go wrong. A sputter. A stall. A moment where the engine would simply give up and leave her stranded halfway to nowhere. It never had. Instead, it had carried her through rain, through mud, through one particularly miserable evening when the road had turned slick and treacherous without warning. The all-wheel drive had caught where it needed to catch. The tires had held. More than once, it had done exactly what she needed when she needed it.

Olivia reached forward and tapped the dashboard lightly. "Don't let it go to your head."

Gus did not respond.

The heater, on the other hand, made its opinion known. It rattled to life with a sound that suggested deep personal offense, then sputtered as if reconsidering its role in the day's events. For a few seconds, nothing happened at all. Then, with a reluctant wheeze, warm air began to push through the vents.

Olivia smiled despite herself. “Good,” she said. “We’re cooperating today.”

The road curved again, steeper this time. Through a break in the trees, Mistwood Lake came into view far below. From this height, the thin ice across its surface looked more solid, a pale expanse stretching between the dark shoreline. The town itself appeared small. Quiet. Tucked into its place as if it had always been there and always would be.

Olivia held the view for a moment, then returned her attention to the road. The climb continued. The trees thinned as she neared the top of the ridge. Snow gathered more heavily here, clinging to branches and piling along the roadside in uneven drifts. The air felt different. Sharper. Cleaner.

Then, as the road rounded one last bend, the lodge came into view. North Star Summit Lodge rose from the ridge with an almost imposing presence. Massive timber beams framed the structure, dark wood set against stone that seemed to have been pulled straight from the mountain itself. The roof stretched wide and high, built to bear the weight of heavy snowfall without complaint. Large windows lined the front, catching the light and reflecting the landscape beyond. Smoke curled from the chimneys.

A wide set of steps led up to the main entrance, flanked by heavy wooden railings worn smooth by years of use.

To the right, the ski slopes spread out in long, open lines, the lifts already in place, cables stretching up the mountain like thin, deliberate threads. Even now, before the full season had begun, a few figures moved along the lower runs, testing equipment, preparing for what was to come.

To the left, the land dropped away, revealing a sweeping view of Mistwood Lake far below.

It was the kind of place built to impress. And it did.

Olivia slowed as she approached the parking area. It was already half-full. Trucks and SUVs lined the gravel lot, their tires marked with mud and early snow. A few vehicles bore the logos of local businesses. Others were unmarked but clearly well-used, the kind that belonged to people who spent more time outdoors than in.

She guided Gus into an open space near the edge of the lot and shifted into park. For a moment, she sat there. The engine idled quietly. The heater continued its uneven battle with the cold. Outside, the air moved in faint, visible currents.

Olivia reached forward and rested her hand on the steering wheel. "You've done your part," she said. "Don't start any trouble while I'm gone."

Gus, as expected, remained silent.

She gathered her bag, opened the door, and stepped out into the cold.

It hit her harder here. The wind moved more freely at the top of the ridge, carrying the scent of snow and pine. It tugged at her coat and slipped beneath her scarf, sharp enough to remind her she was no longer in the relative shelter of town. She shut the door and headed toward the lodge.

The heavy wooden doors opened easily under her hand. Warmth rushed out to meet her.

Inside, the lodge was even more impressive. The main room stretched wide, anchored by a massive stone fireplace that dominated one wall. Flames crackled within it, casting a steady, golden light across the space. Thick wooden beams crossed the ceiling overhead. Comfortable chairs and low tables were arranged in clusters, already occupied by people deep in conversation.

The air smelled of wood smoke, coffee, and something faintly spiced.

Voices carried easily. Laughter rose and fell. It was busy, but not chaotic. Organized.

Purposeful.

Olivia stepped inside and let the door close behind her.

Almost immediately, someone approached. "Welcome," the man said, extending a hand. "You must be Olivia March."

She shook it. "That's me."

"Gerald Huxley," he said. "Owner of North Star Summit." He carried himself with quiet confidence, the kind that came from long familiarity with the place he stood in. His handshake was firm. His smile was practiced, but not insincere.

"Glad you could make it," he added. "We're looking forward to having March House represented."

"Thank you for the invitation."

He nodded, then gestured toward the room. "We're gathering

everyone for introductions shortly. Make yourself comfortable. Meet a few people."

Olivia inclined her head. "I will." He moved on to greet someone else, leaving her to take in the space. She had not gone far before another voice caught her attention.

"Olivia, right?"

She turned.

A woman in a tailored coat approached, her posture straight, her expression composed.

"Cindy Keller," she said. "Mistwood Lake Hotel."

Olivia recognized the name. "Nice to meet you."

"We've heard good things about your coffee shop."

Olivia smiled. "I hope they're true."

"They are," Cindy said. "We may need to talk about referrals. Guests are always looking for places in town."

"That would be great."

Another man joined them, broad-shouldered and dressed in layers suited for outdoor work.

"Mason Reed," he said. "Outfitter."

"Olivia."

He nodded. "You do food?"

"Coffee, pastries. Some catering."

"Good," he said. "People come off the mountain starving. We send them to the local restaurants. It's better if we know special places to send them."

"Then we should definitely talk."

A woman with a bright scarf and a quick smile stepped into the conversation next.

"Darla Bishop," she said. "Snowmobile tours."

"Olivia."

"Coffee is essential to my business," Darla said. "Cold tourists are terrible tippers."

Olivia laughed. "Then I will do my best to keep them warm."

"Please do."

A final voice joined them, quieter but no less steady.

"Tom Granger. Ski rentals."

Olivia shook his hand as well. "Nice to meet you."

He nodded. "We get a lot of beginners. They spend half the

morning falling down. By afternoon, they need somewhere to recover."

"I can help with that."

"Good."

The group shifted as conversations branched and reformed, introductions continuing around her. Olivia moved with it, listening, speaking, and taking mental notes. Names. Faces. Businesses. Connections that might matter later.

It was working. Already, she could see the potential in it. Then, just as she stepped slightly away from the group to catch her breath, she noticed someone standing near the edge of the room. A woman, perhaps in her thirties, held a notebook close to her chest. She was not speaking to anyone. Not really. Her attention drifted around the room, not in the casual way of someone observing, but with a sharper edge. As if she were looking for something specific and not finding it.

Olivia hesitated, then approached. "Hi," she said. "I don't think we've met yet."

The woman turned, startled just enough to be noticeable. "Oh," she said. "No. Sorry. I was just …" She trailed off, then gave a quick, slightly distracted smile. "I'm Cassie. Cassie Greer."

"Olivia March."

Recognition flickered in Cassie's eyes. "March House?"

"That's me."

Cassie said. "The bed-and-breakfast and the coffee shop."

Olivia nodded. "You're here for the summit?"

Cassie shifted her notebook slightly. "Sort of. I'm actually attending on behalf of the historical society."

Olivia tilted her head. "Really?"

Cassie nodded. "I teach history at Mistwood High. The society asked if I could sit in, take notes, and that kind of thing. I've been researching the resort. The mountain. Its early development." Her voice carried a thread of enthusiasm, but something beneath it felt off. Tight.

As if her attention were divided.

"That sounds interesting," Olivia said.

"It is," Cassie replied quickly. "There's a lot that people don't realize about this place. Things that get ... forgotten." She stopped herself, her expression shifting. "Anyway," she added, too lightly. "It's good to meet you."

Olivia studied her for a moment.

Cassie's smile was present, but it did not quite reach her eyes. Her grip on the notebook was too firm. Her gaze flicked past Olivia once, twice, toward the far side of the room. Looking.

Checking.

"Are you okay?" Olivia asked.

Cassie blinked, as if pulled back from somewhere else. "Yes," she said. "Of course. Just ... a lot going on."

Olivia nodded slowly. "Right. First day."

"Exactly." But even as she said it, Cassie glanced over Olivia's shoulder again, her attention snagging on something unseen. Or someone.

Olivia followed the movement instinctively, but saw nothing out of the ordinary. Just more guests. More conversations. The steady, warm life of the lodge. When she looked back, Cassie had already composed herself.

"I should go find my seat," she said. "They're about to start."

"Of course."

"It was nice meeting you."

"You too."

Cassie moved away, slipping into the growing crowd.

Olivia watched her go, a faint unease settling in her chest. Something was bothering her.

Not nerves. Not exactly. Something sharper. Something that did not belong in a room full of business owners discussing winter schedules and tourism numbers.

Olivia let out a quiet breath and turned back toward the center of the lodge. The summit had begun. And already, something felt just slightly off.

CHAPTER FOUR

Questions About the Mountain

The conference room at North Star Summit Lodge smelled faintly of coffee, pine cleaner, and damp wool. Olivia slipped into her seat near the middle of the long table, notebook in front of her, pen poised but idle. Around her, the room filled with the low hum of small-town business politics. Voices overlapped. Chairs scraped. Someone laughed too loudly at something that was not particularly funny.

Through the tall windows lining one wall, the mountain stretched out in a sweep of white and shadow. Snow clung to the pines in thick layers, bending branches under its weight. The ski lifts moved steadily in the distance, carrying early riders up the slope in a slow, silent procession.

Inside, it was warm enough to shed coats. Most had not. At the head of the table, Cindy Keller stood and tapped a pen lightly against a clipboard. "All right, everyone," she said, her voice bright and practiced. "Let's get started."

The room settled. Olivia straightened slightly, shifting her attention forward.

Cindy launched into the agenda with the efficiency of someone who had done this many times before. "Winter tourism projections are strong this year. Bookings are up compared to last season. We want to build on that momentum. The goal of this summit is to strengthen partnerships between the lodge and local businesses."

There were nods all around the table.

Olivia listened, absorbing the rhythm of the conversation. Marketing packages. Shuttle routes from town. Coordinated promotions between the lodge, the ski rental shop, and the restaurants along Main Street.

It was familiar territory. Structured. Logical. Manageable. Safe. She relaxed slightly and began taking notes.

Across from her, Gerald Huxley leaned back in his chair, arms crossed over his chest. He had the air of a man who believed he already knew how things should be done and was waiting for everyone else to catch up.

"Transportation is still the weak point," he said, cutting into Cindy's explanation. "People don't want to drive up the mountain in bad weather. We need more reliable shuttle service."

"Agreed," Cindy said smoothly. "We've been in talks with—"

"We've been in talks for three years," Huxley interrupted. "At some point, we need results."

A few people shifted uncomfortably.

Olivia glanced between them, noting the tension but saying nothing.

Cindy pressed on.

"We are making progress. In the meantime, we can focus on enhancing the experience once guests arrive. That's where our local partners come in."

She gestured toward the group. "This is where ideas matter. Food, events, atmosphere. We want guests to stay longer, spend more, and come back."

Olivia hesitated, then lifted her hand slightly.

Cindy nodded toward her. "Yes, Olivia?"

All eyes turned.

Olivia cleared her throat. "I run the March House Bed and Breakfast," she said. "We've seen a lot of guests who want something warm and simple when they come off the mountain. Coffee, pastries, something quick but high quality." She paused, choosing her words carefully.

"You could set up small coffee stands near the lifts. Not just vending machines. Something curated. Fresh baked goods. Local branding. It gives people a reason to linger instead of rushing back inside."

There was a moment of consideration. Then a few nods.

"That's a good idea," someone said.

"Especially for early morning runs," another added.

Cindy smiled. "I like that. We could coordinate with local bakeries and cafes."

Olivia felt a small flicker of satisfaction.

Huxley grunted, but he did not object.

Encouraged, Olivia continued.

"And catering," she said. "If you're hosting events up here, you could partner with businesses in town instead of bringing everything in-house. It spreads the economic benefits and builds stronger ties."

Cindy made a note. "Excellent point."

The conversation shifted, building on the idea. Logistics. Vendor lists. Seasonal menus.

For a while, it was exactly what Olivia expected the summit to be. Structured. Productive.

Normal.

Then Cassie Greer raised her hand.

Olivia glanced toward her.

Cassie sat a few seats down, posture straight, expression intent. She had been quiet until now, listening with a focus that felt sharper than the rest of the room.

Cindy acknowledged her. "Cassie?"

Cassie folded her hands on the table.

"I have a question," she said.

Her tone was calm, but there was an edge beneath it. Something deliberate.

"It's related to the property itself."

A few people exchanged glances.

Cindy hesitated, then nodded. "Go ahead."

Cassie looked directly at Gerald Huxley. "I've been reviewing some historical records about the land this resort sits on," she said. "I'm curious about the original deeds. Specifically, the boundaries established when the property was first developed."

The room shifted. It was subtle. A tightening. A pause in the air.

Huxley's expression hardened almost imperceptibly. "That's not relevant to tourism planning," he said.

Cassie did not look away. "I think it might be," she replied. "Understanding the history of the land could affect how we present it. There's a story here. People are interested in authenticity."

"That story has already been established," Huxley said, his voice clipped. "This resort was built in the late 1940s. End of discussion."

Cassie tilted her head slightly. "Built, yes," she said. "But the land itself has a longer history. There were transfers before that. Some of them … unusual."

A murmur rippled through the room.

Olivia felt a prickle at the back of her neck.

Cindy stepped in quickly. "Cassie, perhaps we can take that offline—"

"I'd prefer to discuss it here," Cassie said. Her voice remained steady, but the insistence in it was unmistakable. "I'm particularly interested in the original land transfer in the 1940s. There are gaps in the records."

Huxley's chair scraped against the floor as he leaned forward. "There are no gaps," he said.

"There are," Cassie replied. "Several documents are missing. And the boundaries listed in the early filings don't match the current maps."

The room had gone very still.

Olivia glanced around.

People were not just uncomfortable. They were alert. Watching.

Cindy forced a smile. "Historical discrepancies aren't uncommon in older records—"

"These aren't minor discrepancies," Cassie said. She leaned forward slightly. "They suggest that the land may not have been acquired legally."

The words landed like a stone dropped into deep water. Silence spread outward from the center of the table.

Huxley's face darkened. "That's a serious accusation," he said.

"I'm asking a question," Cassie replied.

"No," Huxley said. "You're implying wrongdoing."

"I'm asking for clarification."

"You're disrupting a professional meeting."

Cassie did not flinch. "People deserve to know the truth about this mountain." The sentence hung in the air.

Olivia felt it settle somewhere deep in her chest. Truth about this mountain. It sounded less like a question and more like a warning.

Cindy stepped in again, more firmly this time. "All right," she said. "That's enough. This meeting is about tourism development, not historical investigations."

Cassie's gaze flicked to her, then back to Huxley. "We can't separate the two," she whispered.

"Yes, we can," Cindy replied. "And we will."

Huxley pushed his chair back. "This line of questioning is inappropriate," he said. "If there are concerns, they can be addressed through the proper channels. Not here."

Cassie's jaw tightened. "For over eighty years, no one has addressed it," she said.

The room tensed again.

Huxley stood. "This discussion is over." He did not raise his voice, but the authority in it was absolute.

Cindy nodded quickly. "Let's move on."

But no one moved. The energy in the room had shifted. What had been a routine meeting now felt brittle, as though something had cracked beneath the surface.

Cassie sat back slowly, her expression controlled, but frustration flickered in her eyes.

Olivia watched her, trying to read what lay beneath that calm exterior. This was not a casual question. Cassie had come prepared. And she had expected resistance.

Cindy cleared her throat. "Let's return to the agenda," she said. "We still have several items to cover."

The conversation resumed, but it lacked the earlier ease. The voices were quieter now. More cautious. People avoided looking directly at Cassie.

Huxley remained standing for a moment, then sat again, his posture rigid.

Olivia made a few notes, but her attention kept drifting. Something was wrong. Not just in the conversation, but with the reaction. If Cassie had asked an irrelevant question, it would have been dismissed, redirected, or ignored. Redirected. Ignored. This had not been ignored. It had been shut down.

Forcefully.

Olivia's gaze moved around the room again.

Cindy was speaking, her voice steady, but her smile felt strained.

Huxley stared straight ahead.

A man near the end of the table avoided eye contact entirely.

Two women exchanged a brief glance, then looked away quickly.

Cassie sat very still, her hands folded again, but her fingers tapped once against the table. A small, controlled movement, frustration, and determination.

Olivia leaned back slightly, her mind turning. People deserve to know the truth about this mountain. The words echoed. Truth about what? And why did everyone in this room look like they already knew?

The rest of the meeting passed in a blur of logistics and half-hearted discussion.

Ideas were offered. Notes were taken. But the energy never recovered.

When Cindy finally adjourned the session, chairs scraped back quickly. Conversations resumed in low voices, but they felt guarded now, fragmented.

Olivia closed her notebook and stood. As she gathered her things, she caught Cassie's eye. For a brief moment, something passed between them, Recognition, understanding.

Cassie knew she had noticed. Olivia hesitated, then stepped toward her. "Hey," she whispered.

Cassie looked up.

"You're Olivia March," she said. It was not a question.

Olivia nodded. "I am."

Cassie studied her for a moment, then gave a small, almost wry smile. "You're like your aunt," she said.

Olivia blinked, surprised. "You knew Izzy?"

"Everyone knew Izzy," Cassie said. "She paid attention. That's rare."

Olivia felt a flicker of warmth at that. "She did," she said.

Cassie's expression shifted, becoming more serious. "Be careful," she added.

Olivia frowned. "About what?"

Cassie glanced around the room, then leaned in slightly. "People don't like questions," she said. "Not the right ones."

Olivia's pulse ticked up. "And those were the right ones?" she asked.

Cassie held her gaze. "Yes." There was no hesitation in the answer.

Olivia swallowed. "What are you looking for?" she asked.

Cassie straightened, her expression closing slightly. "The truth," she said. Then, softer, almost to herself: "It's been buried long enough."

Before Olivia could respond, Cassie turned and walked away.

Olivia stood there for a moment, watching her go. Olivia glanced toward the windows.

Outside, the mountain stood silent and still. Snow drifted gently from the sky, soft and harmless on the surface. But beneath it, something was hidden. Something people did not want uncovered.

Olivia closed her notebook slowly. Questions about the mountain.

Cassie had asked them out loud.

And now Olivia could not stop hearing them. Nor could she ignore the way the room had reacted. Whatever truth lay buried here, it was not just history. It was something people were still afraid of. And that, she knew, was never a good sign.

CHAPTER FIVE

The Old Medal

By evening, North Star Summit Lodge had changed personalities. During the day, it had been all business: clipboards and coffee. Forced smiles around a conference table while old tensions slithered beneath polished words. At night, the lodge turned theatrical. Lamps glowed low against knotty pine walls. The great stone fireplace in the lobby threw honey-colored light across rugs woven in red and black geometric patterns. Guests drifted through the public rooms, wine glasses in hand, voices softened by the hour and the weather pressing close outside.

Snow tapped against the tall windows in a steady whisper.

Olivia stepped out of the elevator and paused at the end of the second-floor hall, one hand curled around the belt of her cardigan. She had changed after dinner into dark jeans, boots, and a cream sweater that still carried the faint scent of cinnamon from the kitchen at March House.

The summit attendees had gathered downstairs for drinks and networking, which, in Olivia's opinion, was another phrase for standing around pretending to enjoy yourself while trying to remember who owned which business in town. She had done enough pretending for one day. The meeting that morning still sat badly with her. Cassie's questions had been blunt, yes, but not unreasonable. Yet the room had reacted as though she had marched to the center of the table and accused someone of murder.

Olivia folded her arms and started down the hall. She told herself she was only walking. Stretching her legs. Looking at the lodge. Getting out of her room before she spent another hour replaying every uneasy glance and carefully controlled answer from that conference room.

That was all. Not snooping. Absolutely not.

The hall opened onto an upper balcony that overlooked the main lobby. Below, people clustered in knots near the fire, their laughter drifting upward in warm little bursts. A piano recording played somewhere out of sight. The massive Christmas tree stood in one corner, dressed in white lights, silver ribbon, and over a hundred brightly colored ornaments.

She leaned briefly against the railing and looked across the lobby. A long wall opposite the fireplace held a series of glass display cases. She had noticed them earlier in passing but had not stopped to examine them. Now, with time to spare and an excuse to avoid the social cluster downstairs, they drew her attention.

Historic artifacts from the resort's early days, a sign had said. Olivia went down the wide staircase instead of taking the elevator. The stairs curved with old-fashioned lodge grandeur, polished smooth by decades of boots. At the bottom, she crossed the lobby, keeping just far enough from the larger groups to avoid getting pulled into a conversation. A few people nodded. Someone lifted a glass in greeting. Olivia smiled politely and kept moving.

The display cases lined the wall between the lobby and a smaller sitting room furnished with leather chairs and a pair of taxidermy elk heads that stared down with glassy disapproval.

Overhead, iron sconces cast amber pools of light across the exhibits.

Olivia stopped before the first case.

The lodge had made an effort. She had to give them that. Antique wooden skis with leather bindings rested on brass hooks. Beside them hung an old wool racing sweater in faded red and cream, the fabric worn thin at the elbows. There were sepia photographs of early skiers standing in front of the mountain with expressions of grave determination, as though winter sport were less recreation than moral duty.

The next case held framed posters from North Star Summit's

early promotional years. Cheerful painted figures flew down impossible slopes beneath slogans promising alpine adventure, wholesome air, and modern comforts. Olivia smiled despite herself at one poster featuring a woman in bright lipstick and tailored ski pants looking glamorous enough to pose for a cigarette ad while barreling down a mountain in heeled boots. "That seems safe," she muttered.

She moved on to black-and-white photographs mounted in careful rows. Teams of young men with skis over their shoulders. Winter Carnival queens in fur collars and tilted hats. Snow sculptures. Torch-lit parades. A band playing on a temporary stage while spectators in bulky coats watched from the sidelines.

The whole thing felt frozen in a curated memory of the past, polished until it gleamed. Charming. Picturesque. Entirely harmless.

Except that after that morning, Olivia no longer trusted anything here that looked too polished.

She slowed before the third case. This one was smaller and set slightly apart from the others, perhaps because the objects inside were medals, ribbons, and trophies, each one perched on a velvet riser under a tiny angled light. Brass plates beneath them gave names and dates.

A silver cup from 1928. A pair of tarnished competition badges from 1931. A narrow blue ribbon from a women's slalom event. And there, in the center, mounted upright on dark felt, was a medal that caught the light more sharply than the rest.

Olivia stepped closer.

It was silver, round and heavy-looking, with a laurel border worked around the edge. The ribbon had long since faded from a color that might once have been royal blue. The front of the medal bore a skier in motion, body bent forward, one arm angled behind him in a posture that somehow managed to look both athletic and theatrical.

The plaque below it read: Anton Volkov, 1934 Winter Carnival Downhill Champion.

Olivia frowned. The name was unfamiliar, but the medal had a presence the others lacked. Not magical. Not glowing. Nothing dramatic. It was simply the one object in the case that seemed to command the air around it.

She bent slightly, reading the smaller card beside the plaque.

Anton Volkov was one of North Star Summit's earliest athletic stars, known for his daring downhill runs and charismatic public appearances during the resort's growing years.

"Charismatic public appearances," Olivia murmured. "That could mean anything from charming to completely unbearable."

A couple passed behind her on the way to the bar, whispering. Somewhere near the fireplace, someone laughed too hard again. The piano music drifted on.

Olivia kept staring at the medal. Something about it tugged at her. Not in the awful, cold way haunted objects sometimes did. Not in the frantic, urgent pulse she had felt from darker things. This was different. A prickling interest. A sense of waiting.

The little brass latch on the display door had not been fastened properly. One side sat slightly ajar, probably from a staff member polishing the glass.

Olivia noticed it and should have stepped back. Instead, she glanced over her shoulder, saw that no one was paying the slightest attention to her, and reached out to nudge the door more securely closed.

Her fingertips brushed the medal. The surrounding temperature dipped by ten degrees.

Olivia shut her eyes for one hard blink. When she opened them again, a man was standing at her elbow.

She jerked back so fast she nearly collided with the display case behind her.

The man did not move. He simply looked at her with the calm expectation of someone greeting an admirer who had finally come to her senses.

He was tall and broad-shouldered, dressed in ski clothes from another era. Cream trousers tucked into high lace-up boots. A fitted sweater with a bold diamond pattern across the chest. A scarf looped dramatically around his neck. His dark hair was slicked back in glossy waves, and his jaw was clean-shaven and handsome in a way old movie stars might have killed for. He held a pair of spectral ski goggles in one hand. His posture alone could have been framed and labeled confidence, excessive.

He smiled. "Ah," he said in a rich accent touched with Eastern Europe and decades of performance. "At last."

Olivia stared at him.

He pressed a hand to his chest and inclined his head with a flourish. "Anton Volkov," he said. "Champion. Visionary. The soul of winter competition."

Olivia closed her eyes again briefly. Of course. Of course, the one time she tried to have a ghost-free weekend, she found one in a display case next to the lobby bar.

When she opened her eyes, Anton Volkov was still there, looking pleased with himself.

"No," Olivia muttered.

Anton blinked. "No?"

"No," she repeated under her breath. "Absolutely not. I am off duty."

He frowned lightly, as though she had spoken nonsense in a language he should not have to learn.

"You touch the medal," he said. "You see me. Therefore, fate has introduced us. This is straightforward."

Olivia glanced around. No one seemed to notice her, frozen in front of the display. Good. Wonderful. She was now in public with a ghost athlete from the 1930s, and from every outward appearance, she was just a woman standing alone, glaring at a case of old ski memorabilia.

She lowered her voice. "I am not doing this tonight."

Anton leaned closer, eyes bright. "You were admiring my achievements."

"I was reading a plaque."

"Same thing."

He turned to inspect the display case himself and sniffed. "They polish everything too much. It removes character. In my day, silver was allowed dignity."

Olivia folded her arms. "In your day, people also thought skiing downhill on planks with leather straps was a great idea."

"It was a great idea," Anton said with offense. "It required courage, balance, technique, and thighs forged by the gods. Modern equipment does everything but sing a lullaby to the skier."

Olivia could not help it. Her mouth twitched.

Anton caught it immediately.

"Ah," he said. "You appreciate quality."

"I appreciate not dying."

"Too cautious."

"I am alive. I consider that a strong point in my favor."

He waved a dismissive hand. "Life is temporary. Reputation is forever."

"That sounds exhausting."

"It is glorious."

Olivia rubbed her forehead. She should walk away. That was the obvious solution. Leave the display. Return to her room. Pretend none of this had happened. But Anton drifted a pace beside her as easily as breath, making it clear that walking away would solve nothing.

He studied her face. "You have the expression," he declared, "of a woman with purpose."

"I have the expression of a woman regretting several decisions."

"You are investigating."

Olivia let out a soft, humorless laugh. "I am not."

He gave her a look of indulgent disbelief. "You touched the champion's medal on the evening after a tense public confrontation. You examine exhibits with suspicious focus. You stand alone in the lobby, pretending not to think dangerous thoughts. This is an investigation."

"This is called having eyes."

Anton lifted one shoulder. "Same family."

Olivia started walking toward the sitting room, hoping motion would help. Anton floated neatly beside her, entirely too elegant for a dead man tethered to a sports medal.

"I am not investigating anything," she said.

"Of course you are."

"I am attending a tourism summit."

"Terrible cover."

"It is not a cover."

Anton lowered his voice dramatically. "Do not worry. You may trust me. Every mystery requires observation, strategy, and athletic excellence."

Olivia stopped and stared at him.

"Athletic excellence?"

He nodded once, solemn as a priest. "It's absolutely essential."

"I fail to see how."

He looked offended by the question itself. "Because people reveal weakness under pressure. On slopes. In storms. During competitions. Character emerges."

"This is a lodge meeting, not the Winter Olympics."

Anton's expression turned pitying. "For you, perhaps."

Olivia pressed her lips together to keep from laughing again. That annoyed her. She did not want to enjoy this. She especially did not want to enjoy this while worrying about Cassie Greer's questions and the ugly current running beneath the lodge's polished public face.

Anton, oblivious to all internal conflict, began pacing in front of the photograph wall with his hands clasped behind his back.

"These people," he said, nodding toward the old images, "they understood presentation. Posture. Drama. See that man there? Terrible knees. Weak center of gravity. He must have fallen constantly."

Olivia glanced at the photograph he indicated. It showed a solemn skier from 1932 standing beside a trophy.

"You cannot possibly know that from one picture."

"I know everything from one picture."

"That seems unlikely."

"It is a champion's instinct."

"It is ghostly arrogance."

Anton smiled brightly. "Yes."

A server carrying a tray of drinks passed nearby. Olivia turned away and pretended to study an old poster while Anton moved behind her shoulder and continued his running commentary.

"The woman in the green sweater downstairs," he whispered. "Very poor walking posture."

Olivia did not turn. "There is no green in a black-and-white photograph."

"Not the picture. The real woman. Near the fireplace. She leads with her chin. Dangerous habit."

Olivia glanced across the lobby and spotted the woman he meant.

"She is carrying two martinis," Olivia murmured. "Maybe she is just trying not to spill them."

Anton considered this. “Acceptable temporary adjustment.” He drifted ahead of her toward the lobby entrance, then stopped and examined the long central corridor stretching toward the dining room. His eyes lit.

“This,” he announced, “would make an excellent ski run.”

Olivia stared. “No.”

“Yes. Start from the staircase landing, push off from the balcony, descend with a strong left turn by the registration desk, then straight through here. Fast. Elegant. Memorable.”

“Into the dining room fireplace?”

He tilted his head. “Only if one is careless.”

Olivia huffed a laugh despite herself.

Anton pointed toward the sweeping staircase. “Even better from there.”

“You are the reason safety regulations were invented.”

He looked pleased. “Thank you.”

“I was not complimenting you.”

“Many great truths begin as insults.”

Olivia shook her head and resumed walking. She headed toward a quieter side hall lined with framed photographs and landscape paintings. The farther she moved from the lobby, the softer the sound of conversation became. Lamps glowed in alcoves. Snow whispered at the windows.

Anton followed without an invitation. Of course he did.

Olivia stopped beside a window overlooking the dark slope outside. Snow runs had shut down for the night. The mountain lay pale under the moonlight, beautiful and watchful.

Her smile faded. For a moment, she remembered Cassie’s voice in the meeting room.

People deserve to know the truth about this mountain.

Anton’s expression sharpened as he studied her profile. “There,” he said more quietly. “That face again.”

Olivia kept her eyes on the snow. “What face?”

“The one that says you have seen something crooked and do not intend to leave it alone.”

She let out a slow breath. “I told you,” she said. “I am not investigating.”

Anton came to stand beside her, his reflection absent from the dark glass. “Then why are you thinking so hard?”

Because a roomful of adults had reacted to old land records as though they were dynamite. Because Cassie had looked frustrated, not foolish. Because Olivia had spent enough time around secrets to know when one was being guarded. Instead of saying any of that, she muttered, “Bad habit.”

Anton nodded as though that confirmed everything. “Yes, investigating.”

Olivia turned from the window. “You are impossible.”

“I am observant.”

“You are attached to a medal in a display case.”

He drew himself up. “A champion’s medal.”

“Still a medal.”

“A very distinguished one.”

She sighed. “Fine. Distinguished.”

He softened instantly, as though praise were oxygen. “Thank you.”

Olivia stared at him for a long beat, then laughed quietly under her breath. Not because anything was particularly funny, but because the absurdity of it all had finally tipped past resistance. The mountain was hiding something. Cassie was clearly digging into it. Olivia had promised herself she would stay out of whatever small-town mess had begun brewing under the lodge roof. And now she had acquired a flamboyant dead skier with opinions. Her so-called ghost-free vacation was becoming a joke.

Anton seemed to take her laughter as consent to a partnership she had not offered.

“Excellent,” he said briskly. “We begin with surveillance.”

“We do not begin with anything.”

“We watch people. We assess gait, confidence, and duplicity. It is a science.”

“It is not.”

“It is absolutely science.” He gestured toward the lobby, where summit guests still mingled over drinks and firelight.

Olivia followed his gaze and felt a thread of reluctant amusement pull at the corner of her mouth again.

A vacation without ghosts, she had thought. That had clearly been optimistic to the point of stupidity. She looked at Anton Volkov, champion of 1934, connoisseur of melodrama, critic of modern ski equipment, and entirely uninvited addition to her evening. Then she looked back toward the lodge, toward its warm lights and polished displays and the unease that seemed to linger just below every pleasant surface. Maybe she was not investigating. Not yet. But if she was going to be haunted anyway, she might as well be haunted by someone entertaining.

Anton folded his arms and surveyed the hallway with proprietary disdain. "Yes," he said. "I will be very useful."

Olivia shook her head and started back toward the lobby.

Anton glided after her at once.

As they passed a pair of guests on their way to the bar, he leaned toward her and murmured with grave disapproval, "That man has the balance of boiled cabbage."

Olivia bit the inside of her cheek. Then, despite everything, she smiled. Her ghost-free vacation, she realized, was definitely not happening after all.

CHAPTER SIX

Evening Reception

By the time the evening reception began, the lodge had fully settled into its nighttime rhythm. Firelight dominated the main lobby, spilling out from the massive stone fireplace in a steady glow that softened everything it touched. Shadows gathered in the corners and climbed the timber beams overhead. Outside the tall windows, snow fell in a quiet, constant curtain, turning the mountain into a blurred painting of white and gray.

Inside, warmth and conversation layered over one another. A low hum of voices filled the space. Glasses clinked. Laughter rose and fell in small bursts. Soft instrumental music threaded through the room, barely noticeable but enough to smooth the edges of the noise.

Trays of appetizers circulated through the crowd, carried by staff moving with practiced efficiency. Small plates changed hands. Napkins disappeared. The entire scene carried that careful balance between casual and curated that came from years of hosting events exactly like this.

Olivia stood just off to one side of the main cluster of guests, a glass of sparkling water in one hand and a small plate in the other. She had intended to simply observe. That plan lasted approximately thirty seconds. The moment a tray passed within reach, her instincts took over.

She selected a puff pastry bite first. It was golden, neatly shaped, and visually appealing in a way that suggested it had been assembled to look good under warm lighting rather than to impress anyone who actually knew what they were eating.

Olivia took a bite. She chewed once. Twice. Her expression did not change, but internally she sighed. "Store-bought," she murmured under her breath.

The pastry was uniform. Too uniform. The butter flavor was present but flat. The filling had been piped with a precision that spoke of mass production, not a human hand adjusting texture and seasoning as it went. Fine. Completely fine. Entirely forgettable.

She set the empty shell on her plate and reached for the next offering from a passing tray.

Mini quiche. Again, visually appealing. Again, identical. She took a bite. Reheated. The texture gave it away instantly. Slightly rubbery in the center, the edges were just a touch too dry. The kind of compromise that happened when something was prepared elsewhere, frozen, transported, and then coaxed back to life in a kitchen that had no actual connection to its creation.

Olivia swallowed and exhaled slowly. Still fine. Still acceptable. Still not something anyone would remember a week from now.

A server paused near her with a cheese plate.

Olivia selected a cube of cheddar and a slice of something softer, paired with a cracker that had been arranged at a precise angle. She tasted it. No complaints. Also, no reason for excitement. Her mind, traitorous and automatic, began working.

The room faded slightly as possibilities took shape. Smoked trout tartlets. Crisp shell, light, fresh filling with a hint of lemon. Rosemary mushroom turnovers. Real mushrooms, sauteed properly, not chopped into submission and buried under salt. Cranberry brie pastries. Bright, sharp sweetness cutting through rich cheese, balanced rather than cloying. Miniature savory scones. Flaky, warm, with a depth of flavor that made people pause mid-conversation to actually notice what they were eating.

Her fingers tightened slightly on the edge of her plate. The lodge had the audience for it.

The traffic. The visibility. And from what she had seen so far, the current food program was serviceable. Which meant it could be improved. Significantly. A familiar spark lit in her chest.

Opportunity.

"Tragic."

Olivia did not jump this time. Progress. She did, however, close her eyes briefly before turning her head.

Anton stood beside her, arms folded, expression grave as he surveyed the tray of appetizers passing between guests.

"What is tragic?" she asked quietly.

He gestured toward the food with open disdain. "This," he said. "This is what they offer? These small, sad bites? Where is the substance? Where is strength?"

"It's a reception," Olivia said. "Not a training camp."

"In my day," Anton continued, ignoring her entirely, "athletes required real nourishment. Meat. Bread. Proper sustenance. Not … this." He lifted an invisible quiche between two fingers as though it might offend him by proximity alone.

Olivia took another sip of her water and deliberately did not engage.

Anton moved closer to the passing tray, peering down at it with exaggerated scrutiny.

"Look at this," he said. "So small. How does anyone build power on something this size?"

"They're not building power," Olivia said. "They're networking."

"Networking requires energy."

"So does talking. Yet here you are, doing quite well without food."

He paused, considering that. Then nodded once. "Fair point. I am exceptional."

Olivia bit back a smile. She shifted her attention across the room. Clusters of local business owners had formed near the fire-place and along the edges of the lobby. Conversations overlapped, topics shifting between weather, bookings, staffing, and the general challenges of keeping anything running smoothly in a town that depended on seasons and tourism.

And there, near the center of it all, stood Gerald Huxley. He held a glass of whiskey in one hand and was speaking with a pair of men Olivia vaguely recognized from town. His posture was relaxed now, the rigid tension from the morning meeting softened by the environment and the drink.

This, Olivia thought, was the moment. She set her plate aside on a nearby table, straightened her shoulders, and crossed the room.

Anton drifted after her. "Ah," he said. "You approach an important figure. Good. Observe his stance. Slight imbalance. Too much weight on the right foot."

Olivia kept walking. "I am begging you," she murmured under her breath. "Do not comment on his posture out loud."

"I will be discreet."

"You will not."

"I will try."

That was the best she was going to get. Olivia reached the edge of the group and waited for a natural pause in the conversation. When it came, she stepped forward. "Mr. Huxley?"

He turned, his expression polite and attentive. "Yes?"

"Olivia March," she said. "March House Bed and Breakfast."

Recognition flickered.

"Ah, yes," he said. "You spoke earlier. Coffee stands. Catering."

"That's right."

He nodded once. "Interesting ideas."

Encouraging, Olivia allowed herself a small, professional smile. "The reception looks great," she said. "You've got a good turnout."

"We do," Huxley replied. "This weekend is important for us."

"I can see that."

She gestured lightly toward the circulating trays.

"I was noticing the food," she said.

Anton leaned in at once. "Now we discuss nourishment."

Olivia ignored him.

Huxley followed her glance. "We keep it simple for events like this," he said. "Efficient. Consistent."

"I can tell," Olivia said carefully. She let a beat pass. "I also think you have an opportunity here."

Huxley's attention sharpened slightly.

"How so?"

Olivia kept her tone measured and professional. "March House has a full commercial kitchen, and I am a professionally trained chef," she said. "I'm in the process of expanding beyond the coffee shop side of the business. Catering is a natural next step."

Anton nodded approvingly. "Ambition. Good."

"We focus on fresh, locally prepared food," Olivia continued. "Small plates, pastries, light catering. Things that fit events like this, but with a little more … presence."

Huxley took a slow sip of his drink, considering.

"You're suggesting replacing our current supplier?"

"Not replacing," Olivia said. "Complementing. Elevating." She gestured again toward the trays. "These are fine. But they don't stand out. You're marketing North Star Summit as a premium experience. The food should support that."

Anton made a soft, approving sound. "Yes. Presentation. Excellence."

Huxley's gaze shifted back to her.

"We use a regional supplier," he said. "Reliable. Cost-effective."

"I understand," Olivia replied. "But local sourcing is part of your branding. People come here for the mountain, for the town, for something they can't get somewhere else." She let the idea settle. "I can provide fresh pastries for your cafe," she added. "Cater receptions. Create seasonal menus that tie into what's happening here. It gives guests a stronger sense of place."

For a moment, Huxley said nothing. Then he nodded slowly. "That does align with what we're trying to build," he admitted.

Anton leaned toward Olivia. "He is interested."

"I can see that," she murmured.

Huxley glanced toward the fireplace, then back to her. "We've been discussing ways to expand our local partnerships," he said. "Food is an obvious area."

"It is," Olivia said.

"And you can handle volume?"

"Yes." Confidence, clean and steady.

Huxley studied her for another second, then gave a small, decisive nod. "I'd be happy to discuss it further," he said. "After the summit. We can look at specifics."

There it was. Not a contract. Not a commitment. But an opening. Olivia felt the flicker of something solid and promising settle into place. "Thank you," she said.

Anton straightened beside her. "Victory."

"Preliminary conversation," she corrected under her breath.

"First step to victory."

She did not argue.

Huxley shifted his weight, his expression easing back into its earlier relaxed state.

"Leave your contact information with the front desk," he said. "We'll set something up."

"I will."

They held each other's gaze for a moment longer.

Then, from somewhere behind them, a voice cut through the peaceful rhythm of the room.

"Gerald."

Cassie.

Olivia turned slightly.

Cassie stood a few feet away, her expression composed but intent.

Huxley's shoulders tightened.

It was subtle, but Olivia saw it.

The same man who had been calm, engaged, and open to discussion about pastries and catering now looked guarded.

"Yes?" he said.

Cassie stepped closer. "I was hoping to continue our conversation from earlier," she said.

The air shifted. Not dramatically. Not enough for anyone across the room to notice. But up close, the change was unmistakable.

Huxley's jaw set. "This is not the time," he said.

"It's as good a time as any," Cassie replied. Her voice remained calm, but there was steel beneath it.

Olivia took a small step back, instinctively giving them space.

Anton leaned toward her, intrigued. "Ah. Conflict."

"Not helpful," Olivia murmured.

Cassie met Huxley's gaze directly. "I'd like clarification on the land transfer records," she said. "The discrepancies I mentioned this morning."

"We're not discussing that here," Huxley cut in. His tone had changed completely.

Gone was the relaxed businessman. In his place stood someone defensive, controlled, and clearly unwilling to engage.

Cassie did not back down. "That's exactly the problem," she said. "No one wants to discuss it anywhere."

A few nearby conversations faltered, attention beginning to drift in their direction.

Huxley lowered his voice, but the edge remained. "Miss Greer, I will not have you stirring up speculation at a professional event."

"I'm asking for transparency."

"You're making accusations without evidence."

"I have evidence."

That landed.

Olivia felt it in the air.

Huxley's expression tightened further. "Then take it through the proper channels," he said. "Not here."

Cassie's eyes flashed. "Those channels have been closed for forty years."

The silence that followed was brief but heavy.

Then Cindy Keller appeared at Huxley's side, her smile already in place. "Cassie," she said lightly. "Can we talk for a moment?"

Cassie hesitated. Then gave a brief nod. "Fine."

Cindy guided her toward the hallway leading away from the lobby.

Huxley exhaled slowly, the tension lingering in the set of his shoulders. He turned back to Olivia, but the ease from earlier was gone.

"Excuse me," he said.

"Of course," Olivia replied.

He moved away, disappearing into another cluster of guests.

Olivia stood where she was for a moment, her thoughts shifting.

Anton watched the retreating figures with keen interest. "Very interesting," he said.

"Yes," Olivia agreed quietly. Relaxed when discussing food. Tense when discussing history. The contrast was sharp enough to leave a mark.

Olivia picked up her glass again, though she had no memory of setting it down. "If I land this account," she murmured to herself, "March House could supply the entire lodge."

Anton nodded approvingly. "Expansion. Influence. Good strategy."

"It would be a major step forward," she said.

He gestured toward the hallway where Cassie and Cindy had gone. "And yet," he added, "you are not thinking only of pastries."

Olivia did not answer. Because he was right. She told herself it was just curiosity.

Professional awareness. Nothing more. But the unease from earlier had returned, threading through her thoughts. After a moment, she set her glass aside and moved toward the hallway.

Anton followed instantly.

"Where are we going?" he asked.

"Nowhere," Olivia said. "I'm just …" Her words cut off as she reached the corner.

Voices carried from just out of sight. Cassie. Cindy. Not loud. But sharp enough to catch.

"… not something you can ignore," Cassie was saying.

"This isn't the place," Cindy replied, her tone tight beneath its polite surface.

"It's exactly the place," Cassie said. "It's happening here. On this mountain."

Olivia stilled.

Anton leaned closer, fascinated. "Oh," he said softly. "This is very good."

Olivia held her breath, listening.

"… you're going to cause problems," Cindy said.

"Good," Cassie replied. A pause. Then, quieter: "People deserve to know what happened."

Silence followed. Heavy. Final.

Olivia stepped back before either of them could round the corner and find her standing there. She turned, moving back toward the lobby with careful, unhurried steps.

Anton drifted beside her, practically glowing with interest. "Definitely investigation," he said.

Olivia shook her head once, but the denial felt thinner now. Behind her, the hallway remained quiet. Ahead, the reception continued as though nothing had happened. Firelight.

Music. Laughter. Plates of perfectly acceptable, entirely forgettable food.

Olivia slipped back to the edge of the crowd, her mind returning to pastries or business plans. If she could secure the lodge account, March House would grow. That much was clear.

But something else was just as certain. Before the weekend was over, no one would remember this summit for its catering. And Olivia had the uneasy feeling she was standing at the very edge of whatever would replace it.

CHAPTER SEVEN

The Body on the Slope

Morning arrived with a brilliance that felt almost cruel. The storm had spent itself during the night, leaving the mountain buried beneath a fresh, unbroken layer of snow. Sunlight spilled across the slopes, dazzling and sharp, reflecting so brightly it forced the eyes to narrow. Every pine branch carried a heavy white burden. Every rooftop glittered. The world looked untouched, pristine, as though nothing unpleasant could exist within it.

Olivia knew better. She woke earlier than she had intended. The unfamiliar quiet of the lodge pulled her from sleep. For a moment, she lay still, listening. No wind rattled the windows. No voices drifted from the hallway. Just a deep, muffled stillness, the kind that only came after a heavy snowfall.

Anton was already awake. He hovered near the window, his expression sour as he surveyed the landscape. "It is too clean," he muttered.

Olivia groaned softly and pushed herself upright. "It's snow, Anton. That's what it does."

"In my time," he continued, ignoring her entirely, "snow did not pretend to be innocent. It buried armies. It starved cities. This—" he gestured with disdain "—this is decorative."

Olivia swung her legs out of bed. "You're complaining about snow now?"

"I am complaining about everything," he said crisply. "It is my right."

She smiled despite herself and reached for her sweater. "I'm getting coffee."

"Ah," Anton said, drifting closer. "Yes. Let us see what passes for coffee in this century."

"That sounds ominous."

"It should."

THE LODGE CAFE occupied a wide corner of the main floor, its large windows framing the slopes in blinding white. A few early risers had already claimed tables, wrapped in sweaters and scarves, nursing steaming cups and speaking in low voices.

Olivia joined the line, grateful for the warmth and the scent of brewed coffee. It was strong, at least. That was something. She ordered a simple black coffee and carried it to a small table near the window.

Anton hovered beside her, eyeing the cup with open skepticism. "You will drink this?" he asked.

"I will," she said, taking a cautious sip.

He watched her face closely. "Well?"

"It's fine."

"It is not fine," he said immediately. "It lacks depth. It lacks character. It lacks soul."

"It's coffee, not a personality."

"In Vienna," he began, launching into a lecture she had no intention of hearing.

Olivia tuned him out, letting her gaze drift toward the slopes. Ski patrol had already begun their morning checks. A few figures moved methodically across the terrain, their bright jackets stark against the white.

It looked peaceful. Too peaceful.

She shifted in her seat, an unease she could not quite name settling in her chest.

Then the front doors burst open.

A man stumbled inside, breathless, his face pale beneath the cold. “Manager,” he called out, voice shaking. “We need—there’s—someone down.”

The room stilled.

Conversations cut off mid-sentence. Chairs scraped as people turned. The lodge manager hurried forward. “What happened?”

“There’s a body,” the man said. “On the service trail. Behind the lodge.”

A ripple of shock moved through the room. A few people asked questions.

“What do you mean, a body?”

“Is it a skier?”

“Did someone fall?”

The man shook his head, struggling to catch his breath. “I don’t know. I just—she’s not moving.”

Olivia’s grip tightened around her cup.

Anton went still beside her.

Guests rose, drawn by instinct toward the windows, toward the doors. The fragile calm of the morning shattered in an instant, replaced by a restless, buzzing tension.

Ski patrol moved quickly outside, their pace urgent now.

The manager raised his voice, attempting control. “Everyone, please remain inside. We’ll handle this.”

No one listened.

Olivia stood slowly, setting her coffee aside.

“You’re going,” Anton said.

“I’m looking,” she corrected.

“You are going,” he repeated. “You always go.”

She didn’t argue.

The cold hit her like a wall the moment she stepped outside. The air was sharp, biting through her coat as she followed the small crowd forming at a distance from the lodge. No one dared go too close, but no one stayed away either. Curiosity held them in place.

The service trail curved behind the building, partially shielded by a line of trees. Ski patrol had already roped off the area, their movements efficient and controlled.

Olivia stopped well short of the boundary. She didn’t need to be closer to see. Cassie Greer lay in the snow.

For a moment, Olivia couldn’t reconcile the image before her with the woman she had spoken to the night before. Cassie had been animated and sharp. Her eyes were bright with curiosity. Now she was still. Too still.

Her body lay at an awkward angle near the edge of a wooded slope, one arm partially buried in the snow. A light dusting had already settled over her, softening the outline of her form.

Someone near Olivia whispered, “She must have slipped.”

Another voice answered, “Hit her head, maybe.”

“That happens on these trails. Especially after a storm.”

The explanation moved quickly through the crowd, taking hold with surprising ease.

An accident.

It was simple. Acceptable.

Olivia didn’t move.

Anton stood beside her, his gaze fixed on the scene. “She did not fall while racing,” he whispered.

Olivia frowned. “What?”

“In a race,” he continued, “there is motion. There are marks. Disturbance. This …” he gestured toward the snow “… is wrong.”

Olivia’s eyes sharpened.

She looked again, forcing herself to take in details instead of the whole. Cassie’s boots.

No skis.

Olivia’s stomach tightened. There were no ski tracks. Not around her. Not leading to her.

The snow was smooth, unbroken except for the disturbance where her body lay. Which meant …

“She walked out here,” Olivia murmured.

Anton inclined his head slightly. “Yes.”

Olivia’s mind began to turn, pieces shifting into place. Why would Cassie leave the lodge on foot? In fresh snow. On a service trail. Unless she meant to. Unless she had a reason. Her thoughts flicked back to the night before. Cassie’s voice. Quiet, tense. The argument. Cindy’s sharp tone. Cassie’s refusal to back down.

Something about it had lingered with Olivia, a thread she couldn’t quite pull. Now it tightened. This wasn’t right.

Behind her, someone said, “They’ll call the sheriff.”

“Of course they will.”

"It's probably just a fall."

Probably.

Olivia didn't believe that.

~

THE SCENE GREW MORE CONTROLLED as minutes passed. Ski patrol established a wider perimeter. The manager moved through the gathered guests, urging them back toward the lodge with polite firmness.

"Please, everyone, let the authorities handle this. There's nothing to see here."

There was everything to see. But Olivia stepped back anyway, allowing herself to be guided with the others. She took one last look over her shoulder. Cassie lay where she had fallen.

Or been left. A chill ran through Olivia that had nothing to do with the cold.

Inside, the warmth felt artificial. The lodge buzzed with low voices, speculation already taking shape.

"Poor woman."

"Such a shame."

"Accidents happen."

Olivia returned to her abandoned coffee, though it had gone cold. She wrapped her hands around the cup anyway, more for something to anchor herself than for warmth.

Anton hovered nearby, unusually quiet.

"Well?" she asked after a moment.

He studied her. "You are thinking."

"I'm always thinking."

"Not in this way," he said. "This is the look you have when you decide something is wrong."

Olivia exhaled slowly.

"She wasn't skiing," she said.

"Yes."

"There were no tracks."

"Yes."

"She walked out there."

Anton's expression did not change. "And people who walk into the snow in the early morning do not usually fall by accident."

Olivia met his gaze. "No," she said. "They don't." The noise in the room faded around her. Her mind returned to Cassie's words. To the questions she had been asking. To the unease that had followed her even then. Cassie had been looking for something. And now she was dead.

Olivia straightened. "This isn't an accident."

Anton nodded once, as though he had expected nothing less.

An announcement came shortly thereafter. The lodge manager stood near the center of the room, his voice steady but strained. "Ladies and gentlemen, because of the incident this morning, the summit meeting is suspended until further notice. We ask that you remain available for questions from the authorities."

A murmur passed through the crowd. Disappointment. Concern. Curiosity.

Olivia barely heard it. Her attention remained fixed on the same thought, circling again and again. Cassie walked out there. On purpose. Something had drawn her onto that trail. Or someone.

Anton leaned closer, his voice low. "This is not finished," he said.

Olivia looked toward the windows, toward the blinding white slopes beyond. "No," she agreed. "It's just starting."

CHAPTER EIGHT

The Investigation Begins

The sheriff's truck arrived just before mid-morning. Olivia saw it from the lodge window before anyone else reacted. The vehicle climbed the last stretch of the access road in a slow, deliberate crawl, tires cutting through the packed snow left by the morning crews.

It looked out of place against the clean white landscape. Too dark. Too official. A reminder that whatever had happened outside was no longer rumor or speculation. It was real.

The low murmur inside the lodge shifted as others noticed. Conversations quieted. Heads turned toward the windows. Someone near the fireplace muttered, "That'll be the sheriff."

Olivia didn't move at first. She stood with her arms folded, watching as the truck came to a stop near the edge of the service trail. The engine idled for a moment, then cut out. The door opened. Luke stepped out. Even at a distance, his mood was obvious. He paused beside the truck, scanning the scene with a sharp, assessing gaze. His posture held a familiar tension, one Olivia recognized from their previous encounters. He was already irritated. Not surprised, not uncertain. Irritated.

It almost made her smile.

Anton drifted closer to the window, peering over her shoulder. "Ah," he said. "Authority arrives."

Olivia didn't respond.

Luke spoke briefly with a member of ski patrol, his expression tightening as he listened. Then he turned toward the lodge. Toward her.

"Of course," she murmured under her breath.

Anton tilted his head. "You know this man."

"Unfortunately."

"Good," Anton said. "Then this will be entertaining."

Olivia stepped outside before Luke could come in. The cold struck her again, sharp and immediate, but she barely noticed. Her focus stayed fixed on him as she crossed the packed snow toward the edge of the controlled area.

Luke saw her halfway there. His expression shifted, irritation sharpening into something more pointed. He stopped, planting his hands on his hips as she approached. "Of course you're here."

Olivia folded her arms, matching his stance without thinking. "I was invited."

His eyes narrowed slightly. "Invited."

"Yes," she said. "To the summit. Not the body, in case you're confused."

"I'm not confused," he said flatly. "I'm disappointed."

"In me?" she asked. "Or in your timing?"

He let out a quick breath, something close to a restrained laugh. "In the universe, mostly."

For a moment, they simply looked at each other. There it was again. That strange, unspoken undercurrent that seemed to follow them into every conversation. Friction and familiarity tangled together in a way Olivia wasn't entirely comfortable examining.

Luke broke the silence first. "Are you staying out of this?" he asked.

"No."

"At least you're honest."

"I try."

He studied her for another second, then shook his head and turned away. "Stay back. Let us do our job."

Olivia made no promises.

~

THE SCENE HAD CHANGED SLIGHTLY since earlier. The initial chaos had settled into a controlled rhythm. Ski patrol stood at measured intervals, maintaining the perimeter. A small cluster of personnel worked near Cassie's body, their movements careful and deliberate.

Luke stepped under the rope line, crouching near the edge of the embankment.

Olivia remained where she was, just outside the boundary, but close enough to observe.

She watched him work.

He moved with quiet efficiency, his earlier irritation channeled into focus. He spoke briefly with one of the patrol members, gesturing toward the slope, then leaned closer to examine the ground.

The snow told a story. Not a loud one. Not obvious.But it was there.

Cassie lay where she had fallen, her position unchanged, but the surrounding area revealed subtle disturbances. A shallow indentation along the slope. A faint slide in the snow, as though something had shifted downward.

Luke traced the edge of the embankment with his gloved hand. "Short drop," he said to the patrol officer. "Not enough to kill someone outright."

"Maybe she hit her head on a rock?"

"Maybe," but his tone suggested he wasn't satisfied. He stood, stepping carefully along the edge, scanning the ground with narrowed eyes.

Olivia followed his line of sight. There. A slight break in the snow near the top of the slope. Not a full set of tracks. Just enough to suggest movement. A step. Or a stumble.

Luke noticed it too. He crouched again, brushing away a thin layer of snow to reveal the surface beneath.

"Could have slipped," the patrol officer offered.

Luke didn't answer immediately. "Could have," he said after a moment. "But I don't like could have."

Olivia almost smiled. She waited until he stepped back from the immediate area before speaking.

"Luke."

He glanced up, clearly expecting her to remain silent.

She didn't. "She wasn't skiing."

His expression didn't change, but his attention sharpened. "I noticed," he said.

"No tracks," Olivia continued. "No skis. She walked out here."

"I said I noticed."

"She came out here for a reason."

Luke straightened, brushing snow from his gloves. "Or she stepped outside, wandered too far, and slipped."

Olivia held his gaze. "In fresh snow. On a service trail. Alone."

He didn't respond immediately.

For a moment, the air between them felt heavier than the cold.

"You're jumping ahead," he said finally.

"I'm paying attention."

"That's not the same thing."

"No," she said. "It's better."

His mouth twitched, just slightly, as though he wanted to argue but wasn't entirely sure how. "Stay out of it," he said instead.

Olivia's lips curved faintly. "You know I won't."

"I do."

That was the problem.

Luke turned back to the scene, signaling to the deputy who had just arrived. "Bag everything," he instructed. "Careful with the pockets."

The deputy nodded and moved forward.

Olivia watched as they began a more thorough examination. Gloves. Evidence bags. Methodical, practiced movements. They checked Cassie's hands, her boots, and the area immediately surrounding her body.

Then the deputy reached into her coat pocket. "Got something."

Luke stepped closer. "What is it?"

"Papers. Folded."

"Let me see."

The deputy handed them over.

Luke unfolded the documents carefully, keeping them shielded from the wind.

Olivia leaned slightly, trying to catch a glimpse without crossing the line. Photocopies.

Maps. Even from a distance, she recognized the structure. Clean lines. Grid markings. Parcels divided into measured sections. Land survey maps. Her pulse quickened.

Luke flipped through the pages, his brow furrowing. One page held his attention longer than the others. There was a mark. A note scrawled in the margin.

Olivia couldn't read it clearly from where she stood, but she saw the shape of the letters.

She saw the number. 7B. Her breath caught. Cassie's research. This wasn't random. This wasn't an accident.

Luke folded the papers again, sliding them into an evidence bag.

Then, without comment, he tucked the bag into his jacket. He looked up. Right at Olivia.

He knew she had seen. Of course he did.

She stepped closer, stopping just short of the boundary. "What was that?"

"Evidence."

"I saw the maps."

"That's nice."

"Cassie was researching something," Olivia pressed. "Those aren't random."

Luke held her gaze for a long moment.

"You're not part of this investigation."

"I'm standing in the middle of it."

"No," he whispered. "You're standing near it. There's a difference."

Olivia didn't back down.

"She was asking questions last night," she said. "About Mistwood. About things people don't talk about."

His expression shifted, just slightly.

"What kind of things?"

"History. People. Things that were … forgotten."

Luke's jaw tightened.

"Forgotten on purpose?" he asked.

Olivia nodded.

Silence stretched between them.

Then he exhaled slowly.

"Stay out of it," he said again, but this time the words lacked their earlier edge.

"Tell me that's a coincidence," Olivia said.

"I don't believe in coincidences," he replied. He looked away first.

THE BODY WAS PREPARED for transport shortly thereafter.

Olivia stepped back as the stretcher was brought forward, the careful process unfolding with quiet precision. The onlookers had thinned, most retreating to the lodge, but a few remained, drawn by the gravity of the moment.

Cassie was lifted gently, the snow beneath her disturbed at last. For a brief second, the pristine surface gave way to something harsher. Reality breaking through the illusion of perfection. Then it was covered again. Contained. Managed.

Luke spoke with the coroner, his tone low and controlled. Professional.

Olivia watched him, noting the shift. The irritation was still there, simmering beneath the surface, but it had settled into something more focused. More dangerous. He was thinking.

Good.

Anton appeared at her side again, as though summoned by the conclusion of events.

"Well," he said. "That is not an accident."

Olivia sighed. "You've been waiting to say that, haven't you?"

"Of course," he said. "It is obvious."

"Not to everyone."

"They are fools."

"They're normal," she corrected. "There's a difference."

Anton sniffed. "Normal people miss important things."

"Normal people also don't narrate investigations out loud," Olivia said.

He ignored that.

"She walked into the snow," he continued. "To meet someone. There is intent. There is a purpose."

"I know."

"And then she fell," he said, "or was pushed."

Olivia closed her eyes briefly. "Anton."

"Yes?"

"Stop narrating the investigation."

He looked offended. "I am assisting."

"You are speculating."

"I am correct."

"You don't know that."

"I feel it."

"That's not evidence."

"It is better than evidence," he said. "It is instinct."

Olivia opened her eyes and fixed him with a look. "You are not helping."

He paused. Then, reluctantly, "Fine." A beat. "But it is suspicious."

She gave a quiet laugh. "Yes. It is."

Luke approached a few minutes later.

The scene was nearly cleared. A quieter aftermath replaced the urgency. He stopped in front of her, his expression unreadable. "They're taking her down the mountain," he said.

"I figured."

"We'll run a full examination. See what we're dealing with."

Olivia nodded.

He hesitated. Then, "You said she was asking questions."

"Yes."

"About what?"

Olivia studied him. This was the line. The moment she decided how much to give.

"About something old," she said finally. "Something connected to Mistwood. She didn't say everything, but she was close to something. I could tell."

Luke's gaze sharpened. "And you think that's related?"

"I think she came out here for a reason."

He exhaled slowly. "Stay out of it," he said again.

Olivia smiled faintly. "You're running out of new material."

"I mean it."

"So do I."

Another pause. Then, quieter, "You're going to do what you want, anyway."

"Yes."

He nodded once, as though accepting something he already knew. "Then try not to get in my way."

"Try not to miss anything," she shot back.

A flicker of something passed between them. Respect. Reluctant. Unspoken. Real. Then Luke turned and walked back toward the lodge.

Olivia remained where she was for a moment longer, staring out over the slope. The snow still glittered in the sunlight. Still perfect. Still deceptive. But now she could see the cracks beneath it. Cassie hadn't fallen by chance. She had come here for a reason. And whatever she had been looking for, it had followed her into the snow.

Olivia turned back toward the lodge, her mind already moving ahead. The maps. Parcel 7B. Cassie's questions. This wasn't over. Not even close.

Anton drifted beside her as she walked. "You are going to investigate," he said.

"Yes."

"I will assist."

"No."

"I insist."

"No."

"I am very good at this."

"You are very loud at this."

He considered that. "Fine," he said. "I will assist quietly."

Olivia glanced at him. "You don't know how to do anything quietly."

He smiled. "You will see."

She doubted that. But she didn't argue. Because deep down, she knew one thing with absolute certainty. She would not let it be buried under fresh snow.

CHAPTER NINE

Parcel 7B

Evening arrived slowly at North Star Summit, filtered through a pale sky and heavy clouds that promised more snow. The lodge, so lively the night before, now carried a subdued energy. Conversations were quieter. Laughter, when it appeared, felt forced. Even the fire in the great room seemed to crackle with restraint, as though it too sensed something had shifted.

Olivia stood near the wide windows overlooking the slope, her arms folded loosely across her chest. Outside, a handful of skiers moved cautiously along the groomed trails, their bright jackets muted by distance and the gray light. It should have been beautiful. It should have felt peaceful. It didn't.

Behind her, Deputy Luke Thatcher was already at work. He had chosen a corner of the lodge near the reception desk, positioning himself where he could observe both the lobby and the hallway leading toward the guest rooms. It was not an official interrogation setup. There were no harsh lights or recorded statements. Just a steady, deliberate presence and a quiet series of conversations that no one could easily avoid.

Luke leaned against the edge of a polished wooden table, speaking with a man Olivia vaguely recognized from the reception the night before. His posture was relaxed, but there was nothing casual about him. Every movement was controlled. Every question precise.

She watched him for a moment longer than she had intended.

"Of course you're watching him," Anton's voice drifted near her ear, rich with amusement.

She didn't turn. "I'm watching everyone."

Anton hovered near the window beside her, his form faintly outlined against the glass. His arms were folded in an exaggerated imitation of her own stance. "Ah," he said. "A subtle but important distinction."

Olivia ignored him and focused on the room.

Luke's questioning was methodical. He wasn't pressing too hard, not yet. He asked simple questions. Where were you this morning? Did you know Cassie Greer? Did you notice anything unusual?

It was all very ordinary. But the reactions were not.

A woman near the fireplace fumbled her answer, her voice catching when Cassie's name was mentioned. A man standing by the coffee station stirred his drink long after the sugar had dissolved, his eyes flicking toward the exit more than once. Two attendees spoke in hushed tones near the staircase, breaking apart the moment Luke glanced in their direction.

Nervousness hung in the air, thin but unmistakable.

"They look like runners on the starting line," Anton murmured.

Olivia finally glanced at him. "What?"

He nodded toward the guests. "Athletes before a race. The ones who know they're not prepared. The ones who expect to lose." His expression sharpened. "They fidget. They avoid eye contact. They look for escape routes."

Olivia followed his gaze back into the room. He wasn't wrong. "I suppose even a ghost can learn something useful," she said.

Anton placed a hand over his chest in mock offense. "Madam, I was exceptional in life."

"I'm sure you were."

Luke finished with his current subject and shifted his attention to another group. His eyes flicked briefly toward Olivia, narrowing slightly, as if reminding her without words to stay out of it.

Olivia gave him her most innocent expression. Then she turned and did exactly the opposite. She started with the easiest approach.

Casual conversation. Polite curiosity. The kind of questions no one should feel threatened by.

The lodge's small sitting area provided the perfect setting. A cluster of chairs arranged around a low table. Coffee cups. Half-eaten pastries. The illusion of comfort.

Olivia stepped into the space as though she belonged there. "Mind if I join you?" she asked a pair of attendees seated near the hearth.

They hesitated, then nodded.

She sat, smoothing her sweater, adopting the relaxed posture of someone making idle conversation. "Strange morning," she said lightly.

"Very," one of them replied. "Terrible thing, what happened."

Olivia inclined her head. "Cassie seemed intense. Did either of you know what she was working on?"

The two exchanged glances. "Some kind of research," the second person said. "Local history, I think."

"That's what I heard." Olivia reached for her coffee, taking a slow sip. "She mentioned something odd to me yesterday. Parcel 7B. Does that mean anything to you?"

Both of them shook their heads immediately. "No," the first said too quickly.

"Never heard of it," the second added.

Olivia smiled. "Probably nothing, then." She let the conversation drift, asking about the summit, the lodge, and the weather. Within minutes, she excused herself and moved on.

It was the same pattern again and again. Parcel 7B. A blank look. A denial. Sometimes confusion. Sometimes a flicker of something else. A tightening around the eyes. A pause half a second too long. By the time she crossed back into the main room, Olivia was certain of one thing. People recognized the term. They just didn't want to admit it.

Cindy Keller was standing near the large windows on the opposite side of the lodge, her hands wrapped around a ceramic mug. She wore a fitted wool coat and carried herself with the kind of confidence that suggested she was used to being listened to.

Olivia approached her carefully. "Beautiful view," she said.

Cindy glanced over, offering a polite smile. "It is. When the weather cooperates."

"Do you come up here often?"

"Whenever I can," Cindy's tone was smooth, practiced. "It's good for business. And for perspective."

Olivia nodded, as though that made perfect sense.

"I heard you knew Cassie," she said after a moment.

Cindy's smile thinned. "Knew of her," she corrected. "We crossed paths a few times."

"She seemed very focused on something."

"She was," Cindy said, a faint edge entering her voice. "Unfortunately."

Olivia tilted her head. "Unfortunately?"

Cindy took a slow sip of her coffee before answering.

"She had a tendency to fixate. On things that weren't entirely accurate."

Olivia said nothing, letting the silence stretch just enough to invite more.

Cindy obliged.

"She was convinced there were discrepancies in the resort's land records," she continued. "Old ownership claims. Misfiled parcels. Things that have been settled for decades."

"Parcel 7B?" Olivia asked gently. There it was. A flicker. Small, controlled. But unmistakable.

Cindy recovered quickly. "I don't recall the specific designation," she said. "But yes. That sounds like the sort of thing she would latch onto."

"And it wasn't true?"

Cindy's expression hardened, just slightly. "Cassie was a teacher, not a legal expert. Historical records can be … complicated. Easy to misinterpret."

Olivia observed her. "You think she was wrong."

"I think she was chasing something that didn't exist." Cindy set her mug down with quiet precision. "And I think she let it consume her."

The dismissal was too clean. Too rehearsed. Olivia offered a small nod. "That's a shame."

"Yes," Cindy said. "It is."

But there was no sadness in her voice. Only irritation.

Mason Reed proved more difficult. He stood near the far end of the room, speaking with another attendee when Olivia approached. He was taller than she remembered, broad-shouldered, with a presence that filled a space without effort. When he noticed her, his conversation broke off. "Can I help you?" he asked. His tone wasn't unfriendly. But it wasn't welcoming either.

"I hope so," Olivia said. "I'm trying to understand what Cassie was working on."

Mason's jaw tightened.

"I already spoke with the deputy."

"I know." Olivia smiled faintly. "This isn't official."

"That's what worries me."

She let that pass. "Cassie mentioned something about land ownership," Olivia said. "Old parcels near the summit."

Mason crossed his arms. "My family used to own property up here," he said. "A long time ago."

Olivia's pulse ticked up. "Used to?"

"We sold it." His tone was firm. "Years ago."

"Do you remember the parcel numbers?"

His eyes sharpened. "Why?"

"Because Cassie seemed to think there was a discrepancy," Olivia said. "Something that didn't add up."

"There isn't." The response came too fast.

Olivia held his gaze. "Parcel 7B," she whispered.

Silence. For just a moment. Then Mason exhaled, shaking his head. "Means nothing to me."

It was a lie.

She could see it in the way his shoulders had stiffened. In the way his eyes had shifted, just briefly, toward the window.

"Of course," Olivia said, as though she believed him. "I'm sure it's nothing."

Mason didn't respond. He simply watched her until she turned away.

Olivia returned to the edge of the room, her thoughts moving quickly now, pieces beginning to shift into place.

Cindy knew more than she was saying. Mason definitely did. And neither of them wanted to talk about it.

"Interesting group," Anton said, drifting back into view beside her.

"You noticed that too?" Olivia asked.

"My dear," he said, "I spent a lifetime reading opponents across a field. This is no different." He gestured toward the room. "Fear, denial, calculation. It's all here."

Olivia studied the guests again. "Who?" she asked quietly.

Anton didn't hesitate. "The woman by the window," he said. "Controlled, but annoyed. She resents the disruption."

"Cindy."

"And the tall man." Anton's gaze shifted. "Defensive. Ready to argue before the question is even asked."

"Mason."

Anton nodded. "And there are others. Smaller tells. But those two …" He smiled faintly. "They expect to be challenged."

Olivia considered that. "They expect to be caught," she corrected.

Anton's smile widened. "Exactly."

ACROSS THE ROOM, Luke was watching her again. This time, there was no mistaking it.

He pushed away from the table and crossed toward her, his expression already set in that familiar mix of irritation and reluctant respect. "You want to tell me what you're doing?" he asked.

Olivia lifted a shoulder. "Observing."

"You're questioning people."

"Casually."

"Olivia."

She met his gaze evenly. "Parcel 7B," she said.

Luke went still. Not long. But long enough. "What about it?" he asked.

"You tell me."

His jaw tightened. "Stay out of this."

"That's not an answer."

"It's the only one you're getting."

Olivia held his gaze a moment longer, then stepped back. "Then I guess I'll keep asking questions," she said.

Luke exhaled sharply. "Of course you will."

Anton chuckled softly beside her.

Olivia ignored him. But as she turned back toward the room, one thing was obvious.

Parcel 7B wasn't just a detail in Cassie's research. It was the thread that connected everything.

And someone in this lodge was terrified of where it led.

CHAPTER TEN

The Argument Confirmed

By late evening, the lodge had settled into an uneasy rhythm. People still moved through the great room with coffee cups and lowered voices. Boots thudded across the wooden floor. Firelight danced across the beams overhead. From a distance, North Star Summit could still pass for what it had been: a winter retreat filled with fresh powder, expensive knitwear, and people pretending they had come to the mountains for clarity. Up close, the strain showed.

No one wanted to say the word murder, but it was there anyway, drifting through the lodge as surely as the scent of pine and smoke.

Olivia stood near the reception desk, pretending to study a display of local brochures while she watched the front hall. Guests came and went from the dining room. A pair of lodge employees crossed toward the service corridor carrying folded linens. Somewhere in the back, dishes clattered. A vacuum hummed faintly down a distant hall, then stopped.

She had spent most of the day circling the same thoughts. Cassie had not gone outside to ski. Cassie had gone out to meet someone. And whoever that someone was had known exactly where to find her. The question was no longer whether Cassie's death was an accident. The question was who she had met.

Anton drifted through the stone wall near the front desk as if emerging from fog. He wore his usual air of elegant self-importance, though at the moment even he seemed more thoughtful than theatrical.

"You are prowling," he observed.

"I am standing still."

"You are prowling internally, then."

Olivia glanced at him. "Is that one of your great athletic insights?"

"It is one of my great human insights." He looked toward the dining room. "Anxious people pace. Determined people go still. You are never so dangerous as when you appear calm."

Olivia snorted softly. "Good to know." She let her gaze travel toward the service corridor again.

A young lodge employee had just emerged with an armful of clean glasses balanced on a tray. Olivia recognized him from the evening reception. He had been weaving through the crowd with drinks while everyone laughed too loudly and pretended to enjoy underwhelming hors d'oeuvres. She remembered him because he had nearly collided with Anton, prompting the ghost to launch into a dramatic lecture about the decline of standards in public venues.

Olivia straightened. There. That was someone who might have seen more than the guests realized. She moved before she could overthink it.

The employee was setting the tray down behind a side station near the dining room entrance when she approached.

"Excuse me," Olivia said.

He looked up, startled at being addressed by a guest, then offered a polite smile. He was in his early twenties, with sandy hair and tired eyes that suggested a long shift and not nearly enough pay.

"Can I help you, ma'am?"

Olivia did her best not to react to ma'am. "I hope so. I'm sorry to bother you. You were working the reception last night, weren't you?"

"Yes." His smile faltered almost at once. "Is this about what happened this morning?"

"A little." Olivia lowered her voice. "I'm not with the sheriff's office."

His expression eased, though only slightly. "That's probably for the best. Deputy Thatcher already talked to half the staff."

"I'm not trying to get anyone in trouble," Olivia said. "I just wanted to ask if you noticed anything unusual last night. Around the time of the reception."

He hesitated. That hesitation alone told her he had.

She softened her tone. "Anything seem off to you? Anyone upset? Anyone arguing?"

The employee glanced toward the front desk, then back at her. "I don't know if it matters."

"It might."

He rubbed the back of his neck. "There was a woman and that teacher. Cassie. They were talking near the side hall by the conference rooms."

Olivia's heartbeat quickened. "Talking?"

He gave her a look that said he understood the polite words but did not entirely buy it.

"Arguing," he corrected. "Not shouting, exactly. But tense."

"Which woman?"

"The blonde one. Nice coat. Sharp voice." He frowned as he searched his memory. "Cindy something. I heard somebody say her name earlier today."

Olivia kept her face neutral with effort. "You're sure it was Cindy?"

"Yeah. Pretty sure." He shifted his weight. "Cassie looked upset. Not loud, but upset. The other woman kept telling her to lower her voice."

Olivia pictured the hallway at once. The stretch near the conference rooms, a little removed from the main reception crowd, close enough to remain in public view but private enough for a heated conversation no one wanted overheard. That was exactly where Olivia had heard the murmur of angry voices the night before. Her suspicion settled into something harder.

"Did you hear what they were saying?" she asked.

He shook his head. "Not much. I was carrying trays. I only caught bits."

"What bits?"

He thought for a moment. "The teacher said something about records." He looked uncertain. "Or maybe files. Something being wrong. And the other woman said she didn't know what Cassie thought she was doing."

Olivia's fingers tightened around the strap of her bag. Land records. Cassie had confronted Cindy. Not theory now. Not instinct. Fact. "Did either of them say anything else?"

The employee frowned harder. "Cassie said something about not letting it go. I remember that because the other woman looked ..." He paused.

"Looked what?"

"Nervous," he admitted. "Or angry. Maybe both."

Olivia nodded slowly. "Did you see what happened after that?"

"They split up. Cindy went back toward the reception room. Cassie stayed in the hallway for a minute." He glanced past Olivia as though replaying the scene. "She looked mad. Then she went upstairs."

Olivia let that settle.

Cassie had argued with Cindy over records, likely the land records she had been digging through. She had been upset enough to remain in the hallway afterward, gathering herself. And then sometime later, she had gone outside and wound up dead in the snow. The line between those facts was not yet complete, but it was no longer invisible. "That helps," Olivia whispered.

The employee lowered his voice further. "Do you think that woman had something to do with it?"

Olivia looked at him. "I think Cassie found something important," she said. "And I think somebody didn't want her talking about it."

He swallowed and gave a small nod. "Well," he said, stepping back from the side station, "I didn't see anything else."

"That's all right. You've already helped."

As she turned away, Anton appeared at her shoulder.

"Well done," he murmured. "Subtle. Persistent. Almost graceful."

"Almost?"

"I am trying to encourage growth."

Olivia did not bother to answer. Her mind was moving too fast. Cassie had argued with Cindy. About records. Which meant the unease in Cindy this morning had not been simple irritation. It had been fear.

Cindy Keller had just become much more than an annoying woman with a polished smile and a rehearsed explanation. She had become an actual suspect.

Olivia crossed into the quieter stretch of hallway near the conference rooms and stood for a moment in the same place where the argument had happened. The carpet muffled the sounds from the main lodge. A sconce on the wall cast warm amber light across the framed photographs of old ski seasons. Somewhere overhead, heat clicked through the pipes. She could almost see it.

Cassie planted in the middle of the hall, clutching her notebook or perhaps only her temper. Cindy tried to keep the conversation quiet while panic climbed behind her eyes. The two of them speaking in tense, clipped voices while guests laughed only a room away.

What had Cassie said? I know what you did? I found the records? I'm going public?

Olivia leaned one shoulder against the wall and closed her eyes briefly. If Cassie had uncovered something in the land records, Cindy had motive. Not proven, not yet, but motive. If there was a discrepancy in ownership, or a hidden transfer, or land that had been claimed through fraud, exposure could damage more than a reputation. It could threaten money, business, inheritance, and the resort itself. And if Cassie had threatened to reveal it publicly, perhaps to the historical society, to the town, or to anyone who would listen, Cindy might have panicked.

Panic made people reckless. Panic lured people out into the snow. The trouble was that the rest still did not fit.

Olivia pushed away from the wall and began strolling toward the window at the end of the corridor.

Cassie had argued with Cindy. Fine. Cassie had then gone outside to meet someone. Also likely. But had she gone out to meet Cindy again? Or had the argument triggered something else? Another meeting. Another confrontation. Another person who knew Cassie had gotten too close. The answers kept shifting the moment she reached for them.

"You are frowning with remarkable intensity," Anton said.

Olivia glanced at him. "I'm thinking."

"Yes, I can see that. It is a very dramatic expression on you."

She kept walking. "Cassie confronted Cindy. That much is real."

"And now you suspect the blonde woman."

"I suspect a lot of people."

"Good. Because in my experience, the obvious rival is not always the genuine threat."

Olivia stopped at the end of the hallway and looked out the tall window toward the white slope beyond the lodge. The snow had begun again, softly at first. A drifting curtain across the mountain. "Cassie knew something," she whispered. "Something important enough to argue about."

Anton folded his hands behind his back. "Then the question becomes who feared her most."

LUKE FOUND her twenty minutes later.

She had returned to the great room and was standing near one of the stone pillars, absently watching the front entrance as skiers stamped snow from their boots. She sensed him before she saw him, some part of her now attuned to the particular force of his irritation.

"Walk with me," he said. It was not a request.

Olivia turned. "Why?"

"Because I'd rather not have this conversation in front of everyone."

That alone made her curious enough to comply.

He led her toward a side hall near the administrative offices, out of earshot of the guests. The moment they were alone, he turned to face her, arms crossed. "You've been asking the staff questions." It was not phrased as a question either.

Olivia folded her arms in return. "And?"

"And I told you to stay out of this."

She raised an eyebrow. "You also told me not to jump to conclusions. I'm trying not to."

Luke stared at her for a moment that felt suspiciously close to a sigh held in human form.

"One of the employees told me you were asking about Cassie and Cindy Keller."

"So he talked to you, too. Good to know."

"Olivia."

There was less bite in her name this time. More warning than annoyance. She noticed it immediately.

"I was trying to establish whether the argument I overheard last night was actually between them," she said. "Now I know it was."

Luke's expression shifted, not much, but enough. He knew. Or at least he was no longer surprised to hear it. "You should have brought that to me," he said.

"I just did."

"Before you started playing detective on your own."

Olivia held his gaze. "Cassie was researching land records. She argued with Cindy. Then she went outside and ended up dead. You really expect me to sit quietly by the fire and pretend those things have nothing to do with each other?"

His jaw flexed. "No," he said after a moment. "I expect you not to get yourself into trouble."

The answer caught her off guard, not because of the words but because of the tone. It was still firm, still very much Deputy Thatcher laying down a boundary, but the old flat dismissal was gone. In its place was something more complicated. Concern, maybe. Frustration sharpened because he knew she was not entirely wrong.

Olivia lowered her voice. "Cassie's research may be the key to this."

"I know."

The words landed between them. Simple. Quiet. Real.

Olivia stared at him.

Luke glanced toward the end of the hall, then back at her. "That doesn't mean I need you sticking your nose into every conversation in this building."

"So you think the research matters."

"I think," he said carefully, "that the victim was looking into something before she died, and that's worth examining. What I do not think is that you should be the one chasing it."

"Because I'm not law enforcement."

"Because you have a talent for finding danger and then walking directly into it."

Olivia opened her mouth, then closed it again. That was annoyingly fair.

Luke continued before she could regroup. "Leave Cindy Keller to me. Leave the interviews to me. Leave the evidence to me."

"And what exactly am I supposed to do?"

"Nothing."

She let out a short laugh. "That's not going to happen."

"I know." The corner of his mouth moved, just barely, though it was not quite a smile. "That's what makes this conversation so exhausting."

Despite everything, Olivia felt the faintest tug of amusement. Then she straightened. "You can't expect me to ignore what I know."

"I expect you," he said, "to stop making it easier for a killer to notice you."

The words sobered her at once.

For a heartbeat, the air between them changed. The lodge noises beyond the hall dimmed. The crackle of a distant fire, the muffled sound of voices, and the soft drone of the heating system all seemed to recede.

He was not only warning her off. He was worried.

Olivia looked at him more carefully. At the strain around his eyes. At the controlled set of his shoulders. At the fact that he had taken the time to pull her aside instead of dressing her down in public. "I'm not planning to announce myself with a marching band," she said more quietly.

"With you, I'm not ruling anything out."

She almost smiled. Almost. "Luke."

He waited.

"Cassie went outside to meet someone," Olivia said. "I'm sure of that."

His expression remained unreadable.

"She wasn't skiing," Olivia continued. "She was headed somewhere. Or to someone. And if she'd just argued with Cindy about the records, then either Cindy called her out there, or someone else knew she had."

Luke was silent long enough that she wondered if he would answer.

Then he nodded once. "That possibility is being considered."

It was not a full concession, but it was enough. More than he would have admitted a day earlier.

Olivia took that small opening and pushed once more. "Then let me help."

"No," the answer came immediately, though not harshly.

She exhaled through her nose. "You are impossible."

"I could say the same to you."

"People do."

"I have no doubt."

For a moment, they simply looked at each other, the argument hanging there without heat, tempered now by something steadier. Not agreement. Not trust exactly. But movement.

At last, Luke stepped back. "Stay where other people can see you," he said. "And if you remember anything else about last night, you come to me first."

Olivia considered arguing. Instead, she said, "Fine."

His eyes narrowed, clearly aware that a fine from her could mean almost anything. Then he turned and headed back toward the main part of the lodge.

Olivia watched him go.

Anton slid through the wall beside her the moment Luke disappeared around the corner.

"Well," he said. "That was bracing."

"You were listening?"

"My dear, there are very few entertainments available to the dead."

She rubbed her forehead. "He is not wrong."

"About which part? Your attraction to danger or your inability to obey sensible instructions?"

Olivia shot him a look.

Anton smiled serenely.

~

THAT EVENING, after dinner service had ended and the lodge had quieted again, Olivia found a seat near the window at the far end of the great room with Cassie's notebook open in her lap. She had not shown it to Luke. Not yet. Partly because she did not entirely trust that it would stay in her possession if she did. Partly because she still needed to understand what she was looking at before handing it over.

The pages were worn now from handling. Cassie's handwriting ran across them in tidy lines broken by sharper notes in the margins, ideas added in haste. Land transfers. Parcel numbers. Old survey references. Dates. Arrows. Question marks.

Olivia traced one line with her finger.

Parcel 7B. Transfer irregularity. Cross-check the ownership chain. Meeting? Ask C.K.

C.K. Cindy Keller. There it was again.

Olivia leaned back and looked out at the night beyond the glass, where the slopes glowed faintly under lodge lights and falling snow.

Cassie is researching land records. Cassie arguing with Cindy. Cassie leaving the safety of the lodge to meet someone outside. The chain was there. But the links still did not form a perfect whole. Why would Cassie go at all if the argument had already gone badly?

Unless she thought she was about to get proof. Unless Cindy had promised answers.

Unless somebody else stepped in after the argument and arranged a meeting of their own.

Olivia turned another page. A rough sketch of the area near the trail. Not detailed enough to be an official map, but enough to suggest landmarks. A narrow path. A low embankment. A notation that reads possible line boundary?

Cassie had been connecting the land records to the physical location outside. Which meant that the place where she died may not have been random at all.

The thought sent a chill over Olivia's skin.

If the location mattered, then whoever met her there had chosen it for a reason. She closed the notebook and stared out at the snow.

This was no longer just about a disagreement over old paperwork. There was something buried in those records, something tied to the mountain itself, to ownership, to boundaries, maybe to something that had been hidden or taken or claimed long ago. And Cassie had gotten too close.

Anton appeared beside the window, his form silvered by the reflection from the glass.

For once, he did not launch into commentary immediately. He simply looked out with her at the dark slope beyond the lodge.

The silence stretched long enough to feel companionable. Then he spoke. “In competition,” he said thoughtfully, “the greatest danger is not the mountain.”

Olivia looked over at him. “No?”

Anton shook his head. “The mountain is indifferent. It does not hate you. It does not scheme. It merely exists.”

Olivia followed his gaze back toward the slopes. Snow drifted across the darkness in soft, relentless veils. “Then what is the greatest danger?” she asked.

Anton’s face turned toward the lodge behind them, toward the warm lights, the polished wood, the people moving through the rooms wrapped in comfort and civility. “The other racers,” he said.

Olivia felt the words settle deep. Not the mountain. Not the snow. Not the cold. The people. She turned her head slowly and looked back into the lodge. At the guests seated by the fire. At the staff clearing glasses. At the shadows moving through the hallways beyond the great room. At the smiling faces and guarded expressions, and carefully measured voices. One of them had argued with Cassie. One of them had lured her outside. One of them might have killed her.

Olivia’s grip tightened on Cassie’s notebook. The mountain had not taken Cassie Greer.

Someone inside this lodge had. And somewhere among the soft voices, winter coats, and polished manners, a killer was still walking free.

CHAPTER ELEVEN

Anton's Medal Leaves the Lodge

Morning arrived reluctantly at North Star Summit. The storm had passed in the night, leaving behind a brittle stillness that felt more unsettling than the wind and snow that had come before it. The sky stretched pale and colorless above the ridge, and the lodge, once buzzing with conversation and forced enthusiasm, now moved in hushed, careful motions.

Cassie Greer's death lingered in every corner. Guests spoke in hushed voices as they crossed the lobby. Coffee cups were clutched a little tighter. Eyes avoided the windows that looked out toward the trail where she had been found. Even the fire in the massive stone hearth seemed to burn more quietly, as though it too understood the shift in mood.

The summit was over. Not officially, perhaps. No announcement had been made. No formal closing remarks had been delivered. But everyone knew. People were leaving.

Olivia stood just off the main lobby, near the artifact display lining the hallway leading toward the conference rooms. It was where she had first encountered him. The place where a restless, indignant voice had cut through her thoughts and introduced itself with all the subtlety of a brass fanfare. Anton Volkov.

Now he was pacing beside the display case again, his translucent form moving in sharp, exaggerated strides that passed through the polished wood paneling and back again.

"This," he declared, sweeping an arm toward the glass case, "is unacceptable."

Olivia folded her arms, keeping her expression neutral for the benefit of the living guests drifting past.

"You've said that," she murmured under her breath.

"Have I?" Anton snapped. "Good. It bears repeating." He stopped in front of the display case and glared at it as though it had insulted him. "I was a champion," he said. "A master of speed. A conqueror of mountains. And now I am …" He gestured sharply. "A decorative trinket."

Olivia glanced at the case. Inside, arranged with little apparent logic, were relics of the lodge's early days. Old ski bindings. A cracked leather boot. Yellowed photographs of smiling men and women in wool coats and primitive equipment. And mounted on a small velvet backing was the medal. Anton's medal.

"I wouldn't call you a trinket," Olivia whispered.

"I would," Anton replied. "Look at this presentation. No plaque of proper detail. No recognition of my victory. No mention of my record descent in conditions that would have sent lesser men fleeing indoors."

"You're not helping your case," Olivia said.

"I am making my case," he corrected. "And the case is this: I refuse to remain imprisoned in this … this hallway curiosity cabinet."

Olivia exhaled slowly. "There's a slight problem with that," she said. "It's not exactly mine to take."

Anton turned to her, eyes narrowing. "You have done this before."

"That's different."

"How?"

Olivia hesitated, then said, "Because the objects at March House belonged to my aunt. They're part of the house. I didn't steal them out of a public display."

Anton drew himself up. "Liberation," he said with great dignity, "is not theft."

"Try explaining that to Luke," Olivia muttered.

At the far end of the lobby, Luke stood speaking with one of the lodge employees. His posture was rigid. His attention was sharp.

Even from a distance, Olivia could tell he was still in full investigation mode. He hadn't relaxed for a second since the body had been found.

Anton followed her gaze and scoffed. "That man has the disposition of a poorly waxed ski," he said.

Olivia bit back a smile. "He's doing his job."

"And I am doing mine," Anton replied. "Which is to ensure that I do not spend eternity trapped in a glass box beside a cracked boot and a photograph of amateurs." He leaned closer, lowering his voice conspiratorially. "You will take the medal."

Olivia shook her head. "I can't just walk over, open the case, and pocket it."

"Why not?"

"Because that's stealing."

Anton waved a dismissive hand. "Technicalities."

Before Olivia could respond, a fresh voice entered the conversation.

"Well, I wouldn't recommend smashing the glass," it said mildly. "We just had it replaced last year."

Olivia turned.

Gerald Huxley stood a few steps away, a stack of papers tucked under one arm. He looked tired, though he wore it well. His usual calm confidence was still there, but it had been tempered by the events of the past twenty-four hours.

"Mr. Huxley," Olivia said.

"Please," he replied. "After this weekend, I think we can dispense with formalities."

His gaze flicked briefly toward the display case, then back to her. "Enjoying our little museum?"

"It's charming," Olivia said. "I was just looking at the artifacts."

Anton made a strangled sound. "Charming," he repeated, aghast.

Olivia ignored him. "They're from the early days of the lodge?" she asked.

Huxley nodded. "Before my time, but yes. There was a ski club up here long before the resort became what it is now. A handful of enthusiasts, mostly. They stored everything in a back room for years. When we renovated, we found a lot of it packed away in crates." He gave a slight shrug. "Seemed a shame to throw it out."

Olivia studied the display again, letting her gaze settle on the medal. "It's interesting," she said. "There's a medal here. Downhill champion. Anton Volkov."

Huxley's brows lifted slightly. "You noticed that?"

"It caught my eye."

"That's more attention than it usually gets," he said. "To be honest, we don't know much about him. No records beyond the name and the medal itself. No dates, no confirmed events. Just a fragment of history that never quite made it into the books."

Anton bristled. "Outrageous," he muttered.

Olivia tilted her head. "That's a shame," she said. "He must have been quite accomplished."

"I'm sure he was," Huxley replied. "Anyone who made it up here in those days had to be a little extraordinary." He shifted the papers under his arm and gave a soft, humorless chuckle.

"Though I suppose this weekend will go down in history before anything in that case ever does."

Olivia's expression softened. "I'm sorry," she said. "This wasn't what anyone expected."

"No," he agreed. "It certainly wasn't."

For a moment, the weight of it all settled between them. Then Huxley straightened slightly, as though shrugging it off. "Well," he said, glancing back at the display, "if you're interested in any of it, don't let me stop you."

Olivia blinked. "I'm sorry?"

He gestured toward the case. "The artifacts," he said. "They're not exactly museum quality. No formal cataloging, no provenance to speak of. They were found in storage and put on display to fill space more than anything else." He gave her a sideways smile. "If you want a souvenir of the strangest summit in our history, you're welcome to it."

Olivia stared at him. "I—are you serious?"

Huxley considered it for all of half a second, then nodded. "Why not?" he said. "Better they go to someone who actually notices them than sit here collecting dust." He stepped forward, reached into his pocket, and produced a small key.

Anton froze.

Olivia felt it before she saw it. The sudden stillness in him. The sharp, electric anticipation.

Huxley unlocked the display case with a soft click and swung the glass door open.

"Go ahead," he said.

Olivia hesitated. This was absurd. Convenient. Too convenient. And yet …

She reached inside, her fingers brushing the velvet backing before closing around the medal.

The moment she touched it, a familiar chill ran through her hand. Not unpleasant. Not the sharp, desperate cold of a presence. This was something else. Contained. Focused. Alive.

She withdrew the medal slowly, turning it over in her palm. "Thank you," she said.

Huxley waved it off. "Consider it one less thing for me to worry about this week."

As he turned to leave, he paused. "Though it's funny," he added. "Most of the records from those early days are gone, anyway."

Olivia looked up. "Gone?"

"Storage fire," he said. "Decades ago. Took out most of the old paperwork. Land records, membership logs, event notes. Anything that might have told us more about the people who built this place." He shrugged. "History has a way of disappearing if no one bothers to keep track of it." With that, he nodded to her and continued on his way.

Olivia stood there for a moment, the medal warm against her palm despite the cold that clung to it. Behind her, Anton let out a long, reverent breath.

"Magnificent," he said.

She slipped the medal into her coat pocket. "I cannot believe that worked."

"It was inevitable," Anton replied. "Greatness recognizes greatness."

"Or," Olivia said dryly, "he just didn't care about the contents of a dusty display case."

Anton ignored that entirely. He drew himself up to his full height, chest out, chin lifted.

"You have done a noble thing today," he declared. "A historic act. The liberation of a champion."

Olivia started toward the front doors. "Let's not get carried away."

"I will absolutely get carried away," Anton said. "I have been stationary for decades. I intend to make up for lost time."

"Please don't," Olivia muttered.

They passed through the lobby, weaving between guests who were quietly checking out, collecting bags, and avoiding eye contact with one another.

Luke glanced up as she crossed the room.

His gaze flicked briefly to her face, then to her coat, as though he sensed something had changed.

Olivia kept walking. She pushed through the front doors and stepped out into the cold.

The air hit her sharply, clean and bright after the heavy atmosphere inside. The parking lot stretched ahead, lined with vehicles dusted in fresh snow.

Gus sat where she had left him, solid and dependable and entirely unimpressed by the events of the weekend. Olivia took a few steps forward. Then stopped. Anton was already there.

Standing in front of the Subaru, hands on his hips, studying it with deep suspicion.

Olivia sighed. "Oh, no."

Anton circled the car slowly, his expression growing more critical with each step.

"This," he said at last, "is what you intend to travel in?"

"It's a perfectly good car," Olivia said.

He leaned closer to the front grille, peering at it as though it might reveal hidden flaws under scrutiny. "It lacks elegance," he said.

"It gets me where I need to go."

"It lacks speed."

"It has all-wheel drive."

Anton straightened and looked at her. "I have been liberated," he said gravely. "I will not now be subjected to mediocrity."

Olivia opened the driver's side door. "You're going to have to adjust your expectations."

Anton glanced from her to the car, then back again. "This will require effort," he said.

"I'm sure you'll manage." She slid into the driver's seat, the medal settling securely in her pocket. As she started the engine, she felt it again. That quiet, contained presence. Anton had been loud. Dramatic. Impossible to ignore. But the medal carried more than just his personality.

It carried history. And history, Olivia was learning, had a way of resurfacing when it had been buried too long.

She pulled out of the parking space, the lodge receding behind her.

Beside her in the car, Anton shifted uneasily on the seat, still eyeing Gus with obvious disapproval. "This is going to be a long journey," he said.

Olivia smiled faintly. "Welcome to Mistwood," she replied.

CHAPTER TWELVE

The Drive Back to March House

Olivia smiled and patted the steering wheel as the car remained steady on the road during a tight turn. "Good boy."

Anton, who had somehow settled himself in the passenger seat despite not actually possessing a body, looked from her to the dashboard with astonishment. "You speak to it, and it listens? It is a machine."

"He's Gus."

Anton blinked. "You have named it."

"Of course I named him."

He stared out through the windshield as the defroster continued its battle against the frost. "This century grows stranger by the minute," he muttered.

Olivia prepared to navigate another switchback.

Anton braced himself dramatically against the seat. "You trust this metal carriage to climb mountains?" he demanded.

Olivia scoffed. "We're going down the mountain."

"That was not my point."

"It has done both. Many times."

He looked deeply unconvinced.

The road wound around the mountain, edged by towering pines heavy with fresh snow. Plow trucks had already made a pass, shoving the accumulation toward the shoulder, but the pavement still wore a slick layer of packed white in places. Olivia kept both hands on the wheel and took the descent slowly. There was no sense in hurrying. Not in these conditions. Not with her mind still working over everything she had learned.

The trees were beautiful in the muted winter light. Snow clung to every branch, softening their sharp lines and turning the forest into something almost dreamlike. In the distance, between gaps in the pines, Mistwood Lake appeared and disappeared in flashes of steel blue beneath the pale sky. Smoke rose from chimneys far below, thin and steady. It should have been peaceful.

Instead, the mountain felt watchful. Cassie had come here searching for something. Not gossip. Not harmless local folklore. Something real enough to frighten her. Important enough to keep her digging through records and notes and old fragments of history when most people would have let the past rot quietly in storage.

Olivia tightened her grip on the wheel.

Cassie believed she had found a secret worth uncovering. That much was clear. Maybe it had to do with the land. Maybe with the missing records. Maybe with something that linked the old ski club, the lodge, and the things people in town had chosen not to talk about. Gerald Huxley's casual mention of the long-ago storage fire lingered in her mind. Lost records. Lost land documents and lost history. Convenient, if you were the sort of person who preferred certain truths to remain buried.

Anton shifted beside her, peering at the road ahead. "The mountain is poorly maintained," he announced.

"The road was plowed this morning."

"There should be fewer curves."

"I'll make a note for the county."

"And the guardrails are uninspiring."

Olivia shot him a sideways glance. "What would inspire you? Decorative ironwork?"

"Yes," he said at once. "Or stone pillars. Something with dignity."

She laughed before she could stop herself. The sound surprised her. It felt wrong and necessary all at once. Strange, to laugh on the morning after a murder. Strange, too, how quickly a dramatic dead skier complaining about infrastructure could wedge itself into a grief-heavy silence and crack it open just enough for air to get in.

Anton looked faintly smug. "You see," he said. "My presence improves the journey."

"That's one word for it."

They rounded another bend, and the view opened wide. Mistwood Lake lay below them, broad and cold and reflective. The early winter sky mirrored in its surface. The town spread along the shore in clusters of rooftops and chimneys and narrow streets dusted with snow. From up here, it looked peaceful. Almost picturesque. The sort of place that belonged on a Christmas card sold in a gift shop next to spiced cider candles and handmade ornaments.

Olivia knew better. Small towns had a talent for prettiness. It was one of their more effective disguises.

She passed a snowplow laboring uphill in the opposite lane, yellow lights flashing, blade pushing a curling wave of snow toward the shoulder. The driver lifted two fingers from the wheel in greeting as he went by. Olivia returned the gesture automatically.

Anton frowned at the plow. "That machine is at least built with purpose," he said.

"Don't let Gus hear you say that."

"He is still absurdly named."

Olivia smiled faintly and kept driving.

The further down the mountain they went, the more the familiar pieces of ordinary life returned. Mailboxes half-buried at the ends of long drives. A dog bounding through snow in a front yard. Laundry frozen stiff on a line behind a farmhouse because someone had either faith in the weather or a very stubborn attachment to fresh air. The sight of it all should have grounded her. Instead, it sharpened the unreality.

Someone had been killed only a few miles above this peaceful little town. And now people would go on with their day. They would shovel walkways, make soup, complain about the cold, and stop by the grocery store for milk. They would chat about the weather and whether the school might close if the next storm hit hard enough. All the while, the fact of Cassie's death settled quietly into the foundations of the place, another dark thing tucked beneath its surface.

Olivia thought of March House. Of Lark holding everything together while she had been away. Of the old furnace making noises that never inspired confidence. Of the resident ghosts and their endless opinions. Of the smell of tea and old wood and baking. Home, in the broadest and strangest sense of the word. She was ready to be back.

When they reached the edge of town, Mistwood welcomed them in with the same deceptive calm it always wore so well. Snow softened the rooftops and outlined the bare tree branches along the streets. Storefront windows glowed amber in the afternoon light. Smoke drifted from brick chimneys. The lake beyond the buildings reflected the winter sky in muted silver and blue.

Anton leaned slightly toward the glass, studying the town with interest. “So this is Mistwood.”

“This is Mistwood.”

“It is smaller than I expected.”

“It gets bigger if you count all the gossip.”

He considered that. “Then perhaps it is enormous.”

Olivia snorted.

They drove past the bakery, the hardware store, the diner with its hand-painted sign promising hot coffee and pie. A woman in a red coat trudged along the sidewalk, carrying two grocery bags. A teenage boy in boots too thin for the weather used a shovel to clear the front steps of the pharmacy with the tragic energy of someone who had definitely been volunteered.

Everything looked normal, and that was the strangest part of all.

Olivia turned onto the street leading to March House, and there it was at last, rising from its snowy lot with all the familiar personality of an eccentric elderly relative who disapproved of modern noise but tolerated it for the sake of company.

The old bed-and-breakfast wore winter well. Snow gathered on the rooflines and porch railings, softening the bones of the house without diminishing its character. The windows glowed warmly. Smoke rose from the chimney in a steady gray ribbon.

Relief loosened something in Olivia’s chest. Home. She kept driving. She needed to go to Cassie’s house, and if she stopped home first, she’d be late. Luke would go there as soon as he arrived in town. But it felt good knowing home was close. She also needed to figure out how to introduce Anton to the rest of her permanent houseguests. It was probably a bad idea to bring him home, but like her aunt, when she found a lost and lonely soul, she couldn't just abandon the person if she had the ability to bring them where they could connect with other ghosts.

She pulled Gus into a parking spot and shifted into park. The engine idled for a moment before she turned the key and silenced it. The sudden quiet settled around them.

Anton stared at the dashboard. Then he looked at Olivia with open suspicion. "Is that it?"

"Yes."

"It has stopped."

"That is generally what happens when you park."

He looked toward the hood as though expecting flames to erupt. "And now?"

"Now I need to get into the house because Luke is already here and probably annoyed at having to wait for me."

He frowned. "And the machine will not explode?"

Olivia closed her eyes briefly. "His name is Gus," she said with the patience of a woman drawing very close to the end of hers, "and he's very reliable."

Anton looked offended on behalf of all respectable transportation everywhere. "A vehicle," he said, "should have a more heroic name."

Olivia unbuckled her seatbelt. "What would you have called him?"

Anton did not hesitate. "Thunderbolt."

She thought about the station wagon. At the practical shape of it. The salt on the lower panels. The missing ice scraper cap she kept meaning to replace. The faint smell of coffee and cinnamon gum that permanently lived in the interior, no matter how often she cleaned it. Then she looked back at Anton. "He is absolutely not a Thunderbolt."

Anton seemed pained by her lack of vision. "Something with grandeur," he said. "Something worthy of mountain roads and winter trials. Avalanche. Iron Crest. Storm Runner."

Olivia opened the door. "He's Gus."

She stepped out into the cold, grabbed her scarf, and shut the door. Snow crunched under her boots as she headed for the front walk.

Anton appeared beside the car one last time, giving it a long, dubious look. “I remain unconvinced,” he announced.

“That makes two of us,” Olivia muttered. “I’m still adjusting to you.”

He chose to take that as a compliment.

As she climbed the porch steps, and wondered what was waiting just beyond the front door. Olivia felt the medal in her coat pocket and the strange, invisible thread of everything that had followed her home from the mountain. Cassie’s death. The missing records. The unanswered questions. And now Anton Volkov, self-declared champion, freed from a decorative prison and deeply offended by modern automotive naming standards. March House, she suspected, was about to get louder.

CHAPTER THIRTEEN

Cassie's House

The house sat at the edge of a quiet street, half-hidden behind a pair of snow-laden fir trees that bowed under the weight of the recent storm. It was smaller than Olivia had expected. A single-story structure with faded blue siding and a narrow front porch. A place that blended into the background of a town where everyone knew everyone.

Cassie Greer had lived here alone. The realization settled over Olivia as she walked along the path to the front door. Snow crunched beneath her boots, sharp and loud in the stillness. The air carried that clean, biting edge that came after a storm, when the world felt briefly untouched.

Luke stood near the front gate, hands tucked into the pockets of his jacket, shoulders tight against the cold. He didn't look surprised to see her. That alone told Olivia he'd expected her to come.

"Morning," she said.

"Olivia." His tone held the usual mix of resignation and mild irritation, though it lacked the bite it once had. Progress, she supposed.

Olivia glanced at the house, then back at him. "This is it?"

"This is it."

A beat passed between them, the silence filled with unspoken things. Questions. Warnings. A history of arguments that neither of them felt like repeating.

Luke straightened slightly and stepped toward her, lowering his voice as if the quiet house might somehow overhear. "You're here as an observer," he said. "Nothing more."

Olivia raised an eyebrow. "You've said that before."

"I mean it this time."

"You meant it the other times, too."

His jaw flexed. That familiar tension flickered across his face, but it didn't escalate. Instead, he exhaled slowly, a thin cloud of breath vanishing into the cold. "This isn't your B&B," he said. "This is an active investigation. You don't touch anything unless I say you can. You don't move anything. You don't pocket anything."

"I don't pocket evidence."

He gave her a look.

She lifted her hands. "Fine. I don't pocket evidence anymore."

Luke studied her for a moment longer, as if weighing whether to argue further. Then, with a small shake of his head, he turned toward the house.

"Stay close," he said. "And try not to get ahead of yourself."

Olivia followed him up the narrow path, brushing snow from the railing as they climbed the porch steps. The front door stood slightly ajar, a strip of darkness visible inside.

Luke pushed it open fully. "After you," he said.

Olivia stepped inside.

The house smelled faintly of paper and dust, with a lingering trace of something warmer beneath it. Coffee, maybe. Or old books that had soaked up years of quiet mornings.

The entryway opened into a modest living room. A worn couch sat against one wall, draped with a knitted blanket. A small television rested on a stand in the corner, unplugged. But it wasn't the furniture that drew Olivia's attention. It was the books. They were everywhere.

Stacked in uneven towers on the floor. Lined along shelves that sagged under their weight. Piled on the coffee table, the end tables, even the windowsill. Hardcovers, paperbacks, binders filled with loose pages. History. Everywhere she looked, history.

Luke closed the door behind them, shutting out the cold. "We did a preliminary sweep," he said. "Nothing obviously out of place. No signs of forced entry."

Olivia moved slowly into the room, her gaze sweeping over the stacks. "She wasn't just interested in history," she murmured. "She was buried in it."

Luke followed her line of sight. "Teacher," he said. "Comes with the territory."

"This is more than lesson planning." She reached out, then stopped herself just short of touching a stack of papers. Luke noticed.

"Go ahead," he said after a moment. "Just don't rearrange her life."

Olivia nodded and gently lifted the top sheet. It was a photocopy. A newspaper clipping, yellowed with age even in reproduction. The headline mentioned a land dispute in Mistwood dating back decades. Beneath it, handwritten notes filled the margins in tight, precise script.

Dates. Names. Parcel numbers.

She set it back carefully and moved to the nearest shelf.

Maps were tucked between books, some folded, others rolled. A large one lay partially unrolled across a side table, weighted down by a ceramic mug.

Olivia stepped closer.

It was a map of Mistwood and the surrounding mountains. Not the clean, modern kind you'd find online. This one was older, more detailed in some places, less in others. Sections were marked in pencil. Circles. Lines. Small notations written in the same careful hand.

"She was mapping something," Olivia said.

Luke came up beside her. "Property lines," he said. "Old surveys. We found similar maps in her bag at the lodge."

"This is more detailed."

He studied the markings, his expression tightening slightly. "Yeah," he admitted.

Olivia traced one of the lines with her finger, not quite touching the paper. It led out of town, into the mountains, then circled back.

"Parcel boundaries," she whispered. "Ownership changes."

"You're getting all that from a glance?"

"I worked in a kitchen where the head chef thought mislabeling ingredients was a personal offense against humanity," she said. "Details matter."

Luke huffed a quiet breath that might have been the beginning of a smile. It vanished quickly.

They moved deeper into the house.

The kitchen was small but tidy. A single plate sat in the drying rack beside the sink. A mug rested on the counter, a faint ring of coffee staining the bottom.

Olivia paused there. "She didn't expect to be gone long," she said.

Luke leaned against the counter, crossing his arms. "Or she was used to leaving things this way."

Olivia shook her head. "No. Look at this." She gestured to the mug, the neatly folded dish towel, the absence of clutter. "She finishes things," Olivia said. "Even small things. That kind of habit doesn't disappear overnight."

Luke glanced around the kitchen again, seeing it through her eyes this time. "Okay," he drawled. "So she thought she was coming back."

"Yes."

A silence settled between them, heavier now.

If Cassie had expected to return, then whatever pulled her out into the cold that night hadn't been planned.

Luke stepped back from the counter. "Let's check the rest."

The bedroom told the same story as the living room, only more personal. Books lined the walls here, too, but mixed among them were binders, folders, and stacks of loose papers. A desk sat beneath the window, its surface covered in notes, photocopies, and what looked like survey records.

Olivia stepped closer. "Land deeds," she said.

Luke came around the other side of the desk. "That's what we're thinking."

She picked up one of the documents, scanning it quickly. Names. Dates. Transfers of ownership. Parcel numbers repeated over and over again. "Parcel 7B," she said.

Luke's head lifted. "You've seen that before."

"In her notes," Olivia said. "At the lodge."

He nodded. "It comes up a lot."

Olivia flipped through a few more pages, her brow furrowing. "She was tracking changes," she said. "Comparing older records to newer ones."

"Why?"

"That's the question."

Luke leaned over the desk, studying the papers. "If there's something off in these records," he said, "it could mean fraud. Property disputes. Maybe even something worth killing over."

Olivia didn't answer right away. Her attention had shifted. To the bookshelf beside the desk.

At first glance, it looked no different from the others. Rows of books, some worn with age, others newer. But something about it tugged at her instincts. She stepped closer.

"Something wrong?" Luke asked.

"Maybe," she said. Her gaze moved slowly along the shelf. Most of the books were older. Their spines faded, edges softened by time and use. But one stood out. Near the middle of the shelf, tucked between two thicker volumes, was a book that looked almost untouched. The cover was crisp. The spine was uncreased. New. In a room full of history, it didn't belong. Olivia reached for it, then paused, glancing at Luke.

He gave a small nod. "Careful."

She pulled the book free. It felt heavier than it should have. She frowned and opened the front cover. Inside, the pages had been cut. Not all of them. Just enough to create a hollow space in the center. And nestled inside that space was a small notebook. Olivia's pulse quickened.

"Well," Luke said quietly, stepping closer. "That's not suspicious at all."

She glanced up at him. "You want to take this, or …"

"You found it," he said. "Open it."

Olivia hesitated for only a second before lifting the notebook out. It was small enough to fit in her hand. The cover was plain, unmarked, the edges slightly worn. She opened it.

The first page held a series of photocopies, folded and taped in place. Land deeds.

Older ones. The ink was faded, the text slightly blurred from copying, but still readable.

Olivia flipped to the next page. Survey maps. Hand-drawn overlays marked boundaries and changes, lines crossing over one another in a way that suggested discrepancies.

Luke leaned in, his shoulder brushing hers as he looked. "She was building a case," he said.

Olivia nodded. "She wasn't just collecting information," she said. "She was connecting it." She turned another page. Handwritten notes filled the margins, tighter and more urgent than the ones they'd seen elsewhere. Parcel 7B appeared again and again. Circled. Underlined. Referenced with arrows pointing to different documents. "Everything leads back to this," Olivia said.

Luke's expression darkened. "Then we need to find out who owns it."

Olivia flipped further. More notes. More references. Then she stopped. Near the bottom of a page, written smaller than the rest, almost as if it had been added as an afterthought, were three simple words.

Ask L.W.

Olivia stared at it. "L.W.," she murmured.

Luke straightened slightly. "Mean anything to you?"

She shook her head. "Not yet."

He took the notebook gently from her hands, scanning the page himself. "Could be a person," he said. "Initials."

"Or a place."

"Or both."

Olivia crossed her arms, thinking. Cassie had been careful. Methodical. If she'd written that down, it mattered. "Ask L.W.," she repeated. "She thought this was important enough to hide."

Luke closed the notebook, his grip tightening slightly. "This changes things," he said.

Olivia looked at him. "You believe that now?"

He met her gaze, something sharper and more focused in his expression than she'd seen before. "This isn't just a fall on the ice," he said. "Not anymore."

The words hung in the air between them. A line had been

crossed. Whatever Cassie had been working on, whatever she'd uncovered, it wasn't just history. It was something dangerous.

Something current.

Luke slipped the notebook into an evidence bag, sealing it with careful precision. "We're treating this as a homicide," he said.

Olivia felt a chill that had nothing to do with the cold outside. Cassie had been right.

And it had cost her everything.

As they moved back toward the front of the house, Olivia paused in the doorway of the living room, her gaze drifting once more over the stacks of books, the maps, the notes. Cassie had lived here, surrounded by the past. And somewhere in all of it, she had found a truth that someone didn't want uncovered.

Olivia turned to Luke. "Parcel 7B," she said. "Whoever L.W. is, that's where we start."

Luke nodded once. "Yeah," he said. "That's exactly where we start."

Outside, the snow-covered town of Mistwood lay quiet beneath a pale winter sky.

But Olivia knew better now. Beneath that quiet, something was shifting. And they had just taken the first real step into it.

CHAPTER FOURTEEN

The Historical Society

By the time Olivia pulled Gus into a parking space in front of the Mistwood Historical Society, the sky had turned the pale, washed-out gray that promised more snow by evening. The old brick building sat on a quiet corner just off Main Street, tucked between a law office and a gift shop that sold handmade candles, local jam, and enough pine-scented décor to fumigate a locker room.

A brass plaque beside the door identified the building in elegant lettering. The society occupied what had once been Mistwood's first bank, back when men in wool coats and serious hats had probably stood on these same steps discussing lumber, rail shipments, and whose cousin had lost a finger at the sawmill. Now it houses records.

Olivia climbed out, zipped her coat higher against the cold, and glanced automatically toward the passenger seat.

Anton sat there with his arms folded and his expression deeply offended. "I still object to this machine," he informed her. "It rattles like a kettle about to explode."

"It got you here, didn't it?"

He drew himself up. "That is hardly the point."

Olivia shut the door before he could continue and headed toward the entrance. Snow squeaked under her boots. The wind had picked up since morning, slipping thin fingers of cold down the back of her neck. She ducked inside gratefully.

Warmth met her first, along with the smell of dust, paper, and old wood polish. It was the specific scent of places that stored the past in boxes and expected visitors to handle it gently. The front room was small and neat. Framed photographs lined the walls, showing Mistwood in various stages of its life. A dirt road where Main Street now stands. Men posing with impossible numbers of fish. A parade of smiling townspeople from some forgotten summer festival. A glass display case held antique ski pins, old postcards, and a sun-faded pennant from North Star Summit back when it had been a modest local slope instead of a full resort.

A strange woman sat behind a desk near the back, bent over a stack of papers. Hazel Finch no longer worked for the Historical Society. After Theodore Bramble was arrested, she put in her notice and left at the end of September.

The woman looked up as Olivia entered.

She was in her sixties, maybe older, with silver hair pinned into a tidy twist and half-moon glasses balanced low on her nose. She had the alert, assessing expression of someone who had spent years protecting fragile records from the public. "Can I help you?" she asked.

Olivia stepped forward. "I hope so. I'm Olivia March."

Recognition flickered across the woman's face. In Mistwood, that happened with annoying regularity. "March," she repeated. "From March House."

Olivia gave a small smile. "That's me."

The woman set aside her papers and stood. "Nadine Ellery. I volunteer here three days a week." Her expression softened. "I was sorry to hear about Cassandra Greer."

Olivia nodded. "I was, too."

Nadine clasped her hands lightly in front of her. "She spent quite a bit of time here recently. Very focused. Very determined."

"That's actually why I came."

Nadine's gaze sharpened at once. "You're following her trail."

It was not a question.

Olivia hesitated only a moment. "I'm trying to understand what she was working on."

Nadine studied her with the same careful look Luke used when deciding whether she was about to be useful or troublesome. Olivia had the odd feeling she was being measured for reliability. Apparently, she passed.

"Well," Nadine said, "you'd better come with me." She led Olivia through a doorway into the archive room. It was larger than Olivia expected and much more crowded. Tall metal shelving units filled most of the space, each loaded with document boxes, ledgers, and binders. A long table stood in the center beneath hanging lamps that cast a mellow golden light. Filing cabinets lined one wall. Another wall held framed maps of early Mistwood and the surrounding area, their ink faded to shades of brown and charcoal.

It should have felt cramped, but it felt dense. Not with people. With years.

Old town records. Property ledgers. Family genealogies. Meeting minutes. Survey maps. Tax rolls. Every argument, bargain, marriage, birth, death, and boundary line that had built Mistwood seemed to sleep in this room.

Anton appeared beside a display of sepia photographs and let out an impressed hum.

"At least this place knew how to preserve paper," he said. "Most of the modern world seems determined to erase itself."

Olivia ignored him and followed Nadine to the central table.

"Cassie worked here almost every afternoon for the past two weeks," Nadine said. "Sometimes longer. She asked for early resort records first, then land transfer documents, then anything related to old property boundaries in the north ridge area."

Olivia took off her gloves and tucked them into her coat pocket. "Did she say what she thought she'd found?"

Nadine gave a dry little laugh. "Cassie rarely made a full declaration before she was ready. She liked evidence too much for that." She pulled out a chair and motioned for Olivia to sit. "But she told me something wasn't adding up."

Olivia sat. "What exactly was she researching?"

Nadine moved to one of the shelves and began selecting volumes with practiced efficiency. "The early development of the ski resort," she said. "The original land acquisition, the investors involved, and a series of transfers in the nineteen-forties that shifted several property lines before construction really expanded." She carried the books and boxes back to the table and set them down one by one. "She believed there was a discrepancy in the records."

"Discrepancy" sounded so polite for something that had gotten a woman killed. Olivia rested her hands on the table and looked at the materials in front of her. One large ledger with cracked brown leather. Two archive boxes labeled LAND TRANSFERS, 1931-1949. A binder of copied deeds. A folder of genealogical records tied to early investors. Cassie had gone deep.

Nadine opened the ledger carefully. "The resort did not begin as North Star Summit," she said. "Originally, it was a small private ski club. Locally financed. Half recreation, half ambition. A handful of businessmen wanted to turn the ridge into something fashionable enough to attract winter tourists from Spokane and Boise."

"That sounds optimistic."

"It was. Most early development schemes in mountain towns are equal parts dream and stubbornness."

Olivia glanced down at the page. Names marched in careful script across yellowed paper. Dates. Acreage. Parcel designations. She recognized the rhythm of records now from Cassie's house, though she still could not read them as fluently as someone trained for it.

Nadine tapped a line with one slender finger. "These are the early investors. Some were local. A few came in from outside. Cassie paid particular attention to this group." She flipped through several pages. "And these were the transfers that concerned her most."

Olivia leaned closer. There it was again. Parcel 7B. Not alone, but threaded through the ledger with unsettling frequency. Pieces split off, rejoined, renumbered, then folded into the larger land purchase that eventually established the resort. "That number keeps coming up," Olivia said.

Nadine nodded. "Cassie noticed that too."

Olivia looked up. "Did she say why it mattered?"

"She said the boundary changes were too convenient." Nadine adjusted her glasses. "The original description of the parcel in one record does not quite match later versions. Not enough for an ordinary reader to notice, but enough to shift ownership on paper."

Olivia felt a small, unpleasant twist low in her stomach. "You mean someone changed the boundaries?"

"That was Cassie's suspicion."

Olivia sat back slowly. "And if that happened, someone could have taken land that was never legally theirs."

"Exactly."

The word settled over the table with the weight of a stone.

Olivia stared at the ledger, then at the archive boxes. She could almost see Cassie here in this chair, flipping pages with that same determined intensity, following one line after another until the truth showed itself in the gaps.

"She really thought she'd found fraud," Olivia whispered.

Nadine's face tightened. "I believe she was beginning to."

Olivia reached for the binder of copied deeds. "May I?"

"Carefully."

She opened it. Several documents had been copied onto modern paper, the original handwriting preserved in gray-black ink that had faded at the edges. Legal descriptions filled most of each page in dense blocks of old-fashioned language. Olivia skimmed past those and focused on the bottom, where signatures sprawled in ink.

The first few looked ordinary enough. Flourished, formal, a little pompous. Men from another era who probably thought signing their names with enough confidence made them important.

She turned another page. And stopped.

Something about the signature at the bottom snagged her attention so abruptly that she frowned before she even knew why.

Not that she could read the legal document any better than before. It was something simpler. More instinctive.

The handwriting looked wrong.

Olivia bent closer.

The rest of the document had the smooth, steady flow of practiced script. But the signature was uneven in a way that the others were not. The slant changed halfway through. The pressure seemed inconsistent. One letter looked overly careful, while the next trailed off too fast.

She had spent years piping inscriptions on cakes and writing dessert menus under pressure while trying not to throttle line cooks.

She knew what a practiced hand looked like. She also knew when someone was trying to imitate one.

"Mrs. Ellery," she said, still staring at the page. "Does this look strange to you?"

Nadine came around the table and bent beside her. "Which one?"

Olivia pointed.

Nadine adjusted her glasses and looked. For a few moments, she said nothing. Then she straightened slowly.

"Well," she said, "that is interesting."

"So it's not just me?"

"No," Nadine reached for another folder. "Wait here." She crossed to a filing cabinet and returned with several additional documents. "These are unrelated records signed by the same man over a span of years. Tax correspondence. A town petition. A bank affidavit." She laid them side by side.

Olivia compared the signatures. The difference leaped out now that she had context. On the legitimate records, the man's name flowed in one easy movement. On the deed, it looked forced. Not wildly. Not enough to leap off the page unless you were looking for it. But enough.

Nadine gave a tight nod. "It may be the same name. It is not the same hand."

A cold ripple worked down Olivia's spine. If the signature had been forged, then the deed had not merely been sloppy. It had been false from the beginning. She looked at the copied document again, suddenly seeing it not as a piece of paper but as the first rotten board in a floor that might collapse if someone stepped on it hard enough.

"Cassie saw this," Olivia said.

"She must have," Nadine replied. "I retrieved these documents for her on Tuesday. She spent nearly an hour comparing signatures."

"And she said nothing?"

"She said only that if she was right, it would explain the later boundary changes."

Olivia pressed her lips together. A forged signature on an original land deed. Changed parcel descriptions. Property lines shifting just enough to transfer ownership. Investors. Early development.

Generations of money and local reputation built on something crooked. If Cassie had found proof of that, her research was not just academic. It threatened people. Families. Businesses. Legacies. Possibly the entire legal foundation of the resort itself.

Olivia sat back and folded her arms, the pieces beginning to move together in her mind.

If the original land purchase involved fraud, then later sales and transfers might have been built on false ownership. If anyone discovered that now, there would be lawsuits. Public scandal. Financial fallout. Old names dragged through the mud. Maybe even current owners, suddenly forced to answer impossible questions about land they thought was clean. And Cassie had been digging into exactly that. Someone might have wanted to stop her before she could prove it.

A hush settled over the room. The only sound was the faint tick of an old wall clock and the soft rattle of papers as Nadine replaced the comparison documents in a neat stack.

Olivia stared at the forged signature for a moment longer. "Mistwood likes to act as if its history is all charming festivals and pie socials," she murmured.

Nadine snorted softly. "Every town edits itself."

That felt too true.

Olivia closed the binder carefully. "Did Cassie mention any specific names? Anyone she thought was connected?"

Nadine hesitated. "Not directly. She asked about the Keller family. Then, about the Larkin holdings. And she spent a surprising amount of time tracing the descendants of two early investors whose names no longer appear anywhere in current resort literature."

Olivia's head lifted. "Why surprising?"

"Because those men were involved only at the beginning. Briefly. Then they vanished from the official story." Nadine's mouth thinned. "Cassie thought that the omission was deliberate."

Olivia had heard versions of it all week at the summit. The resort founder cast as some sort of rugged visionary. The old ski club was treated as the romantic beginning of a thriving winter destination. Smiling history polished for brochures and donor dinners. What if the beginning had been dirtier than anyone admitted?

From the far end of the archive room came Anton's sharp voice. "There," he said.

Olivia turned.

He stood in front of a wall display of enlarged historical photographs, one translucent hand lifted toward a framed black-and-white image. He looked almost solid in the dim archive light, his expression intent.

Nadine, of course, did not react. She could not hear him.

Olivia rose from her chair. "Excuse me for a moment." She crossed the room. The photograph showed an early ski club gathering. Men in thick sweaters and caps stood in the snow with wooden skis propped beside them. A few women in belted coats smiled stiffly at the edge of the group. Behind them rose a modest lodge building, little more than a timber structure with ambition.

Anton pointed to a man near the center. "That man was present during my time and discussions about creating a resort," he said.

Olivia stared at the image. The man was broad-shouldered, dark-haired, with a serious face that gave away nothing. He stood slightly behind the others, not central to the photograph, yet somehow impossible to ignore once seen. He looked vaguely familiar.

"You're sure?" she whispered.

Anton gave her an indignant look. "I may be dead, Olivia, but my eyesight remains excellent."

She leaned closer. "Do you remember who he was?"

"No."

She looked at the brass caption beneath the frame. It listed only last names. No first names. No details beyond the date and a bland description of the club's founding members and associates. Her pulse kicked harder.

Anton had just handed her a clue, and it was maddeningly incomplete.

"Of course," she muttered. "Because why would anything in this town ever be simple?"

Anton studied the photograph with a faint frown. "I saw someone who looked like him arguing with a woman at the summit. More than once. And with the scholar."

"Cassie?"

"Yes."

Olivia turned sharply toward him. “You saw Cassie arguing with a man who looked like him?”

“At the lodge. In the hall one evening. Voices were raised. The living often assume the dead are not paying attention.”

“That’s because most of the living are not having conversations with dead Olympic narcissists.”

He drew himself up. “Former Olympian.”

“Still a narcissist.”

Anton seemed to consider objecting, then let it go with surprising grace. “The point remains. He was there.”

Olivia looked back at the caption. Just last names. Her mind raced through everything she knew. Investors. Land transfers. Early resort development. Families whose names remained woven into Mistwood’s present. Any of those surnames might still matter. Behind her, she heard Nadine approach.

“That photograph is from the original ski club,” the archivist said. “One of my favorites.”

Olivia kept her face neutral. “Do you know who all these men are?”

“Some of them. Not all.” Nadine moved beside her and peered at the caption. “Several were investors or local sponsors. Others were club officers.”

Olivia pointed to the man Anton had indicated. “What about him?”

Nadine squinted. “That would be one of the Kellers, I think. Or perhaps a Reed. The caption predates our better cataloging system, unfortunately.”

Of course it did. “Is there a member list somewhere?” Olivia asked.

“There should be. Meeting minutes, club rosters, donation ledgers.” Nadine glanced toward the shelves. “Though it may take a while to find the exact year.”

Olivia nodded slowly. A man connected to the early ski club had argued with Cassie at the summit. Anton was certain of it. And if that man’s family name still carried weight in town, Cassie might have been getting close enough to scare someone. Not proof. Not even close.

But it was something. She looked once more at the stern face in the photograph, then back across the archive room to the table where the copied deed still lay open beneath the warm lamplight.

Forged signature. Boundary changes. Vanishing names. A dead teacher who had kept digging.

The shape of it was forming now, not yet clear enough to see every edge, but authentic enough to cast a shadow. Cassie had not been chasing a harmless historical puzzle. She had been prying at the foundation of the resort itself. And if Olivia was right, that foundation had been crooked from the start.

Nadine touched her elbow lightly. "Miss March?"

Olivia looked at her.

"If Cassandra uncovered what she thought she uncovered," Nadine said quietly, "be careful."

The words settled heavily between them.

Olivia glanced toward the door, toward the gray afternoon waiting outside, toward the town that liked its past tidy and its scandals buried. Too late for careful, she thought. But she only said, "I will."

Anton came to stand beside her, arms folded, gaze fixed on the photograph. "No, you won't," he said.

Olivia sighed.

Unfortunately, he was probably right.

When she stepped back out into the cold, the wind had strengthened, and the first new flakes had fallen, light and dry against her face. She stood on the steps of the historical society for a moment, pulling on her gloves and staring across the street without really seeing it.

Mistwood bustled on around her in that small-town way that pretended life was ordinary. A woman carried a grocery bag to her car. A boy in a knit cap ran past with a sled tucked under one arm. Somewhere down the block, a door opened and shut, releasing a burst of laughter into the winter air. Ordinary. Meanwhile, a forged signature from the nineteen-thirties sat preserved in an archive room behind her, and a dead woman's research was beginning to look less and less academic.

Olivia descended the steps slowly. If Cassie had discovered proof that the resort's original land purchase involved fraud, then this had never been about nostalgia or missing paperwork. It was about motive. And motive, Olivia had learned, was where murder liked to hide.

She headed for Gus as the snow thickened, her mind already turning to Luke, Parcel 7B, and the incomplete last-name clue from the photograph. Somewhere in Mistwood, the past was still protecting itself. And Olivia had every intention of making it very uncomfortable.

CHAPTER FIFTEEN

Ghosts in the Attic

Olivia knew she was home before she even turned into the driveway. Not because of the house. Because of the chaos. March House glowed warmly against the early winter dusk, every window lit, the porch lamps casting soft golden halos onto freshly fallen snow. The place looked like something out of a postcard: welcoming, cozy, perfect. And absolutely not quiet.

Voices spilled out the moment she stepped onto the porch. Laughter. The clinking of mugs. The unmistakable hum of a coffee grinder working overtime.

Olivia paused with her hand on the door, her shoulders sagging in relief. Home. Then she pushed it open and stepped straight into controlled madness. The scent hit her first. Coffee, cinnamon, fresh bread, something citrusy, and beneath it all the faint, ever-present polish of old wood and history. The front parlor was full. Every chair occupied, two guests standing near the fireplace, another leaning against the piano as if that were perfectly acceptable behavior in a Victorian home.

Emma stood behind the coffee station they had set up in the dining room doorway, moving with practiced efficiency. Jess darted between tables with a tray balanced expertly in one hand.

Both of them looked up at the same time.

"Olivia!"

Jess nearly abandoned her tray before remembering she was

holding hot drinks and correcting at the last second. Emma grinned wide enough to light the room.

"You're back!"

Olivia barely had time to close the door before Jess was in front of her.

"You would not believe the week we've had."

"I might," Olivia said, dropping her bag beside the entry table. "Try me."

Emma leaned over the counter. "No disasters. No fires. No angry guests. We even had someone ask about catering."

Olivia blinked. "Catering?"

"See?" Lark's voice floated in from the kitchen, rich with satisfaction. "I told you. All those people at that summit? They eat. Frequently."

Lark appeared in the doorway, wiping her hands on a towel, her layered skirts swaying as she moved. Her silver hair was pulled back loosely, and she looked entirely too pleased with herself.

"There she is," Lark said, spreading her arms. "The conquering heroine returns."

Olivia snorted. "I feel more conquered than anything."

Lark pulled her into a quick hug anyway. "You look exhausted. Which means you've been doing something useful."

"Debatable."

Emma leaned in. "Did you meet anyone important?"

Jess added, "Did you get us catering work?"

Olivia opened her mouth, hesitated, then closed it again.

"Yes," she said finally. "And maybe."

That was enough to send both Emma and Jess into immediate excitement.

Lark beamed. "You see? I knew it. This house is expanding its influence."

Jess and Emma went back to making coffee, chatting noisily as they worked.

Olivia shook her head, a tired smile tugging at her mouth. For a moment, everything felt … normal. Warm. Safe. And the …

"Well, this is intolerably crowded."

Olivia closed her eyes. Of course. She turned slightly, already bracing herself.

Sir Alistair Pruitt stood near the staircase, hands clasped behind his back, his expression one of refined disapproval as he surveyed the room. "This level of noise would have been considered deeply uncivilized in my day."

"You say that every day," Monique replied, appearing beside him in a shimmer of silk and attitude. "And yet, here we are. Surviving."

Olivia exhaled slowly. Home. She bent, picked up her bag, and stepped fully inside.

And then she remembered. Right. Anton. She glanced over her shoulder. "Come on," she whispered. A moment later, Anton stepped through the doorway. The air shifted instantly.

Not colder. Sharper. More … energetic.

The ghosts noticed before Olivia even spoke.

Sir Alistair stiffened. Monique's eyes widened.

Simon appeared near the hallway, his soldier's posture snapping into immediate alertness. "What," Simon said slowly, "is that?"

Anton drew himself up proudly, brushing imaginary snow from his sleeve. "I am Anton Volkov," he declared. "World champion skier."

Silence. Then …

"A foreigner," Simon said flatly.

"Athlete," Anton corrected.

"A nuisance," Sir Alistair added.

Monique stepped forward, her smile turning dangerously interested. "Well now," she said, circling Anton slowly. "A man with confidence. And cheekbones."

Anton turned, clearly pleased. "You recognize greatness."

"I recognize something," Monique said.

Olivia pinched the bridge of her nose. "Oh no," she muttered.

It wasn't long before the others appeared.

Walt walked up to the newcomer and frowned. "Who's this guy?"

Simon scowled, "Another foreigner."

Monique raised an eyebrow and looked offended.

"This is going to be chaos," Olivia said.

Anton had already started talking again.

"I dominated the slopes," he was saying. "Men feared me. Women admired me."

Simon crossed his arms. "What war did you fight in?"

Anton paused. "War?"

"Yes. War."

"I competed," Anton said.

Simon stared at him. "That's not war."

Sir Alistair made a soft, offended noise. "Skiing is not a respectable pursuit."

"It is a test of skill and courage," Anton snapped.

"It is sliding downhill," Sir Alistair replied.

Monique laughed. "Oh, I like him."

"You would," Simon muttered.

The argument escalated almost immediately.

JJ, Daisy, and Flossie stood at the edge of the room, watching the others like spectators ringside at a boxing match.

Olivia backed away slowly. Nope. Not dealing with that right now. She turned toward the stairs.

"Where are you going?" Lark called.

"Up," Olivia said. "If I stay down here, I might lose what little sanity I have left."

Lark frowned. "What did you do?"

"I'll tell you later."

Lark stared for a moment, then nodded.

Olivia took a deep breath and climbed the stairs, the noise of the house following her for a few steps before fading into a muffled hum. The second floor was quieter. Not silent. Never silent. But calmer. She dropped her bag in her room, kicked off her boots, and sat on the edge of the bed for a moment. Her body ached. Her brain felt as if it had been wrung out and left to dry.

The ghosts. Cassie. The lodge. The land records. The feeling that something was just out of reach. She leaned back, staring at the ceiling. And then …

"You're missing something."

Olivia turned her head.

Daisy stood in the doorway, her pressed-flower journal held loosely in her hands.

Olivia sighed. "Hi, Daisy."

Daisy tilted her head slightly. "You're looking in the wrong place."

"Helpful," Olivia said.

Daisy stepped into the room. "Not wrong. Just incomplete."

Olivia sat up. "What am I missing?"

Daisy didn't answer directly. She never did. Instead, she said, "There are boxes upstairs."

Olivia frowned. "Boxes?"

"In the attic," Daisy said. "Your aunt kept everything."

That tracked. Izzy had never thrown anything away. Ever. Olivia stood slowly. "What kind of everything?"

Daisy smiled faintly. "The kind that gets forgotten."

Olivia exhaled. Of course. "Right," she said. "Because this week hasn't been complicated enough." She grabbed a flashlight from her nightstand and headed for the attic stairs. The pull-down ladder creaked in protest as she pulled it open.

Cold air drifted down immediately, carrying the dry, dusty scent of old wood and paper.

Olivia climbed. The attic stretched out above her in shadow and slanted beams. The space was cluttered but organized in that particular way only long-time owners understood. Boxes.

Dozens of them. Some labeled. Most not. She crouched, sweeping the flashlight beam across the nearest stack.

"Okay," she muttered. "Let's see what secrets you've been hiding." She started with the closest box. Old linens. Next. Cookbooks. Next came receipts. So many receipts. She kept going. Time slipped. Dust gathered on her jeans. Her hands grew cold. Then, in a smaller box, carefully sealed, were documents. Older. Much older. Carefully wrapped in tissue paper. Her pulse quickened. She lifted the first bundle. Property records. Handwritten. Ink faded but legible.

Names she didn't recognize. Dates stretching back further than she expected. She flipped through them, her brow furrowing. Land transfers. Boundary changes. Ownership shifts. Her mind immediately connected the pieces. Cassie. The research. The inconsistencies.

"This is what you were looking for," Olivia murmured. She set the papers aside and reached deeper into the box. Her fingers brushed something firm. Flat.

She pulled it out. A photograph. Old. Sepia-toned. Mounted on stiff backing. She angled the flashlight. A group of people stood in front of what looked like an early version of Mistwood.

Families. Children. Men in work clothes. Women in long skirts. A posed moment in time. She leaned closer. Scanning faces. And then … she froze. There, in the second row, was a woman.

She was young with strong features. Eyes sharp, almost amused. Her hair was pulled back loosely.

Olivia's breath caught. "No way," she whispered. She shifted the light, bringing the image into sharper focus. The resemblance was unmistakable. Not identical. But close enough to send a chill through her. Lark. Or someone who could have been her sister.

Olivia's gaze dropped to the bottom of the photograph. A handwritten caption, faded but readable. She leaned in, heart pounding. "Henry Waverly family," she read softly. Her eyes moved along the names. And then stopped. Clara Waverly.

Olivia sat back slowly, the photograph still in her hands. Her mind raced. Waverly. Lark Waverly. She looked back at the woman in the photograph. The resemblance. The name. The timing.

"This … can't be a coincidence." Below her, the house hummed with life, voices, and laughter. The ghosts arguing about skiing versus warfare.

But up here, in the quiet, dust-filled attic, something shifted. The mystery widened and changed shape entirely.

Olivia looked down at the photograph again, her grip tightening slightly. "The Waverlys owned the mountain," she murmured. And if that was true, if Lark was connected to them, then everything Olivia thought she knew about Mistwood's history was about to get a lot more complicated.

She sat there for a long moment, staring at Clara Waverly's face. Slowly, the realization settled in. Not just about the land. Not just about the past. But about Lark. And what Lark might not have told her.

Olivia exhaled. "Okay," she whispered. "Now we're getting somewhere."

CHAPTER SIXTEEN

The Forged Deed

The sheriff's office smelled faintly of stale coffee, damp wool, and old paper. Olivia paused just inside the front door, letting it swing shut behind her with a soft thud. The building was never exactly cheerful on its best days, but this morning it felt especially grim. The sky outside hung low and gray over Mistwood, pressing a cold light through the front windows that did nothing to improve the mood.

The waiting area was empty except for a stack of outdated magazines and a potted plant that looked one missed watering away from death. Somewhere in the back, a printer groaned as if personally offended by its own existence.

Olivia shrugged out of her coat, stamped the snow from her boots, and headed for Luke's office. The door stood half-open. She knocked once against the frame.

Luke looked up from behind his desk, and for a second, she almost laughed. He looked terrible. Not dying-in-a-ditch terrible. More overworked, under-slept, and one misplaced form away from strangling someone with red tape terrible.

His hair was slightly too long again, falling forward as he bent over a stack of paperwork. His jaw was shadowed with stubble, and the muscle there flexed when he saw her, as if even surprise had become irritating lately. "Of course it's you," he said.

Olivia leaned one shoulder against the doorframe. “Good morning to you, too.”

He dropped a pen onto the desk and leaned back in his chair, rubbing a hand over his face. “I didn’t say it was bad.”

“You thought it loudly.”

“That still counts as not saying it.”

She stepped inside. “You look awful.”

“Thank you.”

“You’re welcome.”

His office was a disaster. Folders covered every available flat surface. Reports were stacked in crooked towers on the filing cabinet, with one particularly enormous tower on the corner of his desk. Legal pads sat open in overlapping layers across the desk, and two half-empty coffee cups stood near his elbow in what looked like a long-running experiment in caffeine dependency. His buckskin jacket hung over the back of a chair, and a cardboard evidence box rested on the floor near the wall.

Olivia glanced around. “Should I be worried that these paper towers might collapse and kill you?”

Luke snorted once. “It would be a stupid way to go.”

“I’ve heard of worse ways.”

He gave her a look, but it lacked its usual edge. He was tired, really tired.

Olivia’s humor softened. “Bad morning?” she asked.

Luke let out a slow breath and looked down at the mess on his desk. “Bad week.” That sounded more honest.

She took the chair across from him without being invited. At this point, invitations felt unnecessary. “How bad?”

Luke reached for one of the folders, then seemed to think better of it and let it drop again.

“Cassie’s death is officially being handled as a homicide now,” he said. “Which means a ton more paperwork, outside review, and a whole lot of people suddenly pretending they care about procedure.”

Olivia studied him. He wasn’t just tired. He was wound tight.

“And because the case touches the resort,” she said, “everybody’s nervous.”

Luke gave her a sharp glance. “That’s one word for it.”

“Influential local business owners?”

He laughed without humor. "Even closer to the mark."

Olivia folded her hands in her lap. "How many calls have you gotten this morning?"

Luke stared at her.

She raised an eyebrow. "That many?"

"Three before eight o'clock," he said. "One from a council member, one from a man who thinks owning half the commercial property on Main Street makes him an expert in criminal investigations, and one from a woman who wanted reassurance that winter bookings wouldn't be affected by the phrase 'suspicious death' appearing in regional news."

Olivia grimaced. "Charming."

"People are already worried about the season. The summit murder didn't help. If guests start canceling reservations because they think North Star Summit is cursed or unsafe, the whole town feels it." He said it flatly, but the strain underneath the words was plain.

Olivia glanced toward the badge on his desk, then back at him.

"You're catching heat because you're acting sheriff."

Luke leaned back again, the chair creaking under the shift. "That's part of it."

"Only part?" She waited.

After a moment, he spoke, quieter this time.

"My uncle resigns, suddenly I'm the one in the chair, and half the town can't decide whether to treat me like I'm temporary or incompetent."

Olivia's expression softened.

Luke noticed and frowned faintly, as though he disliked being observed too closely.

"The election's coming," he went on. "Every decision I make gets watched. Every mistake is remembered. There are people waiting for me to do this wrong."

"You haven't."

"That depends on who you ask."

Olivia studied him for a long moment. This was the most he had said about it. About the pressure. About standing in his uncle's place with half the county watching to see whether he stumbled. She thought of the way people in town talked. Friendly to your face, sharp the minute your back was turned. Mistwood had always been good at that particular trick.

"Your uncle left you a mess," she said.

Luke's mouth twitched. "That's a polite description."

"Would you prefer a catastrophic circus?"

He considered it. "Closer."

A smile tugged at her mouth, but it faded quickly. There was too much here to joke away.

She reached into her bag and pulled out Cassie's notebook.

Luke's eyes dropped to it immediately. "That looks familiar," he said.

"It should. It has become very popular lately."

He held out a hand.

Olivia drew it back slightly.

His gaze lifted. "You're not serious."

"I'm serious enough to ask first whether you plan to confiscate it."

Luke sat back, crossing his arms. "You make my job harder on purpose."

"Sometimes."

He stared at her for a beat longer, then sighed. "I'm not confiscating it."

"Good."

She set the notebook on the desk between them and flipped it open to the marked pages.

Luke leaned forward despite himself.

"I've been going through Cassie's notes again," Olivia said. "There are repeated references to Parcel 7B."

His expression changed a fraction. Not surprise exactly. Recognition, maybe.

"You've noticed it too," Olivia said.

Luke did not answer immediately. He looked down at the pages, scanning Cassie's cramped handwriting, the underlined lines, the dates, the arrows connecting names and records.

"Parcel 7B," he said finally, "is old county designation language. It doesn't get used much anymore."

"But it means something."

"It means land."

Olivia gave him a flat look. "Thank you, Sheriff. I was worried it referred to a casserole."

Luke ignored that.

"The old resort acreage got broken into parcels and sub-parcels when the area was first surveyed and transferred," he said. "Most people never see the older designations unless they're dealing with archival property records."

Olivia tapped the page. "Cassie saw them."

"Apparently."

"She was following something."

Luke's gaze moved to another page. "She usually was."

Olivia heard the quiet respect in that and filed it away.

"She linked Parcel 7B to the original mountain transfer," Olivia said. "And to those boundary changes from the 1930s."

Luke exhaled slowly."I know."

She blinked. "You know?"

"Not the whole picture," he said. "But enough to know she wasn't chasing nonsense."

That got her attention.

Luke pushed away from the desk and stood, moving to the filing cabinet behind him. He opened the top drawer, rummaged for a moment, then pulled out a thick file and brought it back.

Olivia sat a little straighter. "What's that?"

"County record copies," he said. "Or the ones we've managed to get our hands on without setting off a riot in three offices." He dropped the folder onto the desk and opened it.

Old photocopies, survey maps, tax references, and transfer forms.

Olivia leaned in.

Luke flipped through several pages until he found what he wanted, then slid one sheet across to her.

"This is a copy of the original deed transferring the mountain land to the first resort developers."

Olivia took it carefully. The paper copy was clean enough to read, though the original had clearly been handwritten in formal script. She recognized the document immediately. Dense legal phrasing. Lines of property descriptions. Names repeated in precise, careful ink.

Her pulse quickened. "So this is it," she murmured.

Luke nodded. "As far as county records are concerned, yes."

Olivia bent over the page.

The landowner's name appeared near the bottom, followed by the signature. Henry Waverly. There it was again. Waverly. She felt a faint jolt, remembering the attic photograph, Clara Waverly's face, the line of her jaw, the resemblance she could not stop seeing when she looked at Lark.

Luke was watching her now.

"What?"

Olivia glanced up. "Nothing."

"That is never true when you say it that way."

She ignored him and looked back down. The signature was elegant enough. Not especially dramatic. Confident, maybe, but something about it made her pause. She frowned.

Luke noticed immediately. "What is it?"

Olivia did not answer right away. Instead, she reached for another sheet from the folder. Then another. "What else do you have from the same period?"

Luke's eyes narrowed. "Why?"

"Because something's wrong."

That got his full attention. He turned, dug deeper into the file, and pulled out several more copies. "Tax record. Boundary declaration. A witness statement tied to a road easement. All the same general timeframe." He laid them out beside the deed.

Olivia moved them around until the signatures aligned in front of her. Then she bent lower. The surrounding office faded. The wheeze of the heater. A distant phone ringing somewhere in front. The groan of floorboards as someone passed in the hall. All of it fell away as she studied the documents and Henry Waverly's signature. Then another, and another. And there it was. She felt it before she could fully explain it. The original deed signature leaned too far to the right. The capital letters were shaped differently. The spacing was off. The hand looked careful in one document and natural in the others. On the tax record, the tail of the y curved sharply back under the name. On the deed, it dropped almost straight down. On one witness statement, the H began with a distinct upward hook. On the deed, it lacked it entirely.

Her skin prickled. "Luke."

He had already leaned forward.

"You see it."

"Yeah," he whispered. "I do." He took the deed copy from her and compared it to the others himself. A long silence stretched. "Finally", he said, "blast it."

Olivia sat back slowly, her heart thudding harder now. "It doesn't match."

"No," he said. "It doesn't." He grabbed another page, then another, laying them side by side in a tighter row as if proximity might somehow make the problem go away. It did not.

If anything, it made it worse. The difference became unmistakable once she saw it. Not glaring. Not cartoonishly bad. The sort of thing most people would miss unless they were really looking.

Cassie had looked.

Olivia thought of the notebook again. The repeated references. The urgency in the notes. The sense that Cassie had known she was circling something dangerous. "She found this," Olivia said.

Luke did not answer. "She had to have." He rubbed a hand over his jaw, staring at the documents.

"If the original deed was forged," Olivia said slowly, "then the transfer of the mountain land to the resort developers may not have been legal."

Luke's expression darkened. "Likely not."

Olivia looked back at the papers. The air in the office suddenly felt thinner.

Outside, a car door slammed. Voices drifted faintly through the window. Normal town sounds. Normal morning. Nothing about this felt normal anymore.

"If this becomes public," she said, "ownership of the entire resort could be challenged."

Luke's laugh was short and grim. "That's the cheerful version."

Olivia lifted her eyes to him.

He leaned back in his chair and looked older than he had when she walked in.

"This doesn't just touch the resort," he said. "It touches the jobs tied to it. The contracts. Vendors. Winter tourism. Property values. Every business in town that depends on ski season traffic. If somebody can prove the land transfer was fraudulent, it opens the door to a legal disaster big enough to swallow half of Mistwood."

The truth of that settled heavily between them. North Star Summit was not just a mountain lodge. It was the engine that kept this town moving through winter. Guests filled the inns. Restaurants stayed alive on resort traffic. Shops counted on the season. Rental cabins, equipment suppliers, shuttle services, grocery orders, seasonal staff, and repair contracts. Everything flowed outward from that mountain.

Olivia knew that. Everyone in Mistwood knew that. And if someone had discovered the foundation was rotten all the way back to the beginning …

Her stomach dropped. "Cassie must have realized what this meant."

Luke nodded once. "And somebody realized she knew."

The words hung there.

Olivia looked down at the deed again, suddenly seeing it not as an old legal document, but as motive. Not old history. Present danger. She thought of Cassie in the archive room. Cassie following land transfers. Cassie looking into Henry Waverly and parcel references and boundary changes. Cassie insisted that something did not add up. And then Cassie died in the snow.

A chill moved down Olivia's spine. "This wasn't just about embarrassing someone," she whispered. "Or exposing a family secret."

Luke's gaze met hers, steady and troubled. "Exactly."

The office was quiet for a moment. Too quiet. Then the printer in the outer room let out a tortured screech and resumed its miserable existence. Neither of them moved.

Olivia looked at Luke more carefully now. The pressure he was under made even more sense. A homicide tied to the resort. Influential business owners. Potential land fraud buried in Mistwood's history. An acting sheriff with an election hanging over his head and half the town ready to question every move he made. No wonder he looked exhausted.

"You're carrying all of this by yourself," she said.

Luke's mouth flattened. "Comes with the desk."

"That isn't the same thing."

He did not answer.

Olivia rested her fingertips lightly on Cassie's notebook. "She died because she found the truth."

"Looks that way."

"And if the forged deed connects back to the Waverly land, then this goes further than the resort board or a modern ownership fight."

Luke nodded faintly. "That's what worries me."

She frowned. "Further, how?"

He hesitated, then said, "Because once people start digging into old fraudulent transfers, they don't stop neatly at one signature. They keep going. Who benefited? Who knew? Who covered it up? And whether later owners were complicit or just inherited the lie."

Olivia thought of Lark and the photograph in the attic. Of Clara Waverly and the mountain that once belonged to the Waverly family. She said nothing.

Luke noticed anyway."What?"

Olivia looked back at the deed. "I found something in the attic last night."

He waited.

"Old family boxes. Records. A photograph."

Luke's brow furrowed. "What kind of photograph?"

"One with the Waverly family in it."

That got his attention. He sat up straighter. "And?"

Olivia hesitated. This was not hers to throw around carelessly. But it mattered. "The woman identified as Clara Waverly looks a lot like Lark."

Luke stared at her. For once, he did not have an immediate comeback. "You're sure?"

"I'm sure enough not to dismiss it."

He leaned back slowly, processing. "Well," he said after a long moment, "that makes things interesting."

Olivia gave him a dry look. "That is one word for it."

He almost smiled. Almost. Then the worry returned. "If Lark's family ties back to the original landowners," he said, "and Cassie found evidence the deed was forged, then this could turn into a very ugly inheritance question on top of everything else."

Olivia exhaled. Ugly was putting it mildly. Mistwood liked its secrets buried deep and decorated nicely. This one had bones under it. She looked again at the line of signatures. Different hands. Different pressure. One real, one not. A lie preserved in county records for decades. "Do you think whoever killed Cassie knew exactly what she had found?" Olivia asked.

Luke's gaze dropped to the deed. "I think they knew enough."

"Enough to panic."

"Enough to kill."

The bluntness of it hit hard, even after everything.

Olivia sat very still. Then she closed the file carefully and slid the deed copy back toward Luke. "So what happens now?"

He gave a tired laugh. "In the official version? I continue the homicide investigation, request a formal review of the record trail, and try not to get buried alive under legal procedure."

"And in the real version?"

His eyes met hers. "In the real version, I need to know who had the most to lose if Cassie went public."

Olivia nodded slowly. The answer to that was probably not one person. It might be a family. A board. A business network. People with money, reputation, and a desperate need to keep the past where they had left it.

Luke reached across the desk and tapped the notebook once. "Be careful."

Olivia looked at him.

"This isn't something to take lightly," he whispered. "This is money, land, and people who think the town can't survive the truth. That makes them dangerous in a different way."

She held his gaze. "I know."

"I mean it, Olivia."

Using her first name landed with more force than it should have. Something in his expression had shifted. Not annoyance. Not skepticism. Concern. Plain and unguarded.

She looked away first, because that suddenly felt easier. "I'm not planning to announce forged deed findings in the middle of Main Street," she said.

"That is not as reassuring as you think."

"It wasn't meant to be."

Luke sighed. Outside his office, the phone rang again.

Neither of them moved for half a second.

Then reality returned. Luke stood, gathering the loose pages into the folder with practiced care. Olivia rose with him, sliding Cassie's notebook back into her bag. At the door, she paused.

"Luke."

He looked up.

"You are experienced enough."

He blinked once, clearly not expecting that.

Olivia kept going before he could interrupt. "Half this town would rather complain than help, and the other half only cares when their wallets get nervous. That doesn't make them good judges of character."

His mouth twitched faintly.

"Is that your version of encouragement?"

"It was downright heartfelt. Don't get greedy."

For the first time since she had arrived, an actual smile threatened at the corner of his mouth.

Then it vanished again under the weight of everything else. Still, the room felt a fraction less heavy. Olivia pulled on her coat. At the threshold, she glanced back once more.

Luke had reopened the file and was staring down at the forged signature, jaw tight, shoulders squared as though bracing against a storm only he could see coming. The forged deed had changed things. Cassie had found the truth, and someone had murdered her to keep it buried.

And if the lie at the heart of North Star Summit came apart, Mistwood itself might crack open with it.

Olivia stepped out into the cold, gray morning with the weight of that knowledge pressing hard against her chest. By the time she reached the sidewalk, she knew one thing for certain. Cassie had not died over an old piece of paper. She had died because that paper had the power to destroy everything built on top of it. And somewhere in town, the person who knew that was still walking around free.

CHAPTER SEVENTEEN

Suspects in Mistwood

Morning settled over Mistwood beneath a sky the color of pewter. Fresh snow clung to the roofs along Main Street, softening the angles of shop fronts and porch railings, turning the whole town into something deceptively harmless. Smoke drifted from the chimneys. Tires hissed over the slush. A woman in a red knit hat hurried across the street with a paper sack tucked under one arm and her shoulders hunched against the cold.

From the outside, Mistwood looked exactly as it should. Peaceful. Picturesque. The sort of town that ended up on postcards beside cheerful little captions about winter escapes and holiday markets.

Olivia knew better. By the time she parked Gus in front of Reed Outdoor Supply, she had already replayed the previous day at least a dozen times. Cassie's notebook. Parcel 7B. The forged deed. Luke's grim face across his desk as the truth began to unfold. A murder that had started with one dead woman on a snowy slope now stretched backward through decades of lies and missing land. Someone in town had profited from that lie. Someone in town had been frightened enough to kill for it.

She shut off the engine and sat for a moment with her gloved hands resting on the steering wheel. Frost still traced the lower corners of the windshield. Her breath fogged the glass in brief, pale clouds.

A faint voice drifted from the passenger seat. "You call this a carriage fit for mountain travel?"

Olivia closed her eyes. The medal tied to his haunting rested in her coat pocket, which meant he was free to accompany her so long as she kept it close. *I've got to remember to leave it at home.* "Good morning to you, too, Anton."

The ghost seated beside her looked thoroughly offended by the Subaru. He wore the same old-fashioned ski sweater and wool trousers he had died in, his translucent form edged with a shimmer that made him seem part mist, part memory. Since leaving North Star Summit, he had taken that freedom as an invitation to criticize almost everything in the modern world. He glanced toward the outfitter shop and sniffed. "If this establishment contains those dreadful boots with the metal bindings, I intend to protest."

"You always intend to protest."

"It is one of my finer qualities."

Olivia grabbed her bag, checked that Cassie's copied notes were tucked inside, and climbed out into the cold. Wind skimmed down the street and found every gap in her coat. She buttoned it higher and headed toward the store.

A brass bell jingled above the door when she stepped inside. Heat wrapped around her at once, tinged with the scents of wool, cedar polish, and damp snow melting from boots. Reed Outdoor Supply was the kind of store that had managed to survive the wave of glossy chain retailers by leaning into what it already was. It had scarred wooden floors with dark beams overhead. Displays built from old pine and iron pipe. Racks of insulated jackets in orderly rows. Wall pegs crowded with hats, gloves, and coils of climbing rope. Snowshoes hung near the back. Skis lined one wall. A rotating rack of trail maps stood near the register, beside a jar of peppermint sticks.

A young couple in matching parkas studied a display of goggles. A man in a camouflage cap compared two pairs of thick wool socks with the concentration of a surgeon choosing instruments.

Anton made a slow turn in the middle of the aisle, his expression one of theatrical disgust. "Snowboards," he muttered. "Ridiculous planks for people who cannot decide whether they wish to ski or fall gracefully."

Olivia kept walking. "Prima donna."

"I heard that," he said.

"That was the point."

One of the customers glanced over. Olivia immediately pretended to cough into her fist and veered toward a display of hand warmers.

Behind the counter, Mason Reed looked up from a clipboard. He was in his late thirties, broad-shouldered, clean-shaven, with dark blond hair that needed cutting and the weathered face of a man who spent a fair amount of time outdoors, whether or not he was technically working. He wore a thermal Henley beneath a fleece vest bearing the store's logo. There was a steadiness to him that most people probably found reassuring. Olivia had once counted herself among them.

Now she was no longer taking anyone in Mistwood at face value.

"Olivia," he said, surprise lifting his brows. "Didn't expect to see you in this part of town so early."

"I heard shocking rumors that Main Street belongs to all of us."

One corner of his mouth twitched. "Can I help you find something?"

"Yes," she said. "Answers."

The twitch disappeared. Mason set the clipboard down with care. "That sounds ominous."

Olivia moved closer to the counter. "I'm asking questions about Cassie."

The shift in him was small, but she saw it. His shoulders tightened a fraction. His gaze flicked past her toward the front window, then returned. "I already spoke to Luke."

"I'm not Luke."

"No," he said. "You definitely are not."

Anton wandered toward a display of brightly colored helmets. "Why would anyone place a bowl on his head before descending a mountain?"

Olivia ignored him and rested one hand on the counter. "I'm trying to understand who might have had a reason to want Cassie quiet."

Mason's face settled into cautious neutrality. "And you came here because?"

"Because Cassie was looking into old land records. Because I've heard your family once owned acreage near the mountain. And because I'd rather ask you directly than listen to three different versions of the same story over coffee."

That earned the faintest exhale, almost a laugh but not quite. He glanced at the few customers in the store, then tipped his head toward the far end of the counter. "Come on."

She followed him past the register toward a quieter section near a wall of fishing gear and avalanche beacons. From this point, the conversation was less likely to drift across the room.

Mason folded his arms. "My grandfather used to say half the mountain belonged to the Reeds before everybody got greedy and started drawing new lines on maps. He was exaggerating, but only a little. We had land up there once. Timber, meadow, access to a stretch of the ridge." He looked toward the hanging snowshoes. "By the time it passed down, most of it was gone."

"Sold?"

"That's the official version."

Olivia watched him carefully. "And the unofficial one?"

His jaw moved. "Cheated, pressured, misled … pick your word."

Outside, a truck rolled past, its tires crunching over snow-packed street edges. Somewhere near the back room, a heater clicked on with a low metallic hum.

She kept her tone easy. "Cassie thought some of the original transfers around North Star Summit didn't add up."

"So I've heard."

"You'd already been looking into them yourself."

Mason gave her a sharp look. "Who told you that?"

"Does it matter if it's true?"

Silence stretched between them for a beat.

Then he blew out a breath and scrubbed a hand over the back of his neck. "Fine. Yes. I started digging around a few months ago. Mostly out of stubbornness. Family stories. Old tax records. A vague suspicion that my great-grandfather got the short end of something. It wasn't exactly a crusade."

"But you found enough to keep going."

"Enough to make me ask questions."

Olivia thought of Cassie hunched over old ledgers, circling parcel numbers in careful ink. Of the note she'd written beside one copied transfer: *same witness again? impossible coincidence.* Cassie had pulled a thread and ended up dead.

"What kind of questions?" Olivia asked.

Mason hesitated. "Whether the Reed land was absorbed legally. Whether somebody used debts and bad timing to force sales that never should've happened. And whether signatures on later documents matched earlier ones."

Her pulse gave a quiet, unpleasant nudge. "And?"

"And I'm not a lawyer, a surveyor, or a forensic document examiner."

"That wasn't my question."

A brief smile crossed his face, thin and humorless. "You really have gotten comfortable in town."

"Occupational hazard."

"You're a chef."

"I'm a chef with trust issues."

Anton drifted back into view carrying nothing, because he could carry nothing, but examining a rack of trekking poles with grave suspicion. "These are all too light. A proper pole should have some dignity."

Mason frowned, "Are you all right?"

She realized she had been staring slightly to the left of his head.

"Fine," she said promptly. "Just thinking."

"About what?"

"How little dignity modern ski poles apparently possess."

His brows knit.

Olivia turned that into a cough. "I mean, legal matters. Obviously."

One of the women near the goggles display shot her a curious glance. Olivia smiled blandly and lowered her voice.

Mason leaned one elbow on the counter behind him. "Cassie came in here once."

That made Olivia raise an eyebrow. "When?"

"About three weeks ago. Maybe a month. She asked if I had any family papers I'd be willing to show her. Old maps, correspondence, land abstracts. She said she was writing something about the resort's history." He looked down for a moment. "I told her I'd check."

"Did you?"

He nodded once. "I found a box in the upstairs storage room. My father kept more than he admitted. There were copies of deeds, survey sketches, and tax notices. A few letters." He lifted his gaze. "Cassie came back. I let her look."

Olivia studied his face. "And you expect me to believe that was the end of it?"

"It was the end of my involvement."

"That sounds carefully phrased."

"It is carefully phrased."

A customer approached the register holding a pair of gloves. Mason excused himself, rang up the purchase, answered a question about waterproofing spray, then returned while the doorbell chimed and cold air swept briefly through the shop.

Once the customer was gone, Olivia said, "You had motive."

He gave a short, disbelieving laugh. "Because my family may have lost land forty years ago?"

"Because if Cassie uncovered proof, it could affect people who profited from it. Lawsuits, public embarrassment, property disputes, old grudges turning into new ones. Motive doesn't have to be simple to be real."

Mason's face hardened. "I didn't kill her."

"I didn't say you did."

"You were thinking it."

Olivia did not bother to deny it.

He looked past her again, but this time she caught the reason. Not nerves exactly. Calculation. He was measuring how much to say and how much to hold back.

"There was a lawyer," he said at last.

Her attention sharpened. "The one involved in the original transfer?"

Mason nodded.

"What was his name?"

"Edwin Hale."

The name meant nothing to her, but the way Mason said it

mattered. Too flat. Too quick. A name delivered with the precision of someone trying not to reveal the weight behind it.

"Do you know much about him?" she asked.

"No."

Anton let out a loud scoff. "Liar."

Olivia pinched the bridge of her nose.

Mason frowned. "Headache?"

"Town life."

He did not look convinced.

She pressed on. "No one just knows the name of some dead lawyer from decades ago and nothing else."

"My father mentioned him."

"Only his name?"

"Pretty much."

Olivia tilted her head. "That's strange."

"Is it?"

"Yes. Men do not spend generations complaining about family land and then casually omit the details."

Something flickered across Mason's face. Not guilt. Irritation, maybe. Or resignation.

"My grandfather hated talking about the actual deal," he said. "He preferred to grumble in generalities. Safer that way."

"Safer for whom?"

"For everybody still living here."

The answer settled between them with a weight that seemed larger than the words themselves.

Across the store, Anton stopped in front of a display of inflatable sleds and stared at them in offended silence, as if the very concept were an insult to sport, to winter, and perhaps to civilization.

Olivia lowered her voice even more. "What aren't you telling me?"

Mason looked tired all at once. Not physically tired. Worn in the way people looked when they had spent years carrying a story that had grown jagged around the edges.

"I found one letter in the box," he said. "Unsigned copy. Typed. It mentioned correcting an irregularity in the chain of title before winter development could proceed. There was a handwritten note at the bottom in my father's writing. Two words. *Hale fixed.*"

Olivia felt a chill that had nothing to do with the weather outside. "Do you still have it?"

"Yes."

"Did Cassie see it?"

"She saw the file. I don't know if she saw that page specifically."

"But you think she might have."

He gave the smallest nod.

"And you didn't mention this to Luke?"

Mason's expression turned guarded again. "Not yet."

"Why not?"

"Because once I hand something like that over, it doesn't stay mine. Because if I'm wrong, I drag my family into old mud for nothing. Because I'd prefer not to wake up and find half the town treating me as the man who set fire to the resort's history."

Olivia folded her arms. "A woman is dead."

His gaze snapped to hers. "I know that."

The words came out harsher than he intended. She saw regret hit him a second later.

He looked away first.

For a moment, the shop fell into a soft hush, broken only by the rustle of fabric hangers and the distant murmur of two customers discussing boot sizes.

Olivia let the silence sit. People often rushed to fill silence with whatever they most wanted hidden. Mason, to his credit or his detriment, managed not to.

Finally, she said, "Did you confront Cassie?"

"No."

"Did you argue with her?"

"No."

"Did you meet her anywhere outside this store?"

"No."

His answers came quickly, but not with the brittle speed of panic. Either he was telling the truth, or he had rehearsed the lie very well.

She changed direction. "Who else knew you were looking into the property records?"

"My father knew. My sister, maybe. I mentioned it once at poker night and got told to leave dead history alone, so a few people heard that."

"Who told you that?"

He paused.

"Mason."

"Several people," he said. "Depends on the week."

She held his gaze until he added, "One of them was Cindy Keller."

That tracked. Cindy had already been circling the case in Olivia's thoughts with increasing insistence. Business owner. Public face. Nerves beneath polish. Too much interest in what Cassie had or had not found.

Olivia filed that away.

At the front of the store, the bell jingled again. Cold light spilled across the floorboards, then vanished as the door swung shut. Someone stamped snow from their boots and greeted Mason by name. He lifted a hand in acknowledgment, but kept his attention on Olivia.

"You think this all connects?" he whispered.

"I know Cassie died because she found something."

"And you think that something was the land."

"I think the land is part of it." Olivia studied him. "I'm still figuring out whether you are."

A huff of reluctant amusement escaped him. "That almost sounded friendly."

"It wasn't."

"Shame."

Anton reappeared at Olivia's elbow. "Tell him his store contains too many gadgets and not enough wool."

"I'm not doing that."

"You never support me when I am right."

She muttered, "You're right far too loudly."

Mason's eyes narrowed. "Who are you talking to?"

Olivia looked up too fast. "Myself."

"Uh-huh."

"It's a long-standing habit. Very efficient."

"Should I be concerned?"

"Only if I start answering."

That got a genuine laugh out of him, brief and surprised. It softened his face and made him look younger, more open, and for one dangerous second, almost entirely innocent.

Olivia did not trust innocence anymore. Not in Mistwood. Not where a forged deed could sit buried beneath town pride for decades while everyone smiled over cider and pie.

She reached into her bag and pulled out a small notebook. "Write down your father's full name, and your grandfather's if you know it. Also, the approximate date of the transfer and anything you remember about that file."

Mason looked at the notebook, then at her. "You taking statements now?"

"Humor me."

After the briefest hesitation, he took the pen she offered and wrote. His handwriting was compact and clean, the letters pressed firmly into the page.

While he did, Olivia let her gaze roam the store. Snowshoes. Lanterns. Waxed canvas packs. Ice cleats. An old framed photo behind the counter showed the shop decades earlier, when the sign had simply read REED'S and the display window held fishing lures instead of ski helmets … a family business with history and grievances. Mason handed it back.

She glanced over the names, then put the notebook back in her bag. "If you still have that letter," she said, "don't leave it where anyone can find it."

His expression sharpened. "You think someone would come looking?"

"I think someone killed Cassie. I'm done ruling out stupidity."

He nodded once, slowly, as if accepting that on some level he had already known it.

"Be careful, Olivia." The warning held no flirtation, no drama. Just sincerity.

That unsettled her more than she liked. She stepped back from the counter. "I'll let Luke know he should speak to you again."

A shadow crossed his face at that. "I was afraid you'd say that."

Anton, drifting toward the door, announced, "At last. I have seen enough insults to winter athletics for one morning."

Olivia headed for the front of the store.

One of the customers moved aside to let her pass, giving her the wary half-smile people used when they were not entirely sure whether the person beside them had been talking to herself on purpose.

She smiled back with all the dignity she could manage.

The bell jingled overhead as she stepped outside into the cold. Wind caught at her hair and stung her cheeks. The street seemed brighter after the warm dimness of the shop. Across the way, someone was chalking a lunch special onto a cafe board while flakes drifted lazily from the low gray sky again.

Anton appeared beside her on the sidewalk, looking deeply aggrieved.

"Those planks," he said. "Those monstrous single planks. And the helmets. Everyone padded and insulated and protected from consequences."

Olivia tucked her hands into her coat pockets and started toward Gus. "You're impossible."

"I am correct."

"You are exhausting."

He smiled, pleased by this.

At Gus, she opened the driver's door but did not get in right away. Instead, she stood with one hand resting on the roof and looked back down Main Street.

Mason Reed had motive. That much was undeniable. Family land lost in a suspicious transfer. Private research into old records. A document he had not yet turned over. Unease whenever the original lawyer's name came up.

Still, unease was not evidence, and suspicion was not proof. And whatever Mason was hiding, it did not yet place him on the mountain with Cassie. It did not explain the timing of her death, the argument Olivia had overheard, or the frantic energy that seemed to ripple outward every time the forged deed surfaced in conversation.

He knew more than he wanted to admit. She would stake good butter on that.

Whether that made him dangerous remained to be seen.

Snowflakes landed on her coat sleeve and melted into dark pinpoints against the wool. Behind her, Anton peered through the truck window at the dashboard with renewed disapproval.

Olivia slid into the driver's seat and pulled the door shut.

One suspect added. More questions than answers, and a lawyer named Edwin Hale whose ghost, if he had one, had had the decency not to show up and complicate her morning.

She started the engine.

"Where next?" Anton asked.

Olivia backed away from the curb, eyes on the white ribbon of street ahead.

"Somewhere people lie better," she said.

CHAPTER EIGHTEEN

Pressure on the Sheriff

The conference room at Mistwood Town Hall had been designed to feel welcoming. Someone had chosen soft lighting, warm wood trim, and framed photographs of the lake in summer, the slopes in winter … the images that suggested steady prosperity and uncomplicated charm. This morning, the room felt neither welcoming nor warm.

Luke Thatcher stood near the end of the long table, one hand resting on the back of a chair he had no intention of sitting in. Outside, snow drifted past the tall windows in slow, steady sheets, blurring the view of Main Street. Inside, the air carried the faint smell of coffee and damp wool, layered over tension thick enough to press against the skin.

He had been in difficult meetings before. This one ranked high. Around the table sat a cross-section of Mistwood's business community. People who had money invested in the town's success. Who depended on winter traffic to carry them through the slower months. People who had attended the summit at North Star and now found themselves facing something far less controlled than a networking event.

Cindy Keller sat three seats down from Luke, her posture perfect, her expression composed in a way that looked practiced. Next to her, Tom Granger from the equipment rental shop tapped his pen against a legal pad with a steady, irritated rhythm. Then came

Gerald Huxley. Across from them, Darla Bishop sat with her hands folded neatly in front of her, her face a study in calm authority, and Mason Reed.

Others filled in the remaining seats. A mix of lodge managers, shop owners, tour operators. Each one with a stake. Each one watching Luke. Waiting.

"Well," Tom said, breaking the silence that had stretched just a bit too long. "Are we going to pretend this isn't a problem, or are we going to talk about it?"

Luke kept his voice even. "We're here to talk about it."

"Good," Tom said. "Because ski season is about to hit full stride, and the last thing we need is headlines about a murder at the resort."

"It wasn't at the resort," Luke said.

"It was close enough," Cindy replied smoothly. "Perception matters."

It always came back to perception.

Luke had learned that quickly once his uncle stepped down and left him holding the badge. The job was not only about doing the work. It was about being seen doing the work. Being trusted. Being judged. "Perception matters," Luke agreed. "So does getting it right."

A few people shifted in their chairs. No one liked that answer.

Cindy folded her hands. "No one is suggesting you cut corners, Luke."

Tom snorted. "I am. If this drags out for weeks, we're going to feel it. Bookings dropped. Cancelations go up. People choose somewhere else because they don't want to ski where someone died."

"People die everywhere," Luke said.

"Not everywhere ends up on the evening news."

Darla spoke for the first time, her tone measured. "We all understand your position. But the town depends on confidence. Visitors need to feel safe."

"They are safe," Luke said.

"They will not believe that if this becomes a spectacle."

Luke let that settle. He could feel the weight of their attention shifting, tightening around him. This was not just about a murder investigation. This was about control. "Here's what I can tell you," he said. "The case is active. We are following leads. We are interviewing witnesses. We are processing evidence. That takes time."

Tom's pen tapped faster. "Time we don't have."

Luke's jaw flexed. "We have exactly as much time as it takes to avoid arresting the wrong person."

Cindy tilted her head slightly. "No one wants that. But efficiency matters. A visible sense of progress matters."

"You'll have that when I have something to share."

"That's not very reassuring."

"It's honest."

A quiet murmur moved around the table. Not agreement. Not quite a disagreement either. Something in between.

Darla leaned forward a fraction. "Luke, you are aware that your position is temporary."

There it was. He held her gaze. "I'm aware."

"The election is not far off," she continued. "The town will be watching how this is handled."

"They should."

"And they will make decisions based on that."

The implication did not need to be spelled out. If he mishandled this, if he appeared weak, indecisive, or out of his depth, someone would step forward. Someone who promised certainty. Someone who promised speed. Someone who might be sitting in this room.

Luke straightened, letting his hand fall from the chair back. "Then they'll see I'm doing my job."

Tom shook his head. "Or they'll see a case dragging on with no resolution while businesses suffer."

"Those are not the same thing."

"They might as well be."

Silence settled again, heavier this time.

Luke looked around the table, meeting each pair of eyes. He saw concern. Frustration. Calculation. In one or two faces, something sharper. Something closer to fear.

"Let me be clear," he said. "I am not rushing this. I am not cutting corners. And I am not making an arrest just to make you feel better about your bookings."

Cindy's smile did not reach her eyes. "No one is asking you to compromise the investigation."

"You're asking me to hurry it."

"We're asking you to be mindful of the impact."

"I am mindful," Luke said. "I am also aware that a woman is dead." That landed harder than anything else he had said. For a moment, the room went still.

Then Darla inclined her head slightly. "Of course."

The meeting unraveled after that. Not abruptly. No raised voices, no slammed doors. Just a gradual loosening as people gathered their papers, exchanged quiet words, and made their way out with polite nods that did not quite hide their dissatisfaction.

Cindy paused beside Luke on her way out. "Do be careful," she whispered. "Pressure has a way of revealing weaknesses."

He held her gaze. "Good thing I don't have any."

Her smile sharpened. "We'll see." Then she was gone.

Luke remained in the emptying room, the hum of the overhead lights suddenly louder without the buffer of voices. Snow continued to fall outside, steady and indifferent.

He dragged a hand down his face and exhaled.

The case had been complicated from the start. Now it was tangled with politics, business interests, and the quiet threat of losing the badge he had not even had time to fully settle into.

He pushed that aside. None of it mattered if he got the case wrong.

BY THE TIME Olivia reached the sheriff's office, the snow had thickened into a steady curtain that softened the edges of buildings and muted the usual sounds of town. Gus handled the roads with steady confidence, tires gripping where other vehicles slipped.

She parked near the curb, grabbed the cardboard tray holding two cups of coffee, and made her way up the steps.

Inside, the office felt warmer than the street, but no less tense. A deputy she recognized gave her a nod. Papers were spread across the front desk. A printer whirred somewhere in the back.

Luke stood in his office doorway, jacket off, sleeves rolled up, a file open in his hands. He looked up when she entered. "Don't tell me you're here to be helpful."

"I brought coffee," Olivia said.

"That's suspicious."

"It should be. It means I want something."

He considered that for a beat, then stepped back to let her in. "Come on."

His office looked exactly as it had the last time she'd been there. His desk was cluttered, but not chaotic. Files stacked in towering piles. A map of the county pinned to the wall with several colored markers indicating locations tied to the case.

Olivia set one of the cups on his desk. "Peace offering."

He eyed it. "What's in it?"

"Coffee."

"I meant, what kind?"

"Black. Because you look like you deserve to suffer."

A corner of his mouth twitched despite himself. He picked it up and took a sip. "Not terrible," he said.

"I aim for adequacy." She settled into the chair across from his desk, studying him over the rim of her own cup. There were new lines at the corners of his eyes. Tension sat in his shoulders, held there with effort rather than ease.

"Rough morning?" she asked.

He gave a short laugh. "That obvious?"

"You look like you just argued with half the town."

"Close. A little more polite than arguing."

"What did they want?"

"A quick resolution. A clean answer. Preferably one that doesn't scare off tourists."

Olivia leaned back. "And you told them no."

"I told them I'm not rushing it."

"How did that go?"

"About as well as you'd expect."

She nodded. That matched what she knew of Mistwood. Friendly on the surface. Demanding underneath.

Luke set the coffee down and leaned back in his chair. "You didn't come here just to check on my mood."

"No," she said. "I came to complicate your day."

"Of course you did."

"I spoke to Mason Reed."

That got his attention.

"What did he say?"

Olivia laid it out, keeping her tone steady and precise. Mason's family land. His research into old property records. The box of documents and the mention of the original lawyer. The letter with the note in his father's hand.

Luke listened without interrupting, his expression tightening as she spoke.

When she finished, he said, "He didn't mention that letter to me."

"He's cautious."

"He's withholding evidence."

"He's afraid of what it means."

Luke exhaled slowly. "I'll have to talk to him again."

"You should."

He nodded once, then studied her. "You think this connects to Cassie?"

"I think Cassie was getting close to proving something about the land."

"And that got her killed."

"Yes."

He leaned forward, forearms resting on the desk. "That's a gigantic leap."

"It's a logical one."

"It's still a leap."

Olivia met his gaze. "You've seen the deed."

"I've seen something that looks wrong."

"You've seen a forgery."

He held her eyes for a moment longer, then looked down at the file in front of him. "Yeah," he whispered. "I have." The admission hung in the air between them. It felt like a shift.

Not dramatic. Not obvious. But real.

"You're not dismissing it," she said.

"No."

"Good."

"That doesn't mean I'm ready to build a case around it."

"It means you're considering it."

"It means I'm not ignoring it."

"That's progress."

He looked back up at her, something almost resembling a smile touching his mouth. "You're very patient."

"I'm very persistent."

"That too."

Outside his office, a phone rang. Someone answered it, voice low and professional. The ordinary sounds of the station continued, grounding the moment.

Luke tapped a finger against the edge of the file. "If the deed was forged, that opens a lot of doors."

"And not all of them are comfortable."

"No," he agreed. "They're not."

"It also gives us motive," Olivia said. "Cassie finds proof that the resort sits on land that was acquired fraudulently. People who benefited from that have a problem."

"People with money," Luke said.

"People with influence."

He thought about that. "Which means pressure doesn't just come from worried business owners."

"It comes from people who want this buried."

He nodded slowly.

For a moment, neither of them spoke.

Then Luke said, "You realize if you're right, this gets bigger than Mistwood."

"I think it already is."

"And you're still poking at it."

Olivia took a sip of her coffee. "I have a habit of not stopping once I start."

"I've noticed."

He studied her again, but this time, there was less irritation in it. Less resistance.

More consideration. "Be careful," he said.

"You first."

"I mean it."

"So do I."

A faint sound came from the corner of the room. A shift in the air, subtle but familiar. Olivia felt it more than heard it. The quiet presence of one of the March house's ghosts. Sir Alistair stood in the office, Bertie beside him, wagging his tail. She touched his pocket watch in her pocket. He was a reminder. She was not alone in this. Not entirely. But the answers would still have to come from the living.

Luke followed her gaze for a fraction of a second, then looked back at her, a question in his eyes he did not voice.

She gave a small shake of her head.

He let it go. "Keep me in the loop," he said. "If you find anything else."

"I will."

"And Olivia?"

She paused at the door.

"Try not to get yourself killed."

She smiled slightly. "That's usually the plan."

"Good."

She stepped out into the main office, then out into the cold once more. Snow continued to fall, steady and relentless, covering tracks almost as soon as they were made.

Behind her, Luke returned to his desk, the weight of the town pressing in from all sides.

Ahead of her, Mistwood waited. Filled with warmth, comfort, and a group of noisy, opinionated ghosts.

CHAPTER NINETEEN

Cassie's Hidden Recording

By the time Olivia reached March House, the snow had settled into a steady rhythm that softened the world without quite silencing it. The lake beyond the back fence lay under a pale gray sky, its surface dull and unmoving, edged with thin sheets of forming ice. Smoke curled from neighboring chimneys. Somewhere in the distance, a dog barked once, then fell quiet.

Inside, the house felt warm but not entirely at ease.

That had become a familiar sensation. Not danger exactly, but a more subtle tension woven through the air, as if the house itself were holding its breath.

Olivia kicked off her boots in the entryway and hung her coat on the rack. The scent of something baking drifted faintly from the kitchen. Butter, sugar, and a hint of cinnamon.

Lark.

Olivia stepped into the kitchen just long enough to confirm it.

Lark stood at the counter, sleeves rolled, gray hair escaping its usual loose tie, hands dusted with flour as she worked dough into careful folds. A low hum escaped her, something soft and tuneless that matched the quiet mood of the house.

"You're back early," Lark said without looking up.

"Field research," Olivia replied.

"Productive?"

"Complicated."

Lark nodded as if that were the only probable answer. "Tea?"

"In a bit. I need to look at something first."

"Try not to frown too hard. It creates wrinkles."

Olivia gave her a look. "I'll risk it." She carried her bag down the hall and into her room, closing the door behind her with a quiet click.

The space felt immediately different. Not colder, but sharper somehow. Focused.

Anton lingered near the window, studying the snowfall with mild disdain. "This weather lacks conviction," he said. "Either snow properly or clear the sky. This half-hearted drifting achieves nothing."

Olivia set her bag on the bed. "You are deeply offended by meteorology?"

"I have standards."

"You have opinions."

"Better than drifting through life without either."

She pulled the notebook from her bag and sat at the small desk beneath the window.

Cassie's handwriting filled the pages in tight, efficient lines. Notes on land transfers. Parcel numbers. Names circled and re-circled. Arrows connecting one piece of information to another. Questions written in the margins, some underlined twice.

Olivia had read through it already. Twice. That did not mean she had seen everything.

She opened to the beginning and forced herself to slow down. No skimming. No jumping ahead. Just a careful, deliberate review.

The room settled into quiet around her. Pages turned. The faint scratch of paper against paper. The distant clink of something in the kitchen. Wind brushing lightly against the glass.

Anton drifted closer, peering over her shoulder with interest. "Does she ever reach a conclusion," he asked, "or does she simply question everything until the end of time?"

"She was getting close," Olivia said.

"Close to what?"

"Something that got her killed."

Anton considered that. "Then she should have written faster."

Olivia ignored him and kept reading. A section on early

investors. Another on boundary adjustments made in the late forties. A list of names with question marks beside several of them. Edwin Hale appeared more than once, always circled, always underlined. She turned another page. Then paused. At the back of the notebook was a small pocket.

Olivia frowned. It was fabric-lined. Something bulged inside. Her pulse ticked up.

"Now that," Anton said, leaning in, "is interesting."

Olivia slid her fingers into the pocket and felt plastic. She drew out a small digital voice recorder. For a moment, she simply stared at it.

"How charming," Anton said. "A device that captures voices. We had something similar once. It was called memory."

Olivia turned the recorder over in her hand. It was scuffed, well-used, the kind of thing someone carried regularly. Not new or decorative, but practical. Cassie had hidden it.

Which meant it mattered.

Olivia pressed the power button. The screen flickered to life, a dim blue glow against the muted light of the room. A list of files appeared, each marked with a date and time.

Her thumb hovered. Then she selected the most recent entry. A soft hiss of static filled the room.

At first, that was all there was. Background noise. The muffled hum of conversation. Distant movement. The faint clink of glassware. It sounded like the lodge during the summit. People talking. Chairs shifting. The low, constant murmur of a gathering in progress.

Olivia leaned forward, listening. The sound shifted. Footsteps. Closer now. Voices became clearer as someone moved nearer to where Cassie must have been standing. Then …

Cassie's voice. Tight. Controlled. Edged with something that had not been there in her earlier conversations. "I have proof that the deed was forged."

Olivia's breath caught.

The second voice came a beat later. Cindy Keller. "You don't understand what you're about to destroy." The words were sharp, but not raised. Not yet. There was tension there, pulled tight between them. "I understand exactly what it means," Cassie said. "People have been lying about this for decades."

"You think exposing that helps anyone?"

"It helps the truth."

A pause. The kind of pause that felt dangerous even through a recording. "You need to let this go," Cindy said.

"No."

"You don't know who this affects."

"I know it's wrong."

"You're going to ruin people."

"They shouldn't have built anything on a lie."

The surrounding noise shifted again. Someone passed nearby. A laugh cut briefly through the tension, then faded. Cindy's voice dropped lower. "You have no idea what you're dealing with."

"I have enough."

"You think this is just about paperwork?"

"It's about fraud."

"It's about everything," Cindy said. "You pull this thread, the whole town starts coming apart."

"Then maybe it should."

Silence. Then, softer now, and that softness made it worse. "Cassie," Cindy said. "Please."

Olivia felt something tighten in her chest. Desperation. It was there in the word. In the way it was spoken. Not anger or arrogance, but fear.

Cassie did not waver. "I'm not backing down."

"You need to."

"No."

The sound shifted abruptly. Approaching footsteps and voices. The recording cut off mid-breath and fell silent.

Olivia realized she had been holding her own breath and let it out slowly. For a long moment, she did not move.

Anton broke the silence. "She was afraid," he said.

Olivia nodded once, her eyes still on the recorder. "Yes."

"Not angry," he continued. "Not defensive. Afraid."

"That's what it sounded like."

He drifted a little closer, his expression thoughtful now rather than critical. "Fear does strange things to people."

Olivia set the recorder down carefully on the desk. “Fear makes people protect what they have,” she said. “Even when they shouldn’t.”

“Especially when they shouldn’t.”

She leaned back in the chair, mind racing. Cindy Keller. Hotel owner. Businesswoman. Polished. Controlled. Directly connected to Cassie’s last confrontation.

Cassie had confronted her with proof. Cindy had known exactly what that meant.

“You’re going to ruin people.”

“They shouldn’t have built anything on a lie.”

Olivia pressed her lips together. Motive. Clear. Immediate. Personal. If the forged deed came to light, everything built on that land would be called into question. Ownership. Value. Legitimacy. Reputation. Cindy’s hotel. Her family name. Her place in Mistwood. All of it balanced on a foundation that might not hold.

Olivia stood and paced once across the room, then back again. “She had motive,” she said.

Anton watched her. “Yes.”

“She had opportunity. She was at the summit. She argued with Cassie.”

“Yes.”

“And she knew exactly what Cassie had.”

“Yes.”

Olivia stopped at the window, staring out at the falling snow. For a moment, the answer felt too simple. Too clean. That alone made her wary. But the recording was real. The fear in Cindy’s voice had been real. The stakes were real. Fear could push someone further than anger ever would. “She thought everything would fall apart,” Olivia whispered.

Anton tilted his head. “Would it?”

“Maybe.”

“Then her fear was not entirely unreasonable.”

Olivia turned back to him. “That doesn’t justify murder.”

“No,” he agreed. “But it explains it.”

She crossed back to the desk and picked up the recorder again. She ran over it again in her mind. Cassie had known. She had pushed and refused to step back. Someone had made sure she never got the chance to take it further.

Olivia slid the recorder into her pocket, then closed the notebook. “Luke needs to hear this,” she said.

Anton gave a small nod. “And what will you do when he agrees with you?”

Olivia paused.That was the question. Because agreement meant action. Action meant consequences. For Cindy. For the town. For everything built on a lie. She reached for her coat.

“We’ll find out what she did next,” Olivia said. “After this conversation.”

“And if the answer is not what you expect?”

Olivia met his gaze, steady now. “Then we’ll keep digging.”

Anton smiled faintly. “Good.”

She headed for the door, the weight of the recorder in her pocket far heavier than its size should allow. Behind her, March House remained quiet. Ahead of her, Mistwood was shifting.

And somewhere in that shift, the truth was getting closer.

CHAPTER TWENTY

Chaos at March House

By the time Olivia returned to March House, the light had faded into that muted gray that came early in winter, when the sun seemed to lose interest long before the day was finished.

Snow clung to her boots as she stepped inside and shut the door behind her. Warmth wrapped around her, carrying the scent of butter and sugar, layered with something citrus beneath it.

Lark was baking again. Of course she was. For a moment, Olivia stood in the entryway and let the quiet settle. Then the quiet broke.

"You call that a proper stance?"

"I call that a tragedy."

"It is not a tragedy. It is a misunderstanding of technique."

"Your technique is outdated."

"My technique is refined."

Olivia closed her eyes. "Absolutely not," she said under her breath. She stepped into the main hallway and stopped.

The ghosts had gathered. Not in their usual scattered way, drifting through the house with their individual habits and routines, but together. Clustered, engaged, and arguing.

Sir Alistair Pruitt stood near the base of the staircase, posture rigid, one hand resting lightly on his watch fob chain as if it were a point of dignity he refused to surrender. His expression carried a deep, unshakable disapproval.

"Skiing," he said, each syllable precise, "is an activity best left to those with a disregard for their own limbs."

Anton stood opposite him, equally firm in his stance.

"Skiing," Anton replied, "is the purest expression of control and grace in motion."

"Grace?" Sir Alistair's brows rose. "Sliding down a mountain at alarming speed is not grace. It is an invitation to disaster."

"It is discipline."

"It is recklessness."

"It is art."

"It is absurd."

Monique Delacroix stood between them, delighted.

"Gentlemen," she said, her voice light and amused, "if you are going to argue, at least make it interesting." She turned her attention fully to Anton, her eyes bright. "You," she said, circling him slowly, "are much more entertaining than the usual company in this house."

Anton straightened slightly, pleased. "I have been told I possess a certain presence."

Monique smiled. "Oh, I can see that."

Sir Alistair made a quiet sound of disapproval that carried more weight than volume.

From the far side of the room, Simon Talbot stepped forward, his Civil War uniform faint but distinct, his expression serious.

"You said you competed," Simon said to Anton.

"I would have," Anton replied. "Had circumstances not intervened."

Simon's gaze sharpened. "On which side?"

Anton blinked. "I beg your pardon?"

"Your loyalty," Simon said. "Where did it lie?"

Anton frowned. "With my country, of course."

"And which country is that?"

Anton hesitated just long enough to be noticeable. "Switzerland," he said at last.

Simon considered that. "Neutral."

Anton lifted his chin. "Strategic."

Simon's expression did not soften. "Convenient."

"I prefer effective."

"Do you now."

The air between them shifted, not hostile, but edged with challenge.

Olivia stepped fully into the room and raised her voice. "Enough."

No one listened.

Walter Hennessey stood near the wall, arms crossed, observing the exchange with the calm patience of someone who had seen far worse arguments in far worse places. Daisy lingered near the doorway, her gaze moving between the others with quiet curiosity. JJ leaned against the banister, cornet in hand, watching with clear amusement.

The house felt full. Too full. Voices layered over one another. Movement overlapping. Energy building in a way that pressed against Olivia's concentration. She rubbed her temples.

"This is not happening," she muttered.

Anton gestured toward an invisible slope only he could see. "The angle of descent must be respected. You cannot simply throw yourself downhill and expect success."

Sir Alistair drew himself up. "I would never throw myself anywhere."

"That is precisely your problem."

"It is not a problem. It is restraint."

"It is hesitation."

"It is prudence."

"It is fear."

Sir Alistair went still.

Monique gasped softly, delighted. "Oh, now it becomes interesting."

Olivia crossed the room in three steps. "Everyone, stop."

They did not.

"Enough," she said again. The noise continued.

Simon had begun questioning Anton about training methods. Monique had drifted closer, her attention fixed entirely on Anton now, her interest unmistakable.

Sir Alistair stood rigid with disapproval that seemed to deepen by the second.

Olivia stared at them. Then she turned and walked into the kitchen. "Tea," she said to herself. Behind her, the argument continued unabated.

~

LARK STOOD AT THE COUNTER, sliding a tray of pastries into the oven. The warm glow of the light reflected off the glass, casting a soft golden hue across the kitchen. She glanced over her shoulder as Olivia entered. “You look overwhelmed.”

“I am overwhelmed.”

“That was quick.”

“It’s been building.”

Lark studied her for a moment, then tilted her head slightly. “Something’s different,” she said.

Olivia paused halfway to the cabinet. “Different how?”

“Busier,” Lark said slowly. “The house feels ... crowded.”

Olivia let out a breath that almost turned into a laugh. “That’s one way to put it.”

Lark wiped her hands on a towel. “Did you bring something back with you?”

“Yes.”

“Something with a powerful presence?”

“Yes.”

Lark nodded, as if that confirmed what she had already suspected. “Well,” she said, “we’ll have to let the house adjust.”

Olivia poured hot water into a mug and watched the steam rise. “Adjust,” she repeated.

“That’s how it works,” Lark said. “Everything finds its place eventually.”

Olivia glanced toward the doorway. The argument had not stopped. “If you say so,” she muttered.

~

IT TOOK NEARLY an hour for the noise to fade into something manageable. Not silence. March House was never truly silent. But the sharp edges of the argument softened. Voices drifted apart. Movement slowed.

Olivia returned to her room with her notebook, the recorder, and the photograph she had brought down from the attic. She spread everything out across the desk in the small office. Focus. She needed to focus.

The recording sat beside her, heavy with implication. Cindy's voice still echoed in her mind. The fear. The urgency. Motive. Clear and immediate. But something still felt incomplete. Olivia picked up the photograph.

The image showed a group of teenagers bundled in winter gear, their faces bright with the careless confidence of youth. Snow beneath their boots. Trees behind them. A moment frozen in time. She studied each face: Mason Reed, Tom Granger, Cindy Keller, and Darla Bishop.

Olivia reached for Cassie's notes and flipped to the section on family connections.

Names. Lines. Arrows. Relationships traced and retraced in careful detail. She followed a single line. Then another. A name surfaced again. Waverly. She flipped back through the pages, scanning quickly now. There. A reference tied to early land ownership. Another linked to a transfer that predated the resort development. A third, barely legible, connecting the name to a boundary dispute.

Olivia's pulse quickened. "No," she whispered. She leaned closer, reading the notes again. The Waverly family once owned land on the mountain. Not a small portion, but a significant section. Land that would have been valuable once the resort was established. Land that had changed hands. Land that might have been part of the forged deed. Olivia sat back slowly.

In the kitchen, Lark moved quietly, the soft rhythm of her work steady and familiar. A faint hum drifted down the hall.

Olivia turned the photograph in her hands. Waverly. She closed her eyes briefly.

Then opened them again. "Lark," she said under her breath.

Anton drifted closer, his expression thoughtful now rather than boastful.

"You have found something," he said.

"Yes."

"And you do not like it."

"No," Olivia whispered. "I don't." She gathered the notes, stacking them carefully.

"If the Waverly family owned that land," she said, "and it was taken through a forged deed ..."

Anton watched her. "Then someone profited from that loss."

"Yes. And if someone were about to expose it ..."

"They would have a reason to stop her." Anton nodded once.

Olivia stood and strolled to the doorway. From there, she could see into the kitchen.

Lark stood at the counter, shaping dough with practiced hands, her movements calm and precise. The oven light cast a warm glow across her face. She hummed softly, unaware of being watched.

Unaware of the past that might be tied to her. Oblivious of what that past could mean.

Olivia felt a weight settle in her chest. If she was right, this was no longer just about Cassie. This was about Lark. About her family. About something that had been buried for decades. And someone had already killed to keep it buried.

Olivia leaned lightly against the doorframe, her gaze fixed on Lark. The house felt different now. Not just crowded. Changed. As if something long hidden had stirred. And there was no putting it back.

CHAPTER TWENTY-ONE

The Family Tree

The house did not settle so much as shift. That was the only way Olivia could describe it the next morning. March House always carried a quiet undercurrent of presence. A constant awareness that she was not alone, even when the halls stood empty and the doors remained closed. But after the previous evening's chaos, something had rearranged itself. The energy had not disappeared. It had reorganized.

Voices no longer overlapped in sharp bursts. Movement did not press in from every direction at once. The ghosts had retreated into their usual patterns, each one reclaiming their preferred spaces, their habits, their routines. It was quieter. Not peaceful. But manageable.

Olivia stood at the kitchen counter, cradling a mug of coffee in both hands, letting the warmth sink into her fingers. Outside, the snow had eased into a fine, steady fall, the kind that softened sound and blurred edges without quite hiding anything.

Lark moved easily around the kitchen, already well into her morning rhythm. Flour dusted the counter. A tray of pastries cooled near the window. A kettle whispered softly on the stove.

"You slept?" Lark asked without looking up.

"Eventually."

"That's something."

"It is."

Lark glanced at her then, eyes narrowing slightly in that way she had when she sensed more than she could see. "You're carrying something," she said.

"I'm carrying several things."

"More than usual."

Olivia took a sip of coffee. "I need to look at Cassie's notes again."

Lark nodded, as if that explained everything. "Then you should."

"I am."

"Good."

That was the extent of it. No pressure. No questions. Just quiet permission.

Olivia set her mug down and gathered her notebook, Cassie's notes, and the photograph before heading back to her room. While Lark continued the morning preparations needed before the coffee shop opened.

THE DESK beneath the window had become her command center. Papers spread in careful layers. Names. Dates. Arrows connecting one point to another. The recorder sat near the edge, silent now but still heavy with what it had revealed.

Olivia pushed everything aside except for Cassie's notebook and opened it to the section marked with a series of tight, deliberate annotations. Genealogy.

At first glance, it looked like a mess. Names stacked over names. Lines drawn between them, then crossed out and redrawn. Question marks scattered through the margins. Dates half-completed, some circled, others scratched through entirely. Cassie had not been guessing. She had been building something.

Olivia leaned forward, tracing the lines with her finger. Henry Waverly. The name sat at the top of the page, underlined twice. Original landowner. From there, the branches spread.

Children. Grandchildren. Marriages. Deaths. Some lines ended abruptly, marked with dates that suggested illness, accidents, or the ordinary attrition of time. Others continued for a while before tapering off. Olivia followed one branch down, then another. Most of them stopped. The Waverly name appeared less frequently as the generations passed. Fewer descendants. Fewer records. Until she found it. A line Cassie had circled heavily, the ink pressed hard enough to leave a faint indentation on the page. One surviving branch.

Olivia's pulse picked up. She pulled the photograph closer and set it beside the notebook.

The image was slightly faded, the edges worn, but the faces were still clear enough. A group gathered outside what looked like an older version of the town. Buildings smaller. Streets less developed. Snow piled higher along the edges. Her gaze moved from one figure to the next.

Then stopped. The woman near the center stood with one hand resting lightly against the back of a wooden chair. Her posture was straight. Her expression was calm. There was something steady about her. Grounded. Cassie had labeled her in faint pencil along the margin. Clara Waverly.

Olivia leaned closer. The resemblance was not identical, not exact, but unmistakable. The shape of the face. The line of the jaw. The way her eyes seemed to hold both patience and quiet strength. Lark.

Olivia sat back slowly. "No," she said under her breath.

Anton appeared beside her, drawn by the shift in her focus. "What have you found now?" he asked.

Olivia turned the photograph slightly so he could see. "That woman," she said. "Clara Waverly."

Anton studied the image. "She has presence."

"She looks like Lark."

He considered that for a moment. "Yes," he said finally. "She does."

Olivia's attention snapped back to the notebook. If Clara Waverly was part of the line Cassie had traced, and if that line continued … She flipped forward through the pages, scanning more quickly now. Cassie had added notes in the margins. Small references to census records. Property listings. Marriage documents.

Olivia reached for her laptop, set it on the desk, and pulled up the local records database.

The screen cast a pale glow across the room. Search Waverly. Results populated slowly.

She filtered by date. Older entries first. Henry Waverly appeared again. Landowner. Property records tied to the mountain. Clara Waverly. Listed in past census records. Olivia scrolled.

A younger brother. Thomas Waverly. She leaned closer. Thomas had not remained in Mistwood.

There was a note showing that he had moved. The records shifted location. A different county. Then another. Marriage. Children. The name continued. Not in Mistwood. Elsewhere. Until …

Olivia's breath caught. The line returned. A later generation. Back in Mistwood. She clicked into the record. The screen refreshed. Name: Lark Waverly. The room seemed to narrow. For a moment, Olivia did not move. She stared at the name, reading it once, then again, as if repetition might change what she was seeing. It did not.

Behind her, Anton let out a low whistle. "Well," he said. "That is inconvenient."

Olivia exhaled slowly. "Inconvenient," she repeated.

"Yes," Anton said. "Though also rather dramatic."

She closed her eyes briefly, then opened them again. Lark Waverly. Not a coincidence.

Not a shared name. A direct line. Thomas Waverly's descendants had left. They had lived elsewhere. And at some point, they had come back. Lark had come back.

Olivia leaned back in her chair, her mind moving through the implications with growing clarity. "If the Waverly family originally owned the land," she said slowly, "and the deed was forged …"

Anton watched her. "Then that land was taken from them."

"Yes. And if Lark is the last living descendant …"

"She would have a claim."

Olivia felt a sharp twist in her chest. Not just a claim. The claim. Everything was built on that land. The resort and the businesses tied to it. The history that everyone accepted as fact. All of it resting on something that might not have been legal to begin with. "Her entire life could change," Olivia said.

Anton's expression brightened. "Oh, I hope so."

She shot him a look. "This is not entertainment. It is significant."

"It's dangerous?"

"It is both."

Olivia stood abruptly, pushing the chair back. "If this comes out," she said, pacing once across the room, "it doesn't just affect the people who benefited. It affects Lark. Her name. Her life. Everything she's built here."

"And the people who stand to lose something," Anton added, "may not appreciate that outcome."

Olivia stopped. That was the center. Cassie had found the truth. And now Cassie was dead.

Olivia looked back at the screen. At the name. Lark Waverly. A quiet presence in a kitchen that smelled of cinnamon and butter. A woman who had spent years caring for a house that did not technically belong to her. A woman who had no idea what her family might have lost. Or what might now come back.

Anton clasped his hands behind his back, his tone taking on a theatrical edge. "The rightful heir returns," he declared. "The mountain awaits its true ruler."

Olivia turned to him. "Stop."

He blinked. "What?"

"Stop making speeches."

"I am not making a speech. I am stating a fact in an appropriately elevated tone."

"You are being dramatic."

"I am being accurate."

"You are being unhelpful."

Anton considered that, then inclined his head slightly. "Very well. I will be quietly accurate."

Olivia pressed her lips together, then let out a breath. She turned back to the desk and gathered the photograph and the notes. This was not something she could ignore. But it was also not something she could rush. If she was right, the truth would not just expose a crime. It would upend a life.

She moved to the doorway and looked down the hall toward the kitchen. Lark stood at the counter, exactly where she had been earlier, shaping dough with steady hands. The soft hum had returned. The oven light cast the same warm glow. Nothing had changed. Everything had changed.

Olivia rested her hand lightly against the doorframe. For a moment, she said nothing.

Then, quietly, to herself, "Someone already killed to keep this hidden."

Anton stepped up beside her, his voice lower now, stripped of its earlier theatrics.

"Then you must decide," he said, "whether bringing it to light will save her … or place her in danger."

Olivia did not answer. She watched Lark move through the kitchen, unaware of the weight of history settling into place around her. And understood, with a clarity that left no room for comfort. This was no longer just about solving a murder. This was about what came after.

CHAPTER TWENTY-TWO

The Lawyer's Legacy

The streets of Mistwood were quiet today. With a fresh blanket of snow, many residents decided today was a good day to stay home by a warm fire. The Mistwood Historical Archive looked abandoned from the outside. It was the sort of place most people forgot existed until they needed something from it. Olivia had begun to appreciate it for exactly that reason.

Inside, the archive felt hushed in a way that went beyond quiet. Shelves lined the walls from floor to ceiling, filled with boxes, binders, and carefully labeled folders. A long table occupied the center of the room, its surface scattered with open records and neatly stacked files. Dust motes drifted lazily in the light.

Mrs. Ellery looked up from behind her desk as Olivia entered. "You're becoming a regular," she said, adjusting her glasses.

"I'm starting to feel that way," Olivia replied.

"Back to the same subject?"

"Yes."

Mrs. Ellery studied her for a moment, then nodded. "The resort records are where you left them."

"Thank you." Olivia moved to the table and set down her bag, pulling out Cassie's notes, her own notebook, and the photograph. The recorder remained tucked safely in her pocket.

Today, she was not looking for broad patterns. She was looking for something specific. A name.

She flipped through Cassie's notes, tracing the references tied to the early land transfer. Parcel numbers. Dates. Witness signatures. And one name that had appeared more than once, always circled, always underlined. A lawyer. Cassie had not written it clearly in every instance. Sometimes it was abbreviated. Sometimes only an initial remained. But the pattern was there.

Olivia turned to the archive files and began pulling the boxes tied to the 1930s development period of North Star Summit. Paper whispered softly as she opened the first folder.

Legal notices. Property filings. Announcements of land sales and development plans. The town's early excitement captured in neat columns of text.

She worked methodically.

One file led to another. A notice referenced a deed. The deed referenced a filing. The filing referenced a legal representative. Olivia's finger stilled on the page. There. Attorney of record. Edwin Hale. She leaned closer, reading it again. Edwin Hale. The name settled into place with a quiet, undeniable weight. Behind her, a chair shifted as Mrs. Ellery stood and moved to another shelf. The soft sounds of the archive continued, steady and unobtrusive.

Olivia sat back slowly. "Hale," she murmured.

Anton appeared at her side, drawn by the shift in her focus. "You have found him," he said.

"I think so," Olivia tapped the page lightly. "Edwin Hale."

Anton nodded. "A respectable name. Or one that wishes to be."

Olivia exhaled slowly. "I know that name. I read it somewhere." She went back through her pile of papers and pulled out the genealogy reports she had printed earlier. It didn't take her long to discover that Edwin Hale was. The connection came immediately. Not distant or obscure, direct. "He's Cindy Keller's grandfather," Olivia said under her breath.

Anton tilted his head. "That explains a lot."

"It explains her reaction," Olivia said. "It explains the fear."

"And perhaps the urgency."

Olivia returned her attention to the documents, flipping to the next page. Edwin Hale's name appeared again. And again. Edwin had been involved in every major filing tied to the early development of the resort. He had handled the legal paperwork. Oversaw the transfer. Certified the documents. He had been at the center of it.

"Convenient," Anton said.

"Too convenient," Olivia replied. She pulled another file closer, this one thicker, its edges worn from age and use. Inside were copies of land sale records. The Waverly property.

Her pulse quickened.

She spread the pages out, scanning quickly. Parcel descriptions. Boundaries. Witnesses. Signatures. She compared them to Cassie's notes. The inconsistencies stood out more clearly now. Dates that did not align. Signatures that varied in subtle but significant ways. References to documents that were not present in the file.

Olivia's gaze sharpened. "Something's missing."

Anton leaned in. "What should be here?"

"A complete chain of transfers," Olivia said. "Every step documented. Every change recorded."

"And it is not."

"No," she flipped through the pages again, slower this time. There were gaps. Not obvious at first glance. Not enough to raise suspicion for someone skimming. But they were there. A document referenced but not included. A signature verified by a witness whose own record was incomplete. A final transfer that relied on earlier paperwork that could not be fully traced.

Olivia sat back, the pieces beginning to align. "The original sale isn't complete," she said.

Anton's expression sharpened. "Incomplete records suggest interference."

"They suggest something was removed," Olivia said. "Or never properly filed."

"Which is it?"

Olivia looked at the name again. Edwin Hale. "I think it was intentional." She reached for a stack of old newspapers and began flipping through them, scanning headlines and reading snippets of articles tied to the resort's development: Mistwood Expands Winter Tourism, New Lodge Planned for North Star Summit, Local Investment Brings Opportunity to Region. The tone was consistent, optimistic, forward-looking, and proud.

Names appeared in the articles. Investors. Developers. Community leaders. And occasionally … legal counsel, Edwin Hale, always in the background, always present.

She found a small notice tucked near the bottom of one page. Legal confirmation of land acquisition. Handled by Edwin Hale.

Olivia studied it. "There's no mention of the Waverly family," she said.

Anton frowned. "That seems unlikely, given their ownership."

"Exactly." She turned back to the land records. If the Waverly family had owned that property, their involvement should have been clearly documented in the final transfer, and it was not.

Olivia leaned forward, her mind moving quickly now. "The land was taken," she said slowly. "Or claimed. Or transferred under conditions that weren't legitimate."

"And the lawyer," Anton said, "ensured it appeared otherwise."

"Yes." She tapped the page again. "Edwin Hale handled the paperwork. He certified the documents. He made it look legal."

"And if it was not?"

"Then he falsified the record." The conclusion settled into place with quiet certainty.

Olivia drew a slow breath. "The developers built the resort believing they had proper ownership," she said. "Or at least believing the paperwork was valid."

Anton nodded. "Which means the fault lies not only with them, but with the man who made it possible."

"Edwin Hale."

"Cindy's grandfather." Olivia leaned back in her chair, the weight of it pressing in. Cassie had found this. Or something very close to it. Cassie had realized that the land transfer was flawed. That the foundation of the resort might not be legal. She had confronted Cindy. "I have proof that the deed was forged." And Cindy had replied, "You don't understand what you're about to destroy."

Olivia closed her eyes briefly. Cindy had known. Not necessarily every detail or every document, but enough. Enough to understand what exposure would mean. Her family name was tied directly to the man who had made it happen. Her business would suffer. The consequences would not be small. Everything would come into question.

Olivia opened her eyes again. "This could destroy her," she whispered.

Anton watched her. "It could."

"And if she believed that ..."

"She might act to prevent it."

Olivia nodded once. "Cassie was going to expose the truth," she said. "Cindy tried to stop her. The argument proves that."

"And when persuasion failed," Anton said, "fear may have taken control."

Olivia gathered the documents, stacking them carefully. Fear of losing everything.

Fear of what would happen when the truth came out.

She slid the papers back into their folders and closed the boxes.

Mrs. Ellery glanced up as Olivia approached the desk.

"Did you find what you needed?" she asked.

"I found more than I expected."

"That tends to happen here."

Olivia offered a small, distracted smile. "It does." She stepped back into the hallway, the door closing softly behind her.

The air outside felt sharper after the stillness of the archive. Snow continued to fall, steady and unrelenting, covering the street in a fresh layer of white. Olivia paused at the top of the steps. The pieces were coming together. The forged deed. Edwin Hale's role and Cindy's reaction. And the quiet truth beneath it all. Lark. The last living connection to the family that had lost everything.

Olivia exhaled slowly, watching her breath drift into the cold air. "If this comes out," she said softly, "nothing stays the same."

Anton appeared beside her, his expression thoughtful. "No," he said. "It does not."

She started down the steps, her mind already turning to what came next. Because understanding the past was only the beginning. The real question now was what someone had been willing to do to keep it buried. And whether they would do it again.

CHAPTER TWENTY-THREE

Reconstructing the Night

The road up to North Star Summit curved through the trees in long, deliberate turns, each one edged with snowbanks that had grown higher with every storm. Gus handled the climb without complaint.

Olivia kept both hands steady on the wheel, her eyes moving between the road and the pale stretch of mountain ahead. The sky hung low and gray, pressing close to the peaks. Snow still fell, though lighter now, drifting across the windshield in soft, irregular patterns.

The road to the summit was quieter than she had ever seen it. The official opening of the ski season wouldn't be until Thanksgiving Weekend. Until then, there was no steady movement of guests coming and going. Just snow and silence.

She pulled into the parking lot and cut the engine. The cold pressed in immediately, sharp and clean, carrying the faint scent of pine and distant wood smoke. For a moment, Olivia sat still.

Then she reached into her coat pocket, feeling the weight of Anton's medal, and stepped out into the snow.

The wind had shifted since the last time she had stood there. It moved across the open space with a low, steady sweep, stirring loose snow into faint, whispering trails along the ground.

Anton appeared beside her, taking in the scene with a measured gaze. "Quieter," he said.

"Yes."

"Better."

"Not really."

He glanced at her. "You prefer noise?"

"I prefer answers." She closed the car door and started toward the trail.

The path leading out from the lodge had been partially cleared, though fresh snowfall had softened its edges again. Beyond that, the marked cross-country route stretched into the trees, a pale ribbon winding between dark trunks and shadows.

Olivia followed it. Each step crunched lightly beneath her boots. The cold settled into her lungs, sharp with every breath. The further she moved from the lodge, the quieter it became. No voices or movement. Just wind, snow, and the faint creak of branches shifting under the weight of ice.

She knew the spot before she reached it. Something about the air changed. Not colder, but heavier. The embankment lay just beyond a bend in the trail. The ground sloped sharply downward where Cassie had been found. Snow covered everything now, smoothing over the details, erasing what had been visible days ago.

Olivia stopped at the edge. This is where it happened. She stood still, letting the scene settle into place around her. Behind her, the lodge. Ahead, the slope. Between them, the narrow stretch of trail where Cassie had stepped out into the dark.

"She came out here on purpose," Olivia said.

Anton nodded. "Not by accident."

"She was meeting someone."

"Yes."

Olivia crouched slightly, studying the ground. The original tracks were long gone. Lost beneath fresh snowfall and time. But the layout remained. The space between the trail and the drop, and the angle of the embankment. The distance a body might fall.

She stood again, turning slowly. Cassie would have walked from the lodge. Out into the cold. To meet Cindy. A faint sound reached her ears. Footsteps. Olivia glanced over her shoulder.

Luke approached along the trail, his jacket pulled tight against the cold, his breath visible in the air. He moved with the steady, purposeful stride she had come to recognize.

He slowed as he reached her. "Of course you're here," he said.

Olivia gave him a small smile. "It's a nice day for a walk."

He looked around at the empty slope. "That's one way to describe it." He stepped up beside her, his gaze moving over the embankment. "You're retracing it," he said.

"Yes."

He did not tell her to leave. That alone marked the change. "What have you got?" he asked.

Olivia studied him for a moment, then turned back to the slope.

"Cassie arranged to meet Cindy," she said. "Out here. Away from the lodge."

Luke nodded slowly. "That matches what we know so far."

"She had proof that the deed was forged."

"I heard the recording."

Olivia glanced at him. "You listened to it?"

"You brought it in. I'm not ignoring something that important."

That, too, was new. "She confronted Cindy," Olivia continued. "Told her what she had. Told her she was going to expose it."

Luke shifted his weight slightly. "And Cindy didn't want that to happen."

"No."

The wind picked up briefly, sweeping across the open space, then settled again.

Olivia stepped closer to the edge of the embankment. "They argued," she said. "Not quietly. Not calmly. This wasn't a conversation. It was a confrontation."

Luke moved beside her, his attention focused.

"She tells Cindy she's going public," Olivia said. "That the truth is coming out. That everything tied to that deed is going to be exposed."

"And Cindy panics," Luke said.

"Yes."

Olivia waved her hand at the surrounding space.

"They're standing here," she said. "Near the edge. Close enough that one wrong step matters."

Luke followed her gesture.

"She tries to convince Cassie to stop," Olivia said. "To let it go. To think about what it would do."

"And Cassie refuses."

"She refuses."

Silence settled for a moment. Then Olivia said, "That's when it changes."

Luke's gaze sharpened. "How?"

"Fear turns into action."

She stepped carefully to one side, positioning herself where she imagined Cassie might have stood.

"Cindy doesn't plan it," Olivia said. "This wasn't premeditated. It's a moment."

Luke watched her closely.

"She shoves her," Olivia said. The word hung in the cold air. "She pushes Cassie," Olivia continued, her voice steady. "Not thinking past that second. Just reacting."

Luke looked down the slope. "And Cassie falls."

Olivia nodded. "The ground drops fast here," she said. "It's not a gentle slope. It's steep enough to throw someone off balance immediately."

Luke stepped closer to the edge, assessing the angle. "She hits her head," he said.

"Yes."

"Hard enough to kill her."

Olivia's expression tightened. "Instantly, most likely."

Luke exhaled slowly, the breath leaving him in a thin cloud.

For a moment, neither of them spoke. The scene settled into place between them.

Not imagined, but reconstructed and real.

"She didn't mean to kill her," Luke said finally.

"No."

"But she did."

"Yes."

He nodded once, as if accepting it.

Olivia stepped back from the edge. "Then comes the next decision," she said.

Luke looked at her. "Which is?"

"Whether to call for help," Olivia said. "Or cover it up."

He did not answer immediately. "She covers it," he said at last.

"Yes."

Olivia turned, walking a few steps along the trail. "She drags the body," she said. "Not far. Just enough to change the position. To make it look like a fall."

Luke followed her.

"But she misses things," he said.

"Yes."

Olivia stopped and faced him. "Cassie wasn't skiing," she said. "No skis. No poles. Just boots."

Luke nodded. "We noted that."

"And the tracks," Olivia said. "Footprints. Not ski tracks."

"Covered by snowfall later," Luke added.

"But still wrong for the story."

He exhaled again, slower this time. "It fits," he said.

Olivia held his gaze. "You believe it."

"I think it's the most coherent version we've got," he said carefully.

"That's not the same as believing it."

"It's close."

She let that sit.

The wind shifted again, colder now, biting at exposed skin. Luke shoved his hands into his jacket pockets. "It explains the argument," he said. "It explains the location. It explains the injuries."

"It explains the fear," Olivia said.

He nodded. "But it's still a theory," he added. "We need something that ties her directly to this spot at that time."

"I know."

He looked at her.

"You're not done," he said.

"No."

"What are you missing?"

Olivia turned back toward the lodge, her eyes narrowing slightly. "Something that places her here," she said. "Not just in conversation. Not just in motive. Physically here."

"A witness," Luke said.

"Or evidence," Olivia replied. "Something she couldn't erase."

Luke followed her gaze along the trail, the trees, and the space between the lodge and the slope. "She was careful," he said.

"Not careful enough."

"You think she left something behind."

"I think she overlooked something," Olivia said. "People always do when they're acting out of fear."

Luke considered that. Then he nodded. "All right," he said. "We keep digging."

Olivia glanced at him. He didn't dismiss her or resist. He just agreed. The shift between them was quiet but unmistakable.

"Good," she said.

They stood there for another moment, the weight of the scene settling into something almost tangible.

Then Luke stepped back from the edge. "We'll go over the reports again," he said. "Look for anything we might have missed."

"I'll go through Cassie's notes again," Olivia said. "And everything tied to Cindy."

Luke nodded. "Be careful," he said.

Olivia gave him a faint smile. "You're starting to repeat yourself."

"Maybe you should start listening."

"Maybe you should worry less."

He almost smiled. Almost. Then he turned and started back toward the lodge.

Olivia remained where she was for a moment longer. The slope stretched out before her, quiet and unchanged. But now she could see it. The entire scene played out before her. She turned at last and followed Luke back up the trail. Behind her, the snow continued to fall. Covering everything. But not enough to hide the truth.

CHAPTER TWENTY-FOUR

The Missing Evidence

By the time Olivia returned to March House, the light had already faded again. Winter days had a way of slipping past unnoticed, swallowed by clouds and snow until evening arrived without warning. The house glowed warmly against the dim gray outside, windows lit, smoke curling from the chimney, the familiar promise of comfort waiting just beyond the door.

Olivia stepped inside and shut the cold out behind her. For a moment, she leaned back against the door and closed her eyes.

The mountain still lingered in her mind. The certainty of what had happened there. A shove, and then a fall. A decision made in fear that could never be undone.

She pushed away from the door and moved through the hallway. The house felt calmer than it had the night before. The earlier chaos had settled into something more familiar. Not silence, but a kind of ordered presence. The ghosts had retreated into their usual rhythms, their movements no longer colliding in sharp bursts.

Anton followed her, quieter now, his earlier bravado tempered by the weight of what they had pieced together.

"You are certain," he said.

"About what happened on the slope?" Olivia replied.

"Yes."

She nodded once. "Yes."

"And yet you are not finished."

"No," she said. "I'm missing something."

He tilted his head slightly. "Then we find it."

Olivia did not answer. She stepped into the kitchen long enough to nod at Lark, who stood at the counter arranging pastries onto a cooling rack.

"You're back," Lark said.

"For a bit."

"You look like you're chasing something."

"I am."

Lark smiled faintly. "You always are."

Olivia gave a small shrug and continued down the hall to her room.

THE DESK WAITED. Papers where she had left them. Notes stacked in careful order. The photograph was set aside but not forgotten.

Olivia pulled out Cassie's notebook and spread it open again. "One more time," she said.

Anton drifted closer. "You have already examined this several times."

"I missed something."

"Or you are looking for confirmation."

"Both." She flipped through the pages slowly. Not scanning, but reading. Cassie's notes were no longer just information. They were a trail. A path Cassie had followed step by step, each piece leading to the next. Olivia needed to follow it the same way. Parcel references. Boundary disputes. Names tied to land transfers. Edwin Hale circled again and again. Waverly noted in the margins. Connections drawn. Questions asked. Olivia turned another page. Then another.

She slowed. A section near the back. Less organized. More hurried. Notes written at sharper angles, the pen pressed harder into the page. Cassie had been close here. Very close.

Olivia leaned in. A line in the margin caught her eye. Small. Almost easy to miss.

"Original contract ... Keller family files."

Olivia stilled.

Anton leaned over her shoulder. "What is it?"

She tapped the line lightly. “This.”

He read it. “The original contract.”

“Yes.”

“And it is with the Keller family.”

“That’s what Cassie thought.”

Olivia sat back slowly.

“That means she found it,” she said.

Anton’s gaze sharpened. “Or believed she had.”

“No,” Olivia said, shaking her head. “Cassie didn’t write guesses like this. She noted only things she could confirm or trace directly.”

“She located the document.”

“Yes.”

Olivia’s mind hurried now, the pieces aligning with a clarity that made her pulse quicken. “If the original contract exists,” she said, “and it was falsified, then it would have to be somewhere controlled. Somewhere it wouldn’t be questioned.”

“The family of the man who created it,” Anton said.

“The Keller family.”

Olivia stood and began pacing. “That means Cindy,” she said. “Or her father. Or someone in that line kept it.”

“And if they kept it,” Anton added, “they knew.”

“Yes,” Olivia stopped. Cindy’s voice echoed in her mind. “You don’t understand what you’re about to destroy.”

“You think this is just about paperwork?”

“It’s about everything.”

Olivia exhaled slowly. “She knew,” she said.

Anton nodded. “For some time, I suspect.”

Olivia turned back to the desk, her thoughts sharpening.

“Cassie must have found a reference to the contract,” she said. “Tracked it to the Keller family and realized what it meant.”

“And confronted Cindy.”

“Yes.”

“And Cindy,” Anton said, “had already discovered it.”

Olivia’s gaze lifted. “That’s it,” she said.

“She found it years ago,” Olivia continued. “Sorting through family papers. Old records. Something that didn’t quite make sense.”

"And instead of exposing it—"

"She hid it."

Anton inclined his head. "A practical decision. If one values stability over truth."

"It wasn't just stability," Olivia said. "It was everything. Her name. Her business. The hotel. Her family's reputation."

"And if the truth came out," Anton said, "it would all collapse."

Olivia nodded.

"Cassie threatened that," she said. "Not just the past, but the present and the future."

Anton folded his hands behind his back. "Fear again."

"Yes."

Olivia looked down at the notebook. Cassie had found the path. And she had followed it straight to Cindy. "That's why Cindy reacted the way she did," Olivia said. "She wasn't just defending her family. She was protecting a secret she already knew existed."

"And one she had chosen to keep."

Olivia closed the notebook. "She couldn't let Cassie expose it," she said.

"No, not after hiding it for so long." Anton's expression shifted slightly, thoughtful.

"There is something else," he said.

Olivia looked at him. "What?"

He hesitated, then continued.

"The night of the summit," he said. "Before everything … ended."

Olivia's attention sharpened. "You saw something."

"I observed," Anton corrected. "I was near the outer path. Watching the slope. Evaluating conditions."

"Of course you were."

"I saw her," he said.

Olivia went still.

"Cindy."

He nodded. "She was leaving the lodge. Moving quickly. Not toward the parking area. Toward the trail."

Olivia felt a quiet surge of confirmation. "You're sure."

"Yes."

"What time?"

"After the gathering had begun to disperse," Anton said. "Before the full darkness settled."

Olivia nodded slowly.

"That fits," she said. "Cassie would have arranged to meet her after the main event."

Anton's gaze held hers. "She was not calm."

"No."

"She moved with purpose," he said. "And urgency."

Olivia turned away, pacing once across the room. "She went to meet Cassie," she said. "Already knowing what Cassie had found."

"And already afraid of what it meant."

"Yes."

Olivia stopped. The pieces were no longer scattered. They formed a line, clear and direct.

Cassie confronts Cindy. Cindy, already aware, panics. The argument escalates. The shove. The fall. The cover. Olivia turned back to Anton. "That's it," she said. "That's the sequence."

"And now?" he asked.

Olivia's gaze hardened. "Now we prove it."

Anton's expression brightened slightly. "Ah. The most troublesome part."

"Yes."

Olivia moved to the desk and gathered the key pieces. Cassie's notebook.

Her own notes. The photograph. Everything that pointed in one direction.

"We don't have the contract," she said. "Not yet."

"But we know where it should be."

"Yes."

"And we know who has it."

"Yes."

Anton smiled faintly. "Then we apply pressure."

Olivia nodded. "Publicly," she said.

He raised an eyebrow. "Bold."

"Necessary." Olivia reached for her phone. "Cindy has managed this quietly so far," she said. "Contained it. Controlled it."

"And you intend to remove that control."

"Yes." She scrolled to Luke's name and paused. "This doesn't work in private," she said. "She can deny it. Deflect. Walk away."

"And in public?"

"She has nowhere to hide."

Anton inclined his head. "A confrontation."

Olivia tapped the screen and lifted the phone to her ear.

Luke answered on the second ring. "Olivia."

"I have a plan to get the conclusive proof we need," she said.

"Am I going to like this?"

"I need you to bring everyone together," Olivia said. "The summit attendees. The ones connected to the land. The ones who were there."

A pause. "For what?"

"A meeting," she said. "At the lodge."

Another pause.

"You're serious."

"Yes."

"Why?"

Olivia glanced down at the notes spread across her desk. "Because I know what happened," she said.

Silence on the line. Then … "You're sure."

"Yes."

"And you can prove it."

"I can get us there."

Luke exhaled slowly. "All right," he said. "I'll set it up."

"When?"

"Tomorrow evening," he said. "Sooner is better."

"Yes," Olivia agreed. "It is."

He hesitated, then added, "You're stepping into something big that could make or break both of us."

"I know."

"Make sure you're ready."

Olivia looked toward the doorway, down the hall where Lark moved quietly in the kitchen, unaware. "I am," she said. She ended the call and set the phone down.

Anton watched her. "You have set the stage," he said.

"Yes."

"And now?"

Olivia met his gaze. "Now we see who's willing to lie in front of everyone," she said.

"And who breaks first?"

Olivia turned toward the door. Beyond it, the house waited. The ghosts watched. The truth stood just within reach. And for the first time since this began, she was ready to bring it into the light.

CHAPTER TWENTY-FIVE

Setting the Trap

By the time Olivia reached North Star Summit again, dusk had already settled across the mountain. The lodge stood against the fading light, its windows glowing warmly against the deepening gray of evening. Snow continued to fall in fine, steady sheets, softening the edges of the building and muting the world beyond it. The parking lot held only a handful of vehicles.

Enough.

Olivia stepped out of Gus and closed the door, the sound dull beneath the weight of snow. The air felt sharper here than in town, cleaner, carrying the faint scent of pine and distant cold.

Anton appeared beside her, his expression keen. “Back to the scene,” he said.

“Not the scene,” Olivia replied. “The stage.”

He smiled faintly. “Even better.”

She adjusted her coat and headed toward the lodge. Inside, the warmth hit immediately, along with the familiar scent of wood smoke and polished timber. The main room had been cleared of most of its casual clutter. Chairs arranged. A long table was set near the center.

Luke stood near the far end of the room, speaking quietly with one of the lodge staff. He looked up as Olivia entered. “You made it,” he said.

“I said I would.”

His gaze lingered on her for a moment, assessing. "You're sure about this?" he said.

"Yes."

"That's not an answer."

"It's the only one you're getting."

A corner of his mouth shifted, not quite a smile. "They're here," he said.

Olivia followed his gaze.

Cindy Keller stood near the windows, her posture as composed as ever, her coat still on, her hands loosely clasped in front of her. Her expression was calm, controlled, unreadable to anyone who did not know what to look for.

Mason Reed leaned against one of the chairs, arms crossed, watching the room with quiet focus.

Darla Bishop sat at the table, flipping absently through a folder she had not been reading.

Gerald Huxley stood near the fireplace, his back straight, his expression impatient.

Tom Granger hovered closer to the door, shifting his weight from one foot to the other.

Five people. Five threads connected to the same place. The same history and secrets.

Olivia felt the weight of it settle around her.

"Everyone's here?" she asked.

Luke nodded. "The ones you asked for."

"Good."

Anton drifted a few steps ahead, surveying the room with interest. "They look uncomfortable," he said.

"They should. Now, please keep quiet. I need to concentrate and do this right."

Olivia moved toward the table, setting her bag down with deliberate care. The room quieted as she did. Conversations that had been murmured fell away. Movements stilled. Attention shifted. All of it focused on her.

She took a breath, glanced around the table, and began. "Thank you for coming," she said. Her voice carried easily in the room. Clear. Steady. "We all know why we're here."

No one answered. They did not need to.

Olivia rested her hands lightly on the edge of the table. "Cassie Greer didn't die by accident," she said. That much was already understood. But saying it aloud changed the air. It made it real.

"She was investigating the history of this mountain," Olivia continued. "Specifically, the land it was built on." A faint shift moved through the group. Not obvious, but there if you knew what to look for.

Mason's shoulders tightened slightly. Darla's fingers stilled on the folder. Tom looked down, then quickly back up. Cindy did not move.

Olivia noticed.

"She believed something was wrong with the original land transfer," Olivia said. "That the deed used to establish the resort didn't hold up under scrutiny."

Gerald let out a quick breath. "That's a serious claim."

"Yes," Olivia said. "It is."

"And you're saying she was right?" Darla asked.

"I'm saying she found evidence that supports it."

Olivia reached into her bag and pulled out copies of Cassie's notes, placing them on the table. "She traced the ownership back to the original landholder," Olivia said. "Henry Waverly."

At the mention of the name, a ripple moved through the room.

"She followed the records," Olivia continued. "The transfers. The legal filings. The changes made over time."

Mason shifted slightly. "And?"

"And the records don't line up," Olivia said. "There are gaps. Missing documents. Inconsistencies in signatures and dates."

Gerald frowned. "That doesn't prove anything."

"It proves something is wrong," Olivia said. She let that sit. Then added, "And it points to one person who handled those records."

A pause. Olivia looked up. Let her gaze move across the room. Then settle. "Edwin Hale."

The name landed. Cindy's reaction was immediate. Small, but unmistakable. Her posture tightened, and her shoulders drew in by a fraction. Her gaze flickered, just once, before she caught it.

But Olivia saw it. So did Luke.

The room seemed to narrow around that moment. Gerald's

brows rose. Darla looked from Olivia to Cindy and back again. Mason's expression sharpened, something like recognition settling in. Tom shifted again, more noticeably this time.

"Edwin Hale?" Gerald said. "That name sounds familiar."

"It should," Olivia said. She did not look away from Cindy. "He was the attorney of record for the land transfer that made this resort possible," Olivia said.

Silence followed, heavy and awkward.

Cindy's voice came, controlled as ever. "And what does that have to do with anything?" she asked.

Olivia met her gaze. "Everything," she said. She stepped slightly closer to the table.

"Edwin Hale handled the legal paperwork for the transfer of the Waverly land," Olivia said. "He certified the documents. He ensured everything appeared legitimate."

"Appeared?" Darla echoed.

Olivia nodded. "Because the original transfer was not complete," she said. "Key documents are missing. References exist to paperwork that isn't in the official record."

Gerald's expression shifted from impatience to something more serious.

"You're suggesting fraud," he said.

"I'm stating it," Olivia replied.

Another silence.

Cindy did not move. But the calm she wore had begun to thin.

Olivia continued. "Cassie found those inconsistencies," she said. "She followed them back to the source. To the Keller family records."

That was when Cindy's composure faltered. Not completely, but enough to be seen.

Her fingers tightened where they rested against her coat. Her breath caught, just for a second.

The others saw it.

Olivia knew they did. "She found the original contract," Olivia said.

No one spoke.

"She knew what it meant," Olivia continued. "That the land this resort sits on may not have been legally transferred."

Mason straightened. "If that's true—"

"It changes everything," Olivia said.

"Yes," Mason whispered. "It does."

Darla looked toward Cindy now, uncertainty in her eyes.

"Cindy?" she said.

Cindy did not answer. Her gaze remained on Olivia. Steady, but no longer unshaken.

Olivia took one more step forward. "Cassie confronted you," she said.

The room stilled. Every movement ceased. Every breath seemed to hold.

Olivia's voice did not waver. "She told you what she had found," she said. "She told you she was going to expose it."

Cindy's lips parted slightly. Then closed.

"She gave you a chance," Olivia continued. "To come forward. To tell the truth."

Cindy said nothing. But her control was slipping.

Olivia could see it now. In the tension around her eyes. In the way her shoulders no longer held perfectly still. In the faint tremor that moved through her hands before she stilled them again.

Olivia held her gaze. "Cassie Greer discovered the truth about the mountain," she said.

The words settled into the silence. "And you knew she was right."

Cindy's expression changed. Not all at once. Not in a way anyone could deny. The calm fractured, and fear surfaced.

Luke shifted slightly, his attention sharpening.

No one else spoke. No one moved. The room held its breath. And in that silence ... the truth stood on the edge of being spoken.

CHAPTER TWENTY-SIX

The Truth Comes Out

The room held its silence. It was not an empty silence. It was the kind that pressed inward, heavy with expectation. Every person knew that something had shifted, and there was no easy way back from it.

Cindy Keller still stood near the windows, the last traces of composure still clinging to her expression, though they no longer fit as cleanly as they had moments before.

Olivia did not look away.

Neither did Luke. He remained near the back of the room, arms relaxed at his sides, his attention fixed, his presence steady without being intrusive. Watching. Waiting. Letting it unfold.

That, more than anything, told Olivia she had been right to do this here. At the resort and in the open. Where nothing could be quietly dismissed or reshaped. Up front, where everyone could see and hear.

Olivia drew a slow breath. Then she continued. “Cassie didn’t just suspect something was wrong,” she said. “She proved it.” Her voice carried clearly, cutting through the tension without strain. “She traced the ownership of this land back to the beginning,” Olivia said. “Back to the Waverly family.”

Mason’s gaze sharpened. Darla’s fingers tightened against the edge of the table. Gerald shifted his weight slightly, his earlier impatience replaced by something more attentive.

Tom said nothing, but his eyes had not left Cindy.

"Henry Waverly owned the mountain," Olivia continued. "Not a portion of it. Not a disputed section. The land that became this resort." She paused, letting that settle. "Decades ago, developers wanted it," she said. "They saw the potential. The slopes, the access to the town, and the profitability of a ski resort near a town that already had destination tourism possibilities with its location next to a picturesque lake.

Gerald nodded faintly. "That much is history."

"Yes," Olivia said. "It is." She took a step closer to the table. "But the way they got it isn't." Silence again. She let her gaze move across the room, then return to Cindy. "Edwin Hale handled the transfer of that land," Olivia said. "He prepared the documents. He certified the sale. He ensured everything appeared legal."

Gerald frowned. "You keep saying that. Appeared."

"Because it wasn't," Olivia said. The words landed harder this time and more direct. "The deed transferring ownership of the Waverly land was forged," Olivia said.

No one spoke or interrupted. The weight of the statement held them still.

"The original contract was incomplete," Olivia continued. "Supporting documents were missing. The signatures did not match earlier records. References pointed to paperwork that no longer exists in the official archive."

Mason let out a quiet breath. "So the land was never legally transferred."

"Not in a way that holds up," Olivia said.

Gerald shook his head slightly. "If that's true …"

"It changes everything," Darla finished.

"Yes," Olivia said. "It does."

She did not look away from Cindy.

"The land was taken," Olivia said. "And the man who made that possible was Edwin Hale."

Cindy's expression tightened again. This time, she did not recover as quickly.

Olivia saw it, and so did the others.

"And if the truth comes out," Olivia continued, her tone steady, "it doesn't just stay in the past." She let the implications settle before she spoke them. “It affects the present,” she said. “Ownership. Legitimacy. Every business tied to this land. Every structure built on it.”

Gerald’s posture stiffened. “You’re talking about lawsuits.”

“Yes.”

Gerald took a deep breath. “Disputes over property.”

“Yes.”

Gerald’s hands were shaking. “And the financial collapse of the investment partnership that owns the resort.”

Olivia did not soften it. “Yes.”

The room seemed to contract.

Darla’s eyes moved from Olivia to Cindy, uncertainty giving way to something sharper.

“Cindy,” she whispered.

Cindy did not answer. Her gaze remained fixed on Olivia with anger that was controlled, but barely.

Olivia took another step forward. “Cassie discovered this,” she said. “Not just the inconsistencies. Not just the gaps. The truth. She found the connection to the Keller family; that Edwin Hale was your grandfather.” Olivia continued. “She traced the documents. She understood what it meant.”

Cindy’s lips parted slightly. Then pressed together again.

“She confronted you,” Olivia said. The words were softer now, but no less direct.

“She told you what she had found,” Olivia said. “She told you she was going to expose it.”

“No,” Cindy said. The word came quickly. Too quickly.

Olivia did not react.

“She told you the truth was coming out,” Olivia said.

“That’s not what happened,” Cindy said, her voice tightening.

Olivia held her gaze. “Then tell us what did.”

Silence.

Cindy’s jaw set. “This is speculation,” she said. “You have theories. Assumptions. Nothing more.”

Olivia nodded once. Then continued anyway. “You met her on the mountain,” Olivia said.

“I didn’t—”

“You met her outside the lodge,” Olivia said, her voice cutting cleanly through the denial. "She asked you to come. Or you followed her when you realized what she knew."

Cindy's hands tightened at her sides. The room held still.

"You argued," Olivia said. "She told you she was going public. That she had proof."

"That's not—"

"You told her she didn't understand what she was about to destroy," Olivia said.

Cindy froze.

The words hung in the air.

Mason's gaze snapped toward her. Darla's breath caught. Gerald straightened fully now, his attention locked in place.

Luke did not move.

But Olivia could feel his focus sharpen.

"You told her it wasn't just paperwork," Olivia said. "That it was everything."

Cindy's control slipped. Just a fraction, but it was enough.

"You were there," Olivia said. "You knew what she had. You knew what it meant."

"I didn't kill her," Cindy said.

The words came out fast. No one had said she had. The silence that followed was absolute.

Olivia let it stretch. Let it press in before she spoke again. "You panicked," she said.

Cindy shook her head. "No."

"You realized she wasn't going to stop."

"No."

"You realized everything your family had built could collapse."

"No."

"You realized your grandfather's name—your name—would be tied to fraud."

"No."

The last denial broke. It cracked at the edges. Fractured.

Cindy's breath came sharper now, her composure unraveling in visible pieces. "You don't understand," she said. The words trembled from the strain.

Olivia did not move. "Then help me understand," she said.

Cindy's hands clenched. "You think this is simple?" she

demanded. "You think you can walk in here and unravel decades of history with a few notes and a theory?"

"It's not a theory," Olivia said.

"It is," Cindy snapped. "It's incomplete. It's dangerous. It's—"

"It's true." The word landed with quiet finality.

Cindy's expression shifted. Her anger flared. Hotly and suddenly. "You have no idea what this town went through to build that resort," she said. "You don't know what it took. The risks. The sacrifices. The years of work to make something out of nothing."

Olivia held her ground.

"You're talking about something that happened before any of us were born," Cindy continued. "And you want to tear everything down because of it?"

"I want the truth," Olivia said.

"The truth?" Cindy laughed once, sharp and bitter. "The truth doesn't fix anything. It destroys things."

"It reveals what's already broken."

"It ruins people."

"It holds them accountable."

"It takes everything away," Cindy said.

The room was no longer silent. It was charged and alive with tension. And with the slow dawning and understanding of what Cindy was saying. What she was admitting. "She was going to destroy everything," Cindy said. Her voice had changed now. No longer controlled, raw.

"She didn't understand what she was doing," Cindy said. "She didn't understand what would happen if that came out."

Olivia's voice remained steady. "And you did."

"Yes," Cindy said. The word slipped out before she could stop it. She froze. The realization hit her a second later. Too late.

Olivia did not look away. "You knew exactly what it meant," she said.

Cindy's breath came fast now. Her composure was gone. In its place was something far more dangerous. Fear.

"She wasn't going to stop," Cindy said. "No matter what I said. No matter what I tried."

The room felt smaller. Every person in it drawn toward the center of the moment.

Olivia's voice softened. But did not waver. "And that's when you decided to stop her."

Cindy did not answer. But she did not deny it either, and that was enough.

Luke shifted slightly at the back of the room, his presence steady and ready. Waiting for the last bit of truth to surface. It was no longer willing to stay buried.

CHAPTER TWENTY-SEVEN

The Confession

No one moved. Cindy walked to the center of the room, her breath uneven now, her composure stripped down to something fragile and raw. The careful control she had maintained for years had cracked, and what remained beneath it was no longer contained.

Olivia did not speak. She didn't need to. The silence pressed in, demanding an answer.

Cindy closed her eyes briefly, as if trying to gather what was left of herself. When she opened them again, something had shifted. Not calm, but acceptance. "I found it years ago," she said. Her voice was quieter now, but it carried. Every word landed. "In my grandfather's papers," she continued. "Boxes no one had touched in decades. Old files. Legal documents. Things my father didn't even know we still had."

Olivia held her gaze. "You recognized what it was," she said.

Cindy nodded once. "At first, I didn't want to believe it," she said. "I thought it had to be a mistake. Missing pages. Misfiled records. Something that could be explained if I just looked hard enough."

"But it couldn't," Olivia said.

"No," Cindy said. The single word held weight. "I kept digging," Cindy continued. "Comparing records. Looking at the official filings. The copies in the archive." Her hands tightened slightly at her sides. "And the more I looked, the clearer it became," she said. "The deed wasn't right. The transfer wasn't clean. My grandfather … made it look that way."

The room remained still.

Mason's jaw tightened. Darla stared at Cindy as if seeing her for the first time. Gerald's expression had gone rigid. Tom said nothing, but his attention had not wavered.

"My grandfather falsified the documents," Cindy said. "He created a chain of ownership that didn't exist." She swallowed. "The land was never properly transferred," she said.

Olivia did not interrupt. She let Cindy continue.

"The developers built the resort believing everything was legal," Cindy said. "Or choosing to believe it. I don't know which. But the paperwork was there. Signed. Certified. Filed."

"By your grandfather," Olivia said.

"Yes," Cindy's voice wavered slightly, then steadied again. "Everything that came after," she said. "Every business, every expansion, every season that brought people here … it all rests on that." She looked around the room. At the others. At the space they occupied. "On this," she said. The silence that followed was heavy and unavoidable.

"And if the truth came out," Olivia said, "the ownership would all be called into question and the ski resort could close."

Cindy nodded. "My family name would be tied to fraud," she said. "Not suspicion. Not rumor. Fact." Her gaze dropped for a moment, then lifted again. "The hotel," she said. "My business. Everything I've worked for. Everything my parents built. It could all collapse under that."

"And the town," Gerald whispered.

Cindy looked at him. "Yes," she said. "The town." Her voice strengthened slightly.

"People here depend on this ski resort," she said. "On the tourists. On the winter season. On everything that comes with it. If that foundation is shaken … if ownership is disputed … if lawsuits start …" She shook her head. "It wouldn't just be my family," she said. "It would be all of us."

Olivia spoke then. "And you decided that was more important than the truth."

Cindy's expression tightened. "I decided it was more important than destroying everything," she said. The words landed without apology, hesitation, or softness.

Olivia held her gaze. "And Cassie?" she asked.

Cindy's composure faltered then, just slightly, enough. "She found it," Cindy said.

Her voice dropped. "She found the same documents I did," she continued. "Or enough of them to understand what they meant. She traced the connections. The missing records. The inconsistencies."

"She contacted you," Olivia said.

"Yes," Cindy's hands clenched. "She said she wanted to give me a chance," Cindy said. "To explain. To come forward. Before she made it public."

"And you agreed to meet her."

"Yes."

The room felt smaller now. Every detail drawing in tightly.

"Where?" Luke asked quietly from the back.

Cindy glanced toward him. "Outside," she said. "Near the trail."

"The slope," Olivia said.

Cindy nodded. "The slope."

Olivia could see it again. The path with its edge and drop. "You went out there knowing what she had," Olivia said.

"Yes."

"And hoping to stop her."

"Yes," Cindy's voice broke slightly on the last word. "I thought I could make her understand," she said. "I thought if I explained what it would do … what it would cost …"

Olivia did not move.

"But she wouldn't listen," Cindy said.

"She listened," Olivia said. "She just didn't agree."

Cindy shook her head. "She didn't care," she said. "Not about the consequences. Not about the damage. She kept saying the same thing over and over." Her voice tightened, echoing the memory. "The truth matters, the truth matters more than anything." Her words hung in the air.

"She wasn't wrong," Olivia whispered.

Cindy's eyes flashed. "Maybe not," she said. "But she didn't have to live with what came after."

The silence deepened.

"What happened next?" Luke asked.

Cindy's gaze shifted back to Olivia.

Olivia did not look away. "Tell us," she said.

Cindy drew a breath. Then another.

They argued. Olivia thought. *Say it.*

Cindy's voice came low. "We argued," she said. She looked past Olivia for a moment, as if seeing it again. "She told me she was going to release everything," Cindy said. "That she had enough. That she could prove it."

"And you asked her to stop," Olivia said.

"I begged her," Cindy said. The word settled heavily. "I told her to think about what it would do," Cindy continued. "To the town. To the people who live here. To everything built on that land."

"And she refused."

"Yes," Cindy's hands trembled now. The control she had rebuilt was slipping again. "She wouldn't listen," she said. "She just kept pushing. Kept insisting. Kept …" Her voice broke. For a moment, she said nothing. Then … "I lost control," she said. The words were quiet. But absolute.

Olivia felt the room tighten around them.

"What happened?" Luke asked.

Cindy swallowed. "We were standing near the edge," she said. "She turned away. I reached out. I pushed her." Silence. "I didn't mean to …" Cindy stopped, her breath catching. "I didn't think …"

"You pushed her," Olivia said. Cindy nodded, her eyes fixed somewhere beyond the room. "She slipped," Cindy said. "The ground was uneven. The snow … she lost her footing."

Olivia could see it. Cassie stepped back to balance herself. Her boot slipping on the sloping snow, and then the fall.

"She went over the edge," Cindy said. "I heard … the impact." Her voice dropped to almost nothing. "And then there was nothing."

Darla's hand flew to her mouth.

Mason looked sick.

Tom stood there with his mouth open.

And Gerald was shaking his head.

The weight of it held them in place.

"You went down to her," Luke said.

"Yes."

"And she was already dead."

Cindy closed her eyes. "Yes." The word barely made it out.

"What did you do?" Luke asked.

Cindy's eyes opened again. "I panicked," she said. "I didn't know what to do. I knew what it looked like. What it was." She shook her head. "I couldn't let it be that," she said.

"So you staged it," Olivia said.

Cindy nodded. "I moved her," she said. "Not far. Just enough. I thought … if it looked like a fall …"

"You thought it would be treated as an accident," Luke said.

"Yes."

"But you missed things," Olivia said.

Cindy's gaze flickered.

"She wasn't wearing skis," Olivia said. "There were footprints. Not tracks."

Cindy closed her eyes again. "I know," she said.

The room remained silent. No one tried to interrupt. No one tried to defend her. The truth had settled into place.

Luke stepped forward then. The movement was quiet. Measured. But it shifted everything.

"Cindy Keller," he said. His voice was calm and controlled. "You are under arrest for the murder of Cassandra Greer."

The words echoed softly in the stillness.

Cindy did not resist. She did not argue. She did not look surprised. She simply stood there for a moment, as if the weight of everything had finally caught up to her, and she cried.

Luke stepped closer, taking her wrist and guiding her hands behind her back. The sound of the cuffs was sharp in the quiet.

They were all frozen in place, watching as Cindy Keller was led toward the door.

Olivia felt sick. She had solved the murder, but at what cost? Nothing was hidden anymore.

CHAPTER TWENTY-EIGHT

The Mountain's Secret

The story did not break all at once. It spread. Through conversation first. Quiet exchanges over coffee. Low voices at the grocery store. A question asked too casually to be casual at all. A name spoken and then repeated, each time with a little more certainty. Then it moved faster.

By the end of the second day, it had a shape. By the third, it had a direction. By the fourth, it had reached every corner of Mistwood.

Olivia stood at the window in the front parlor of March House and watched the town absorb it. Snow still covered everything, but something else had replaced the stillness of winter. Movement. Conversation. People gathering in small clusters outside shops, their voices carrying in the cold air. Heads turned when someone new joined. Hands gesturing. Eyes narrowing.

The mountain had always been there. Now that the winter ski season was due to open in another week, the ownership of the ski resort was in question. People had already bought season ski tickets. The rental shops had reservations for everything from cross-country skis to snowmobiles. The hotel's reservations were full. Even March House was fully booked through New Year's.

The words drifted up from the street in fragments when the wind shifted just right. Forgery. Waverly. Keller. Lawsuit.

Olivia stepped back from the window. Behind her, the house remained steady. The same walls. The same rooms. The same quiet undercurrent of presence that never truly left. But even here, something had changed. The truth had a way of doing that.

~

LUKE DID NOT SEEK ATTENTION. That alone set him apart from most people who found themselves at the center of something this large.

Olivia saw it in the way he moved through town now. The same measured pace. The same steady focus. No attempt to claim credit. No attempt to control the narrative. He simply did the work. And people noticed.

At first, it was cautious. A nod held a second longer than usual. A greeting that carried a hint of respect, where before there had been skepticism. Conversations that shifted when he approached, not to hide things, but to include him. By the end of the week, it had settled into something more solid. Trust. Not loud. Not declared. But present.

Olivia saw it when she stopped by the sheriff's office and found him at his desk, surrounded by files, his attention fixed on a report while two business owners waited patiently nearby, instead of pressing him for answers.

She saw it when someone thanked him quietly on the street. The words simple but sincere. She saw it in the way no one mentioned the election out loud anymore. Not yet. But the question had answered itself.

~

THE CONVERSATION with Lark could not be delayed any longer. Olivia knew that the moment she stepped into the kitchen in the late afternoon.

The coffee shop was closed for the day. Thanksgiving was next week, and most people were preparing things at home and didn't want to go out in the questionable weather. It was the usual calm before the tourists descended and took over throughout the holiday season.

Lark stood at the counter, rolling dough with the same steady rhythm she always used. The scent of vanilla and butter filled the room, warm and familiar, grounding in a way Olivia had come to rely on.

For a moment, she watched her. The way she moved. The quiet certainty in each motion. The ease of someone who had spent years in this space, shaping it into something that felt like home. Unaware. That was what made it harder.

"Lark," Olivia said.

Lark glanced up, her expression open.

"That sounds serious."

"It is."

Lark set the rolling pin aside and brushed her hands together, clearing flour from her fingers.

"Then we should sit," she said.

They moved to a small table in the solarium. Outside, the snow had begun to fall again, light but steady, with the promise of much more to come as the evening grew colder.

For a moment, neither of them spoke.

Olivia chose her words carefully.

"This isn't just about Cassie," she said.

Lark's gaze sharpened slightly. "I gathered that."

"It's about the mountain," Olivia said. "The land the resort sits on."

Lark nodded once. "That's what people are saying."

"They're only partly right," Olivia said.

Lark leaned back slightly, her attention fully focused now.

"Tell me the rest."

Olivia drew a breath.

"Decades ago, that land belonged to a family here in Mistwood," she said. "The Waverly family."

Lark's expression did not change. The name did not land. Not yet.

"They owned the mountain," Olivia continued. "Or at least the section that became the resort. When the developers came in, they needed that land."

"And they bought it," Lark said.

"That's what everyone believed," Olivia said.

"And now?"

Olivia held her gaze.

"Now we know the deed transferring that land was forged."

The words settled into the space between them. Lark did not react immediately. She did not interrupt. She simply listened.

"The lawyer who handled the transfer," Olivia said, "falsified the documents. Made it look legitimate. Made it appear as if ownership had passed cleanly from the Waverly family to the developers."

"But it didn't," Lark said.

"No."

Lark's hands rested lightly on the table, still.

"And the Waverly family?" she asked.

"Most of that line died out," Olivia said. "Or moved away. Over time, the name disappeared from the town."

Lark nodded slowly. "That happens," she said.

"Yes," Olivia paused. Then continued. "But not entirely."

That was when Lark looked at her more closely.

"What do you mean?"

Olivia reached into her bag and pulled out the photograph, placing it gently on the table between them.

"This is Clara Waverly," she said.

Lark leaned forward slightly. Her gaze moved over the image. The room seemed to quiet further, the small sounds of the house fading into the background. For a long moment, she said nothing. Then … "She looks familiar," Lark said.

Olivia did not speak. She let Lark see it. Let her recognize it. The shape of the face. The line of the eyes. The quiet strength in the expression. Recognition came slowly. Then, all at once.

Lark's breath caught. "That's …" she began, then stopped. She looked up at Olivia. Then back at the photograph. Then at Olivia again. "No," she said.

Olivia's voice was gentle. "Yes."

Lark shook her head slightly, as if trying to push the thought away before it could settle.

"That's not possible," she said.

"It is."

Lark's hands tightened on the edge of the table.

"How?" she asked.

Olivia pulled out her notes, turning them so Lark could see.

"Cassie traced the family line," she said. "From Henry Waverly down through the generations. Most of it ends. But one branch continues."

Lark stared at the page. Her eyes drifted over the names. Then stopped. "Thomas Waverly," she said. "My grandfather's name was Thomas. He left," Lark said. "Moved out of the area."

"Yes."

Her finger traced the line downward. Children. Grandchildren. The name shifted, then returned. Then … her own name, Lark Waverly. She went still.

The sound of the oven clicking off in the background felt distant. Irrelevant.

"That's not …" she began.

"It is," Olivia whispered.

Lark's gaze remained fixed on the page. For a long moment, she did not move.

Then she leaned back slowly, as if the weight of what she was seeing had finally reached her.

"I didn't know," she said.

"I figured that."

Lark let out a breath that trembled slightly at the edges. "My family never talked about it," she said. "We didn't keep records like this. We didn't … I didn't …" Her voice trailed off.

Olivia waited.

Lark looked up again. "If this is true," she said, "then that land …"

Olivia nodded. "Yes."

Lark shook her head again, more firmly this time. "No," she said. "No, that doesn't make sense."

"It does," Olivia said.

"It can't," Lark said. "The resort has been there for decades. The town depends on it. People built their lives around it."

"I know."

"You're telling me that all of that might be built on something that wasn't legal to begin with."

"Yes." The word settled heavily.

Lark pressed her hands flat against the table, grounding herself. "That would change everything," she said.

"It could."

"It would cause chaos," she said. "Legal disputes. Ownership claims. People losing businesses. Jobs."

"Yes."

Lark's gaze dropped back to the photograph. To Clara Waverly. To the past that had been hidden. "And you think …" she began, then stopped.

Olivia finished it for her. "I think you're the last living descendant of that family," she said.

Silence followed.

Lark sat there, the weight of it settling over her in layers. Not just surprise, but responsibility. "That's not something I want," she whispered.

Olivia did not answer immediately. "I know," she said at last.

"I didn't ask for this," Lark said.

"No."

"And if it's true …" She looked up again, her expression more focused now, though the shock had not entirely faded. "It could hurt people," she said.

"Yes."

"It could hurt the town. It could hurt March House."

"Yes."

Lark leaned back in her chair, her gaze moving to the window.

Snow continued to fall outside, soft and steady, covering everything in a clean, unbroken layer.

"It could help some people, too," Olivia whispered.

Lark did not look at her. "Maybe," she said. "But not without a cost."

"No," Olivia said. "Not without a cost."

They sat in silence for a while after that.

Lark's hands rested in her lap now, still. "I need time," she said.

"You have it."

Lark nodded. "Good," she said.

Olivia stood slowly, gathering the photograph and the notes. She did not push further.

There was nothing more to say right now. Some truths require space. As she moved toward the doorway, she glanced back.

Lark remained at the table, her gaze distant, her thoughts clearly elsewhere. Maybe she was thinking of the mountain, or perhaps her family. Or maybe she was thinking about everything that might come next.

Olivia stepped into the hallway, the house quiet around her.

Behind her, the kitchen remained still. And ahead, well, that depended on an eccentric lady in her seventies, who liked to bake and drink tea.

CHAPTER TWENTY-NINE

Lark's Decision

The house felt quieter in the days that followed. Not empty. Never that. March House carried too many memories, too many presences, to ever feel empty. But the sharp tension that had lingered after the truth came out had softened into something more thoughtful. More measured.

Even the ghosts seemed to sense it. They moved through their usual routines with less interruption. Fewer arguments. Fewer sudden bursts of commentary that pulled Olivia out of her thoughts. It was not peace, exactly. More of a pause. As if the house itself were waiting.

Olivia found Lark in the solarium late in the evening, seated near the wide glass windows that overlooked the lake. Snow lay untouched across the yard, the fence marking a clean line between the property and the frozen edge of the water. The yard was illuminated by many fairy lights that Emma and Jess had wrapped around the trees and bushes in the front. They said it would give the late afternoon customers something to look at, now that it was dark so early.

Lark held a mug in both hands, though the steam had long since faded. She did not look up when Olivia entered. "I was wondering when you'd come in here," Lark said.

Olivia moved closer, taking the seat across from her. "I didn't want to rush you."

"You didn't," Lark said. "That was wise."

Silence settled between them for a moment.

Then Lark drew a slow breath and set the mug down. "I've been thinking," she said.

"I assumed so."

"That's dangerous in itself," Lark said lightly.

Olivia smiled faintly. "It usually is."

Lark's expression softened for just a moment, then steadied again. "I know what you found is real," she said. "The records. The photograph. The family line. It all fits too cleanly to ignore."

Olivia nodded. "Yes."

"And I know what it means," Lark continued. "Or at least, I understand enough of it to see where it leads." Her gaze drifted briefly toward the lake, then returned. "It means that land was never truly given up," she said. "It was taken. Quietly. Permanently. And everyone who came after built on that without knowing."

"Or without questioning," Olivia said.

Lark inclined her head slightly. "That too." She folded her hands together on the table.

"And now," she said, "it circles back."

Olivia waited.

Lark's gaze held steady. "To me."

"Yes," Olivia said.

The word did not feel heavy anymore. It simply was.

Lark nodded once, as if confirming something to herself. "I've had a few days to sit with that," she said. "To think about what it would mean to do something with it."

Olivia leaned forward slightly. "And?"

Lark's lips curved into a small, almost amused smile. "And I've decided I don't want to disrupt everything, but I don't want the theft to disappear without consequences."

Olivia blinked.

"I want a settlement," she said. "I want a trust set up, and the money used to pay for scholarships for the children in this community. Scholarships for college or trade school or anything that can improve the economy of this town." She shook her head gently. "I don't want to spend the rest of my life fighting over something that was lost before I was even born," she said. "And I certainly don't want to tear apart a town to get it back. I think this would be a suitable compromise."

Olivia studied her. "You're sure?" she asked.

"Yes."

"No hesitation."

Lark's smile faded into something more thoughtful. "There was hesitation," she said. "At first." She glanced down at her hands. "It's not a small thing," she said. "To realize your family might have been wronged on that scale. That something that should have been yours was taken."

"No," Olivia said. "It's not."

Lark lifted her gaze again. "But that was a long time ago," she said. "And what exists now matters too. The town, its people, and the lives built here." She gestured lightly toward the window, toward the lake, toward everything beyond it. "My family helped shape this place once," she said. "I don't want to be the one who breaks it."

Olivia felt something ease in her chest. "That's a generous decision," she said.

"It's a practical one," Lark replied.

"It's both."

Lark considered that, then gave a small nod. "Maybe," she said. She leaned back slightly, her shoulders relaxing for the first time since the conversation began. "That doesn't mean I want the truth buried again," she added.

Olivia's attention sharpened. "No?"

"No," Lark said firmly. "What happened still matters. What my family lost still matters. And what was done … that shouldn't just disappear."

Olivia nodded slowly. "I agree."

Lark's expression shifted, something more certain settling into place. "I don't want the mountain," she said. "But I want the truth acknowledged."

"How?"

Lark thought for a moment, then said, "Something simple."

Olivia waited.

"A plaque," Lark said. "At the lodge. Or somewhere visible.

Something that tells the actual story. That honors the Waverly family and makes it clear what actually happened."

Olivia felt a quiet sense of rightness settle over the idea. "That would matter," she said.

"It would," Lark agreed. "It wouldn't undo the past. But it would stop pretending it didn't exist."

Olivia smiled slightly. "I think that's a good way to handle it."

Lark returned the smile, softer this time.

"Good," she said. "Because I'm not changing my mind."

"I wouldn't expect you to."

They sat in companionable silence for a moment, the weight of the decision settling into something steadier.

Outside, the snow continued to fall, slow and quiet.

The doorbell rang.

Lark glanced toward the hallway. "That'll be Luke."

Olivia stood. "I'll get it."

LUKE STOOD ON THE PORCH, a light dusting of snow on his shoulders, his breath visible in the cold air.

"You always pick the worst weather to visit," Olivia said as she opened the door.

"I like to keep things interesting."

"You're succeeding."

He stepped inside, brushing snow off his jacket.

"Lark around?" he asked.

"In the solarium."

"I'll catch her in a bit." He looked at Olivia, his expression shifting slightly. "Can we talk?"

She nodded. "Of course."

They moved into the kitchen, the warmth wrapping around them again. The scent of earlier baking still lingered faintly in the air.

Luke rested one hand against the back of a chair, not sitting. "I wanted to update you," he said.

"About Cindy."

"Yes."

Olivia crossed her arms lightly, waiting.

"She's been formally charged," Luke said. "Murder. The confession holds. The evidence supports it. There's no question about what happened."

Olivia exhaled slowly. "Good," she said.

"It is," Luke agreed. He studied her for a moment. "You were right," he said.

Olivia lifted a brow. "Careful. That sounds almost like praise."

"It is praise."

"I'll try not to let it go to my head."

He scoffed. "Too late for that."

She smiled faintly.

Luke's expression softened slightly in response. "There's something else," he said.

"What?"

He shifted his weight, just slightly. "People are talking," he said.

"They've been doing that all week."

"About you."

Olivia stilled. "Oh?"

Luke nodded.

"They know you helped put this together," he said. "That you found the connections. That you pushed where others didn't."

Olivia looked away briefly, then back. "I didn't do it alone," she said.

"No," Luke said. "But you started it. And you didn't let it go."

She shrugged lightly. "Bad habit."

"Useful one," he said.

She pretended to consider that. "I suppose it has its moments."

Luke's gaze lingered on her a second longer than usual. "Thank you," he said.

The words were simple. But they carried weight.

"For what?" she asked.

"For not backing off," he said. "For sticking with it when it got complicated. For helping me see what I was missing."

Olivia met his gaze. "You would've gotten there," she said.

"Maybe," he said. "Not as quickly."

She tilted her head slightly. "You're improving."

"At what?"

"At admitting things."

He almost smiled. "I'll try not to make a habit of it."

"Shame," she said. "It suits you."

The moment stretched. Quiet. Comfortable in a way it hadn't been before. Something had shifted between them. Not dramatically or all at once, but steadily. Trust, where there had been resistance. Understanding where there had been friction.

Luke straightened slightly, breaking the moment before it settled too deeply. "I should check in with Lark," he said.

"You should."

He paused at the doorway, then glanced back. "Try not to start another investigation tonight," he said.

Olivia smiled. "No promises."

He shook his head, but there was no real disapproval in it anymore. Only something warmer. He moved down the hall toward the solarium.

Olivia remained where she was for a moment, the quiet of the kitchen settling around her again. Then she reached for a clean mug and poured herself more coffee.

"That young man is growing on me. Although he is still in desperate need of a good tailor. Sir Alistair stood in the doorway. "I do believe we will be seeing more of him in the future."

Olivia smiled. "I hope so."

Outside, the snow continued to fall. Inside, the house held steady. And for the first time since the mountain had given up its secret, things felt almost settled.

CHAPTER THIRTY

Life at March House

Winter did not arrive quietly. It marched into town, dropped its suitcases on the floor, and put its feet up on the coffee table. Snow layered itself over Mistwood in thick, steady waves, smoothing rooftops, softening roads, and turning the lake into a pale sheet of ice that reflected the sky in muted shades of gray and silver. The air carried that familiar crisp edge, sharp enough to wake the senses with every breath. And with it, the town came alive.

Tourists arrived in steady streams, their cars filling the streets, their laughter carrying across sidewalks and through open shop doors. Skis and snowboards appeared in clusters outside restaurants and other eating establishments. Boots stamped snow at the door. Conversations rose and fell in a constant rhythm that replaced the quieter pace of early winter. Mistwood had shifted back into motion, and March House followed.

Olivia stood behind the counter in the kitchen, sliding a tray of pastries onto a cooling rack as the bell at the front door chimed again.

"Another round," one of the baristas called from the adjoining space.

"Already on it," Olivia replied.

The kitchen moved with purpose. Butter, flour, sugar, and heat worked together in practiced harmony. The scent of fresh pastries filled the air, rich and warm, drawing guests from the dining room and visitors from the street.

Lark moved easily beside her, plating scones with careful precision, her movements calm despite the growing demand. "We're nearly out of the cranberry ones," Lark said.

"I've got another batch coming up," Olivia said.

"You always do."

Olivia smiled faintly. That was the rhythm now. Busy with constant customers. The house was truly alive.

The dining room and solarium buzzed with conversation. Cups clinked against saucers. Chairs shifted. The low hum of voices filled the space, blending into a steady, comforting sound.

For the first time since she had inherited March House, it felt exactly the way it was supposed to.

THE CALL from Gerald Huxley came just after noon. Olivia stepped into the hallway, wiping her hands on a towel as she answered.

"Huxley," his voice came, direct as ever.

"Good afternoon," Olivia said. "I wasn't expecting to hear from you."

"I imagine not," he said. "Given everything that's happened."

"That's one way to put it." A brief pause.

"I haven't forgotten our conversation at the summit," he said.

Olivia leaned lightly against the wall. "Neither have I."

"I meant what I said," Gerald continued. "About the food. About the opportunity."

Olivia's interest sharpened. "You're still interested in moving forward," she said.

"Yes," he said. "The situation doesn't change the fact that the lodge needs quality catering. If anything, it reinforces it. We'll need to restore confidence. That includes the experience we offer."

Olivia considered that for exactly one second. "I can do that," she said.

"I thought you might."

"What are you looking for?" she asked.

"Pastries to start," he said. "A continental breakfast service.

Hors d'oeuvres platters for evening events. Possibly expanded menus as we move forward."

Olivia's mind was already moving through possibilities. Seasonal flavors. Presentation. Logistics.

"I can put together a proposal," she said.

"Do that," Gerald said. "And Olivia?"

"Yes?"

"You handled yourself well," he said.

The words were simple. But they carried weight.

"Thank you," she said.

"I'll expect your plan by the end of the week."

"You'll have it." The call ended.

Olivia stood there for a moment, the quiet of the hallway a sharp contrast to the energy in the kitchen. Then she smiled. "Lark," she called as she stepped back into the room.

"Yes?"

"We just landed the lodge."

Lark looked up, a knowing glint in her eye.

"I thought we might."

THE GHOSTS HAD OPINIONS. They always did. But today, they had more than usual.

"This was clearly a coordinated effort," Anton declared from his position near the center of the kitchen. "A strategic application of observation, timing, and intellectual superiority."

Sir Alistair stood near the doorway, his expression deeply unimpressed. "You stood in corners and made commentary," he said.

"I provided insight," Anton replied.

"You provided noise."

"I provided brilliance."

"You provided disruption."

Monique drifted closer to Anton, her smile bright with amusement. "I think he provided entertainment," she said. "Which is far more valuable."

Anton inclined his head slightly. "At last, someone who understands."

Monique's gaze lingered on him. "Oh, I understand many things."

Simon stepped forward, arms crossed. "You take credit quickly," he said.

"I take credit where it is due," Anton replied.

"And where is that?"

Anton gestured broadly. "Here."

Walter let out a low, amused breath from his place near the wall. "Kid thinks he solved the whole thing himself," he muttered.

JJ leaned against the counter, cornet resting loosely in his hand. "I'll give him this," JJ said. "He's committed to the story."

Daisy smiled faintly, her attention moving between them. "It's a lively version," she said.

"It's inaccurate," Sir Alistair replied.

"It's inspiring," Anton countered.

"It's insufferable."

"It's undeniable."

Olivia pressed her lips together, focusing carefully on the tray in front of her. "Not today," she muttered under her breath.

"What was that?" Lark asked.

"Nothing."

The argument continued. Voices overlapping. Opinions clashing. Monique laughing softly as Anton elaborated on his "crucial role." Simon questioned every detail. Sir Alistair was growing increasingly exasperated.

The kitchen filled with it. Energy. Noise. Life, well, afterlife.

Olivia set the tray down and straightened. "Enough," she said.

No one stopped.

She closed her eyes briefly. Then opened them again. "Everyone, be quiet."

They did not.

She reached for the counter, steadying herself. "Of course they don't," she muttered.

Lark glanced at her, a faint smile touching her lips.

"Crowded day," she said.

"That's one way to describe it."

Later, as the rush eased and the afternoon settled into a quieter rhythm, Olivia stepped back from the kitchen. The house moved around her. Guests lingered in the dining room, their conversations softer now, punctuated by the occasional laugh. The baristas worked steadily, refilling cups and clearing tables. The warmth of the house wrapped around everything, holding it together.

Olivia leaned lightly against the doorway and let herself take it in. The sounds of her coffee customers and the baristas. The conversations of the bed-and-breakfast guests. The ghosts gathered at the bottom of the stairs. The balance of it all. This was what she had been building. Not just a business, but a place to call home.

For the first time since she had arrived in Mistwood. The dream she had for the place had become a reality. She let out a slow breath.

Anton drifted up beside her.

"You see?" he said. "A champion investigator always triumphs."

Olivia didn't look at him. She just rolled her eyes. "You're impossible."

"I am exceptional."

"You are exhausting."

"I am victorious."

She glanced at him then, a faint smile breaking through. "You are lucky I'm too busy to argue with you."

"A wise decision," he said.

Behind them, the ghosts resumed their debate with renewed enthusiasm.

Sir Alistair's voice rose in precise irritation. Monique laughed again. Simon challenged another point. JJ added commentary from the sidelines. The noise returned, the chaos of constant motion.

Olivia shook her head slightly. Then turned back to the kitchen. There was work to do.

There were guests to be served. There was a life here now. And she had no intention of stepping away from it. Because if there was one thing she knew, in Mistwood, quiet never lasted. Peace never stayed for long. And sooner or later, another mystery would find its way to her door.

~

IF YOU LOVE MYSTERIES, noisy and opinionated ghosts, great

pastries, and a slow-burn romance, join Olivia March and company for another mystery coming in November 2026.

JOIN my newsletter and stay up-to-date on upcoming releases and sales. You will also learn fun and interesting things about Mistwood, along with sneak peeks of future stories, background information, and special insights into my unique characters.

https://augustinavanhoven.com/join-newsletter/

www.ingramcontent.com/pod-product-compliance
Lightning Source LLC
LaVergne TN
LVHW010055110826
845155LV00028B/350

* 9 7 8 1 9 5 1 5 3 4 4 1 7 *